The God of Mischief

The God of Mischief

PAUL BAJORIA

SIMON AND SCHUSTER

For Verity and Dominic

SIMON AND SCHUSTER
First published in Great Britain by Simon & Schuster UK Ltd, 2005
A Viacom company

1 3 5 7 9 10 8 6 4 2

Simon & Schuster UK Ltd
Africa House
64-78 Kingsway
London WC2B 6AH

A CIP catalogue record for this book is available
from the British Library

ISBN 1 416 90112 4

Printed and bound in Great Britain by
Mackays of Chatham plc, Chatham, Kent

CONTENTS

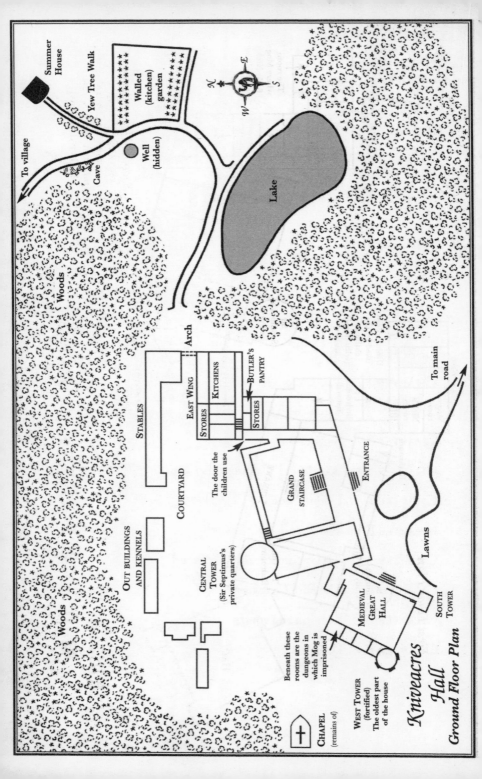

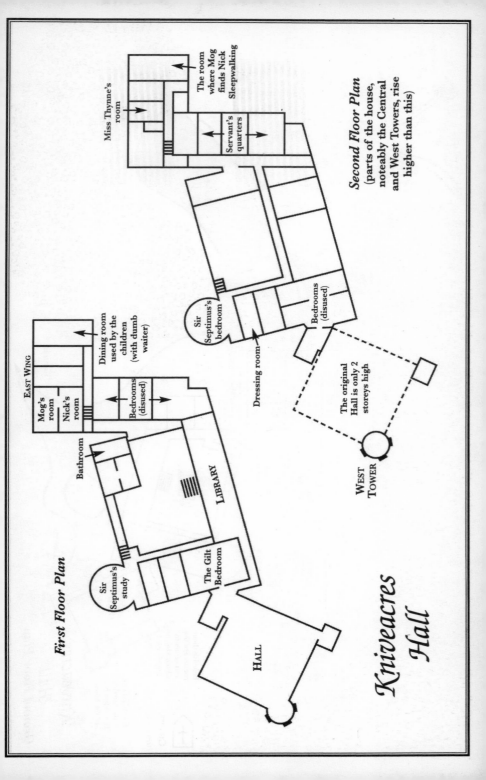

First Floor Plan

EAST WING

Mog's room

Nick's room

Dining room used by the children (with dumb waiter)

Bathroom

Bedrooms (disused)

Sir Septimus's study

LIBRARY

The Gilt Bedroom

HALL

Second Floor Plan (parts of the house, noteably the Central and West Towers, rise higher than this)

Miss Thynne's room

The room where Mog finds Nick Sleepwalking

Servant's quarters

Sir Septimus's bedroom

Dressing room

Bedrooms (disused)

The original Hall is only 2 storeys high

WEST TOWER

Kniveacres Hall

PROLOGUE

. . . apart from some doses of physic of Mr Varley's which I privately confess have done nothing to improve my condition. Disease is rife whence we have come, and, despite individual kindnesses, the arrangements on board since we left have been insanitary and unnourishing. Whatever the truth, the Good Lord attends, and it befits us not to question His motives. The one vital duty of my last days remains to be discharged, and it is in pursuit of this, principally, that I have written to you.

You will be surprised and, I fear, aghast, at the request I make of you. Yet I beg you to give this letter your fullest attention, and to consider with the utmost care how you might execute my will. As I have explained, I am delivered of two beautiful children, and in being taken from them I leave them utterly alone and helpless. If I am taken, my sole desire in departing is to know that the warm and desperate little souls to whom my transgression gave life will be spared, and will be able to live, and grow, and laugh, and learn. It is my dying wish that they be cared for, together or separately, in the best circumstances which may be afforded, and that every effort be made to bring them up in virtue and in health.

I hope I am not mistaken in assuming that you have the means to oversee such an upbringing, and I pray that, with goodwill and modest financial aid, nature may in time be allowed to heal where she has so mercilessly hurt. My dear, I beg you not to spurn my entreaty in this matter, much as your first instinct may be to do so. I charge you with this solemn duty not because I wish to burden your remaining years but because I trust you with all my being. Whatever the imminent fate of the soul, it would indeed be too cruel if the still-innocent flesh begotten of my misdeed were made to suffer.

I know of nowhere else to turn. I feel so helpless, my dear, and I pray that you will not feel equally so, upon being charged with the care of these precious infants. I would not blame you. Your first instinct may very well be to enlist help, and even to seek out those who are closer to them in blood. Yet I would be in dereliction of my duty if I did not prepare you for the difficulty, perhaps the impossibility, of ever doing so. You would be attempting to conduct your inquiries in a country where letters are rarely answered, and where there are no formal records of people's names, histories, births, deaths, professions or whereabouts. I fear it will not be possible to reach Damyata now.

I can say no more; and I am feeling weak. Please God this letter reaches you, and that you do not think too ill of me to grant some mercy to the gentle, perfect creatures who accompany it. My dear, goodbye, and with all the remaining life in my body, I thank you.

Your undeserving
Imogen

CHAPTER 1
A BURIAL

The chanting grew gradually louder. I was frightened. I was being swung round, by my feet, by two big grim-faced girls who held on to my ankles with a grip far tighter and more cruel than necessary. Their faces, the only still points in a whirl of figures and furniture, broke into sadistic grins as I stared at them. I was already dizzy and was beginning to feel sick, my short filthy hair feeling the breeze as my head just missed the wall or the edge of a desk by a matter of inches. I kept my arms pulled in tight against my chest to stop them smashing into something and, with clenched fists, I silently begged them to stop. Round and round I went, faster and faster; the girls couldn't possibly keep control of my whirling body for much longer, and I knew if they carried on I was going to hurt myself badly. A few times I tried to shout at them to stop, but they were making too much noise for my voice to be heard; and anyway, I knew from experience that crying out only made them whirl you more violently and gleefully.

As suddenly as the game had started, it was all over. The lookout's warning – "Mrs Muggerage!" – was taken up by the rest of the girls, until it was simply a general loud hissing sound throughout the room; the girls let go of me and dispersed to the four corners, leaving me spinning on my back, my hair grinding into the filth of the floor, my limbs sprawling.

A terrible silence descended. A huge figure was standing in the doorway. Only gradually did I realise who it was, though at the back of my head was the troubling sense that something was wrong; that this couldn't really be happening. I struggled to sit up, the room continued to spin, and I felt the awful, inescapable sensation of my breakfast trying to escape. As the walls and floor whirled around my head, I brought up a great splattering stomachload of acidic, watery porridge.

A choir of angels couldn't have been more innocent than that roomful of children pretended to be right then. Whether Mrs Muggerage was fooled, I never knew – if she was, I couldn't understand how – but there was only one child in the room who wasn't sitting bolt upright, with their hands by their sides, looking wide-eyed and morally horrified at what they could see in the middle of the floor. And that was me. Just who else had been involved, it was impossible to tell; but plainly I had been at the centre of things, because there I was on the tiles, propped up on one arm, retching.

"Mog Winter," said Mrs Muggerage, in a tone of grim pleasure at the prospect of being able to mete out some punishment. Her black boots echoing on the bare floor, she walked slowly over to me. There were a few seconds' grace as I wiped my mouth and lifted my dizzy head to look up at her. She stood above me, a woman of awesome bulk and power, a grimy cloth in her hand. She was blocking out most of the light, but gazing up at her shadowy outline I could tell her expression was without compassion, even slightly sneering with revulsion at my sickness. Then she grasped me by the collar and yanked me to my feet with a single, violent motion. I hung there from her fist like a marionette, weakened, close to tears.

"Mog Winter," she said again. "I coulda guessed. Before I walked in, I coulda guessed."

She turned around, slowly, holding me out to exhibit me to the rest of the children. There was complete silence as they stared at me. I registered the faces of my chief tormentors among the group, and they were looking at me with disdain, as though they were genuinely as disgusted with me as Mrs Muggerage was.

"What have you got to say fer yourself?" she snarled at me.

"This ain't right!" I said, struggling. "You're not meant to be here."

"No good," Mrs Muggerage was saying, "can ever come to those what misbehaves. Lord knows if we don't try 'ard enough, girls and boys, to make it plain. Lord knows if I don't teach the same lesson day after day. No good will ever come to those what can't behave. And Lord knows if, day after day, some dreadful boy or girl don't completely ignore the lesson, so's I'm 'bliged to teach it all over again. *Well.*"

That "*well*" was calculated to send a shiver of fear into every young heart in the room. Although only a single word, it was stretched so it lasted as long as a whole sentence, and it contained more misery in its elongated syllable than any complete sentence you could possibly think of.

She dropped me. Because she'd been holding me up with my

feet off the ground, I had to put my hands out to break my fall, and as I tumbled to the floor again my palms went straight into the pool of vile porridge I'd left beneath me, smearing it further and sending it splashing up my arms and across my cheek. Without intending it, but unable to prevent myself, I swore – using a word I'd heard the other children use several times a day. The moment I heard myself say it, I knew my fate was sealed.

Their hearts in their mouths, the other children watched me crouching there, and waited to see what Mrs Muggerage was going to do.

She said nothing for a long time, while my unguarded oath resonated in our terrified souls. She said nothing, just stared down at me, for what seemed an eternity. The walls towered around us, cold, dirty and cracked, with barred windows in them so high above our heads that all we could ever see through them was the sun, the clouds, or the night sky. They were that high up on purpose, of course, to prevent us from seeing what was outside and dreaming or devising plans for escape; but quite often, when we were unsupervised, we used to form acrobatic towers by climbing on top of one another. Four children standing on one another's shoulders meant that the person on top could grasp the bars and peer out over the wide sill, and we used to take it in turns to be the one on top. Looking down, we could see the flagstones of the dank little orphanage yard far below, and part of the high brick gateway which led to the outside world; but of much more interest to us was the roofscape, at eye level: the vista of chimneys and church spires receding into the distance and, beyond the city's rooftops, a glimpse of hills to the north. We didn't know any names for the places we were looking at: it was just "Out". When we scrabbled our way up to look through the grimy window, we could see Out; we dreamed constantly of being Out, and staying Out, and never coming back.

And, although I thought about it almost every minute of every day, I had never longed more to be Out than I did at that moment.

Her teeth bared, Mrs Muggerage leaned slowly down and pressed her incensed face into mine.

"Do my ears deceive me?" she hissed. Some other child in the room echoed her hiss with a sharp, frightened little intake of breath. The huge, terrible woman clenched the foul wet rag she'd been holding in her left hand; and which, I now saw, was smeared and dripping with the contents of whatever disgusting corner of the orphanage she'd just been cleaning. It only seemed to occur to her at this moment that the rag was just the object she needed to make her point, and humiliate me at the same time.

"A mouth as filthy as that," she snarled, "wants a good clean."

"*Don't*," I moaned, "don't . . . *please* don't . . ." But there was no escaping it, and the next thing I knew she had grabbed me by the back of the neck with a claw-like hand to stop me moving my head, and the vile-smelling thing was thrust into my face, and squeezed hard until it oozed its slime between my lips and into my nostrils and made me choke and gag.

"*Don't!*" I repeated. "*Please* don't . . . *please* don't . . ."

"Mog," said a familiar voice, "Mog, it's me. Mog! Wake up!"

There still seemed to be something tremendously wet in my

face, but, as I came to, I realised it was the eager tongue of my dog Lash; and the voice was that of Nick, my twin brother, sitting on my bed looking down at me with an expression of urgency in the yellow light of a flickering lamp.

"What's the matter?" he asked.

I reached up my hands in relief, and grabbed my dog's furry head on both sides, both to greet him and to pull him away. His long snout continued to sniff excitedly at my face and I had to strain with all my strength to hold him back from licking me more.

"*Stop* it," I said, "you *ridiculous* dog."

Lash was as ridiculous and loveable a dog as a child ever owned, a gangling golden-haired mongrel with a huge smile and a long tail which was never still, and curly blond eyelashes so prominent they had given me no choice as to what to call him. I ruffled his head as I blinked in the lamplight and exhaled with relief at the discovery that I wasn't in the terrible orphanage after all.

"I was dreaming again," I said to Nick. "Sorry."

"Must have been a bad one," Nick rejoined, "to make you squeal like that. It sounded like you were being murdered. I came in as fast as I could, but you were going the right way to wake up the whole house."

I was still coming to. "I was in the orphanage," I said, the full horror of the dream coming back to me. "I was being whirled round and round . . . and Nick, guess who was there? Mrs Muggerage!"

"Well that *was* a nightmare then," said Nick with sympathy.

We may have been twins, Nick and I, but we hadn't known

one another all our lives by any means. We had been born at sea, on a voyage back from India, to the most beautiful and virtuous mother who had ever lived. I had always thought of her this way; and, although she had died when we were just two weeks old, I had pictures of her in my head and some small mementos of her which had always been the most precious things I owned. I was named after her: Imogen was my full name, and I had only acquired the abbreviated name of Mog in the loathsome orphanage to which I was taken as a baby. I lived there until I was six or seven, when I had the good fortune to be taken away. The streets of London were no place for a little girl, on her own with no one to support her; but there was no shortage of work for boys, and because I'd always looked like a boy, I got a job as a printer's devil for Mr Cramplock, in Clerkenwell. It was a happy life and it contained lots of adventures, which are another story altogether. But ever since I left the orphanage, I'd had dreams like the one from which I'd just awoken, and for several years I'd lived in constant terror of being discovered and dragged back there.

Nick, meanwhile, had somehow become separated from me in our tiniest infancy, and had grown up completely separately. For as long as he could remember, he'd lived among the criminals and sailors of London, looked after by a violent ship's bosun who passed himself off as his father, and by Mrs Muggerage, the dreadful woman in my nightmare. Together they treated him even worse, if possible, than I was treated in the orphanage. We had only met for the first time – completely by accident – last year, when we were both twelve. It turned out we'd been living less than a mile apart, both of us making our way in the crowded

9

streets of London without knowing one another. Neither of us had any inkling we had a brother or sister at all, let alone that we were *twins*, living so close together all this time.

Of course, we'd been together ever since, Nick, myself and Lash. I'd never known anything you might call a family, in my entire life; dreams and contemplations of my mother had been the most comfort I could hope for. Now, for the first time, I was getting used to the idea that I wasn't alone. It meant more to me than anything else in the world; and, to be honest, I still lived in fear of waking up one morning and finding it had all been an impossible dream.

I held Lash's soft head firmly between my hands and gazed into his face, pretending to be stern with him.

"You know," I said, "I don't think it would matter how far away Lash's face was, he could still stick out his tongue and lick my nose. How long do you think it is?"

"It probably never ends," said Nick. "He could sort of *launch* it out of his mouth and lick absolutely anything at all, on the other side of the room, or on the other side of the street. It probably curls up inside his mouth and down his throat and goes on for ever, like a kind of snake."

"What time is it?" I asked.

"It's the middle of the night," said Nick, and his voice was suddenly low and quiet as though he'd just remembered how late it was, and how dark.

"Did I wake you up?"

"Yes . . ." He hesitated. "I was dreaming too," he admitted. "I was glad to be woken up, actually." We had both been having especially vivid dreams in the past few weeks, and when we described our dreams to one another it seemed we were both dreaming very similar things, again and again: dreams of being pursued, dreams in which people we knew were in danger and we were powerless to help them.

"Can you hear something?" I asked suddenly.

"I can hear the wind," said Nick.

"No, there's something else," I said, straining to listen.

I stopped making a fuss of Lash, and got out of bed, and went over to the window. There was no curtain or blind, and the window didn't quite fit the frame properly, which meant if it was windy it often used to rattle and keep me awake. Nick had tried to fold some paper to the right thickness to make a wedge to hold the window shut, but it had never really worked, and the wind still used to whistle through the gap in an eerie way.

"Can't you hear it?" I asked him. "A sort of – crying sound."

"It's just the wind," said Nick, yawning.

"It's not," I said. The wind certainly was hissing violently through the trees tonight; and this house had turrets, and gables, and roofs which sloped at crazy angles to one another, all of which hooked and snagged the wind and could make it sound like thunder. But what I could hear was distinct from all that, like a sporadic distant sobbing. "There!" I said. "It's someone crying, Nick. A girl, or a woman." We both listened hard, and every now and again I was sure it was there – somewhere amid the wind, beyond the windowpane, or perhaps in another part of the house. But I could see from Nick's face that he didn't believe me.

I climbed onto the window-seat to look outside, but the only thing I could see in the darkness was my own reflection.

"Put the lamp out," I said to Nick.

Now, the scene outside emerged. There was a bright three-quarter moon tonight, which only occasionally appeared between scudding clouds. From where we slept we could see the central tower of the castle, with seven tall chimneys in a row jutting out behind it like a lower jaw against the sky. Rooks' nests poked out from between and inside them, and at dusk the rooks would circle and screech for an hour or more in great excitable flocks. This late at night, they were all roosting, oblivious to the wind which stirred their stiff feathers as they huddled among the chimney stacks. If I craned my neck to peer over the sill, I could see the pale gravel of the courtyard at the foot of the tower. Behind that were the low stable buildings and the coach-house on the far side, and beyond them the darkness of the forest. Everything was disappointingly calm and normal. I couldn't even hear the sobbing any more.

"There's no sign of—" I began. But as my eyes grew accustomed to the dark outside, I could see the faint glow of lamplight in one of the windows in the tower, immediately opposite.

"Nick, there's a light!" I whispered.

It was Sir Septimus's study. From this bedroom there was a perfect view across the courtyard into the side of his big oriel window, and Nick and I could often see him sitting there at his desk, in profile, sometimes working, sometimes talking, often just appearing to stare into space ahead of him; and, coming and going, the loyal dark figures of his servants Bonefinger and Melibee. Like a pair of old black ravens, they attended quietly to his wishes, kept the affairs of the house in order, and were rarely far from his side. As I peered out into the night, there was no sign of Sir Septimus in his customary chair, but tall shadows seemed to be moving in the lamplit tower room.

"I can't see him," I said, "but there's *someone* in there."

"He's not normally up as late as this," said Nick. He was kneeling on my bed watching me, still yawning. "Maybe he heard you crying out, and he's got up to investigate."

"Come and *look*," I said, impatiently. "It might be a robber." And I pressed my face back to the cold pane.

The shadows continued to grow and shrink on the study wall; occasionally the curtain moved; but no one came close enough to the window to be identifiable. I was beginning to wonder if we should go and wake someone up, to tell them there was someone in Sir Septimus's study.

"There's *definitely* someone in there," I said. "Do you think we ought to—?"

But as I spoke, the lamplight was suddenly snuffed out; and now the tower was as dark as the rest of the house, the only light coming from the moon flickering behind the thin, fast-moving clouds.

I suppose I should explain that, though Nick and I had both grown up in London, we didn't live there any more. Some months ago, in the dreary dying months of last winter, a stage-coach had brought us the long day's journey northward, to live with our distant relative, Sir Septimus Cloy, here at Kniveacres Hall. It had seemed like a magnificent adventure. We were sorry to be leaving London, the streets and the crowds and the sights and smells, the people who'd looked after us, our friends, and our whole way of life there; but discovering we had a long-lost relative who lived in a tall, partly-ruined medieval castle hidden deep within woods, and that we were on our way there to start a whole new life, was too exciting to begrudge for long. Neither of us had many possessions, and everything both of us owned was packed quite easily into a small wooden chest, which sat on top of the coach by our feet as we travelled.

When we arrived, we found all sorts of things were just as we had imagined them, and plenty of others were quite unexpected. I've said Sir Septimus lived in a castle, and you might have seen enough real castles to know the difference; but we hadn't, and as far as we were concerned Kniveacres was as close to a genuine storybook castle as you could get. It had towers and turrets and crenellations and high chimneys, and crumbling old outhouses, and massive stone fireplaces, and staircases which led nowhere, and rooms into which we weren't allowed to go. It had a big, echoing hall with a wooden ceiling like the hull of a ship turned upside down, and beams on which so many generations of woodworm had feasted it looked as though it might collapse at any moment. It had a long library full of dark oak furniture and more books than either of us had ever imagined existed, let alone actually read. We each had our own room in the east wing, above the kitchens and close to the quarters set aside for the servants. They were huge, with high ceilings and tall mullioned windows, furnished with high-backed benches, chests of huge deep drawers, and beds made of oak with sides which stood up around the mattress, so that it was like falling asleep in a big farm cart. Outside, there were gardens which had gone to rack and ruin, a chapel which had all but fallen down, a gigantic green and stagnant lake, a boathouse, a mysterious cave, and an overgrown old summerhouse, where we'd spent long spring days clearing away the ivy and weeds which had all but enveloped it. The house sat amid dense woods, where you could get hopelessly lost just by turning around twice, and where there were enough rabbits and pheasants and squirrels to drive Lash mad with the excitement of constant chasing.

But we soon discovered there were less palatable things about life here too. It had still been winter when we had arrived, and Kniveacres was dark, and uncomfortable, and freezing cold. Our bedrooms had ill-fitting windows, huge gaps under the oak doors, and open fireplaces which, most of the time, just acted as channels for cold and noisy draughts. Right from the beginning Sir Septimus was – well, he wasn't what you'd call warm either. His few servants looked after him, and the castle, just as they had for decades; but none of them went out of their way to make us welcome, or to light fires, and whenever we dared ask for anything we found we were treated with gruff resentment. The food we were given in the castle was meagre, and the only way Lash got enough to eat was by occasionally catching some of the wildlife he chased in the surrounding estate, much to the displeasure of the servants. Gradually, as the months went by, we became friendly with the kitchen servants and found we were able to persuade them to slip us a bit extra from time to time; but it wasn't always enough to prevent us feeling hungry.

I shivered. I'd been kneeling here on the wooden window-seat for several minutes now, and the wind was still whistling through the gap in the window-frame. The summer was over, and it was getting too cold at night to be able to stay out of bed for long. There was no more sign of light in the tower, now, and no more sobbing. I was beginning to think Nick might be right: that someone had been woken up by my shouting in my sleep, and whoever it was had now gone back to bed.

Nick had retreated under the covers of my bed, to stay warm while he watched me. "Come on, Mog," he said, "there's nothing more to see."

But suddenly, through the noise of the wind, there came a distinct dull thud from below, like a heavy door being pulled shut. I pressed my face to the dark window again.

"Just a minute," I said. "Keep quiet."

Now, a figure was crossing the courtyard below: hunched over, head down into the wind, with thin legs and a big cloak over his back like the carapace of a beetle. In the moonlight I could make out lots of small objects whirling around him; fallen leaves, swept up by his cloak as it moved across the ground. The sound of footsteps crunching on the gravel rose on the air; and, amid the whistling of the wind, the faint sound of the jangling of keys. There was no mistaking him.

"Where's *he* going at this time of night?" I whispered.

"Bonefinger?" Nick whispered. Without looking away from the window, I nodded.

Bonefinger. The most faithful and ancient of Sir Septimus Cloy's servants, grey and gaunt, sharp-eared and sharp-tongued, a man with even less warmth than Sir Septimus himself, if such a thing were possible. He was the kind of man who, having one moment been nowhere to be seen, could the very next be standing by your side as though he'd been there all along. His ability to suddenly appear in the same room, without being summoned and without our noticing, had caused us quite a few shocks in the months we'd known him, and several uncomfortable moments when we'd been discovered doing something we shouldn't. We had spent a great deal of time and energy trying to anticipate his movements and work out his routes through the castle, but they still baffled us as completely as they had when we first arrived. Now, under cover of night, here he was scuttling around, long after the rest of the household had gone to bed.

Lash came to join me on the window-seat, his nose against the cold pane, and as I reached out to ruffle his coat I could feel his hackles go up.

"I *bet* it was him in Sir Septimus's room," I whispered. "What do you suppose he was doing there?" Nick didn't answer, and I peered out again into the dark courtyard below. "He's going to the stables," I whispered.

"Fine," said Nick, and yawned. He pulled the woollen blanket from my bed tighter around himself. "Do you mind if I go back and lie down?" he asked.

"Nick, wait a minute, he's coming out again."

Below, Bonefinger's cloaked figure emerged from the dark archway of the stable; and this time he was carrying something.

"He's got a stick, or a staff," I observed to the indifferent Nick. "No – it's not, it's – it's a *spade*."

"Maybe he's going to kill some rats," said Nick.

"He's going down towards the lake," I said. I jumped down off the window-seat. "Nick, I'm going to follow him."

"You're *what?*"

"I'm going to follow him. Are you coming?" I reached hastily for a heavy coat I thought I'd hung on the back of a chair earlier in the day; but found myself scrabbling at bare wood.

"Have you moved my coat?" I asked.

"Mog, it's the middle of the night," protested Nick. "This is no time for playing spies." He knew it was a waste of his time trying to get me to listen to him; but he never stopped telling me I was too inquisitive for my own good, and that the scrapes I got myself into were nearly always my own fault.

Feeling my way around the room, I found the coat I was looking for folded up on a low chair by the window-seat.

"I'd better leave Lash here," I said, "because I want to be quiet. Sorry, boy, but I can't have you giving me away. Nick will look after you."

"No. No, wait." Nick had slid off the bed and was looking for some clothes to pull on. He was in too much of a hurry to go back to his own room for his own things. "I don't know what you think we're going to see," he muttered, "but I'll come with you."

I opened a cupboard and pulled out an old pair of boots for him.

"My breeches are over there," I said, "and my other coat."

"Sometimes I think it's a miracle you're still alive, Mog," he grumbled.

We left Lash in my room, locking the door behind us; and tiptoed down the stone stairs in the darkness. By the time we emerged into the courtyard Bonefinger had disappeared, of course, and we had more or less to guess where he'd gone; though I'd seen him striding with some determination under the courtyard gate and out in the direction of the walled garden and the lake. It was cold, and we quickly realised that neither of us had really put on enough clothes for scurrying around in the dark and the howling wind. We moved fast, and close together.

As we got a little further down the track between massive beech trees which led to the lake, the wind blew a cloud clear of the moon and lit up a long straight stretch of the path – and there he was, far ahead of us, still moving quickly, though without the urgency of someone who feared being followed. We often used to imitate Bonefinger's affected gait, to amuse ourselves. Half walking, half dancing, he placed one foot before the other with a mincing precision which he probably thought made him seem more genteel. But now, out in the blustery night, with no one around to impress, the prancing was replaced by a kind of purposeful stalk. We hurried to close the gap a little, while taking care to stay some distance behind in case he should turn around unexpectedly. But he never looked back once, until, a few minutes later, he arrived at the top of an avenue of yew trees which led down towards the walled garden. Here he paused, and began to look around.

Just twenty yards or so behind him now, Nick and I pressed ourselves into the hedge without a word. The coats we'd pulled on were hopelessly insufficient to shield us against the prickly undergrowth, and the tentacles of brambles snagged themselves around my bare calves, drawing blood. I swore under my breath. Maybe this hadn't been such a great idea.

"Ssssh," hissed Nick shortly.

Among the varied things Nick had done as a kid in London was a good deal of thieving, and spying, over many years; and his instinct for remaining unseen and unheard was still acute. Even though he hadn't wanted to come out tonight, he was now fully alert, and his hand was clasped around my upper arm as if to stop me doing anything foolish. We suffered the blackberry wounds in silence, and watched.

Bonefinger was deliberating, moving slowly between the yews with his eyes on the ground. He kept running the toe of his boot over the earth, as though testing whether it was firm or soft. He stopped. Briefly, he looked around him in every direction. And then he began to dig. Down here near the wall of the garden there was more shelter, and the noise of the wind wasn't nearly so great. We could hear the slice and suck of each stroke of the spade, as he dug deep into the wet earth. He kept digging, without pausing, for several minutes; then he stood up to exhale noisily and stretch his back; and then he was bent again, digging more, slinging the soil away to his right, moving slowly around to create a hole of the size and shape he needed. He was an old man, but he certainly didn't lack stamina. Catching a glimpse of Nick's breathless, moonlit face beside me, I could see he was as transfixed as I was by Bonefinger's determined, unflagging work rate.

After a while I was so cold I'd lost all contact with my feet, and had moved so close to Nick I was more or less enveloped in his coat as well as my own. Occasionally Nick's fingers found a ripe blackberry on the brambles around us, and he'd lift it in his cupped hand to my lips in the dark. We'd rather lost track of time, but we must have stood there for the best part of an hour, freezing, saying nothing, sustaining ourselves only by letting the occasional fat blackberry melt on our tongues. At last Bonefinger seemed satisfied with what he'd done, stopped digging, and began walking around the hole, surveying it in the moonlight, making sure it was deep and long enough. Despite our distance from him, we worked out from his movements that he'd created quite a narrow trench, probably about six feet long and quite deep enough for his spade to disappear into it right up to the handle. He rested, now, looking around, enjoying the chance just to stand there, and stretch his old muscles, and listen. We were sure we were well hidden; but still we didn't dare breathe.

Finally he stabbed the point of his spade into the soil so it stood up on its own, and moved off into the shadows to his left. I felt Nick's grip tightening on my arm: a signal not to move just yet. Bonefinger could easily be coming back towards us, or passing very close to our hedge on the other side. The slightest rustle, or whisper, might make him suspicious. Only when he'd been gone for three or four minutes did we dare move, disentangling ourselves cautiously from the painful brambles.

And almost immediately we had to dive back into them; because we could hear him now, coming back through the undergrowth. At least – we thought it must be him, though there was something different about the sound this time. It was more of a slow slithering, like something being dragged. As we listened, and it came closer, I felt the hairs on the back of my neck standing up. I don't like this, I wanted to say to Nick, let's run. But I kept my mouth shut.

And, suddenly, there he was, emerging into the patch of moonlight by the yew tree where he had been digging. And he *was* dragging something. Something huge.

He stood up, holding his back, breathing heavily, for about a minute. And then he bent down to lift one end of the big bundle again. It appeared to be wrapped in cloth or old rags, but it was heavy enough to make him grunt as he staggered with it towards the trench. We craned our necks from our prickly hiding place: what on earth *was* it?

And then – as he dragged it fully into view, and we saw its shape, and how heavy and limp it was, and how it bent roughly in the middle as he struggled with it – Nick's grip on my arm tightened so much he was surely leaving fingermarks in my skin, and my heart came up into my throat and I nearly cried out in panic.

Bonefinger was burying a corpse.

He rolled it into the trench with his foot, and then picked up the spade and seemed to use it to manoeuvre the horrible heavy thing into place, down in the grave. Grunting with the effort, he manhandled it to his satisfaction so that it was eventually completely within the trench; and now he began to pile the soil back on top. He moved the loose earth quickly, efficiently, scooping it back over the rag-covered body, his breath coming heavily as he worked. He was tired now. He used the side of his boot to shift mounds of soil back over the grave, and scraped at the surface with the spade to smooth it all over. He walked back and forth on top of it to press it all down; then he covered his bootmarks with more soil, more spadework. I was so tired I was beginning to wonder if I was hallucinating; any minute now I might find I was actually standing here completely alone, or else I'd wake up in my bed just as I had a couple of hours ago after the orphanage nightmare. But no – Nick was here, warm against my aching back; Bonefinger was here, prowling now around the site of his night's work; the grave was almost completely covered up, and it was all over.

This time he didn't carry the spade; he dragged it, its blade trailing in the soil and the long grass, all the way back to the castle. And we followed him, numb with cold and horror, at a greater and safer distance than before.

The routines of Kniveacres Hall were ageless, and irreversible. Depending on what day of the week it was, the same things happened at the same time every day, and had been doing so for centuries. Everyone knew what was supposed to happen, and when; and everyone's actions were completely determined by the convention. Suggesting things should be done differently, just for once, just for a day, was as unthinkable as suggesting that the sun shouldn't come up, or that a mighty river should stop flowing towards the sea and start receding towards the hills, for a change.

So, our breakfast of poached eggs, left to go cold on a silver serving-plate, and a dish of almost-solid porridge under a kind of glassy skin, was there, waiting for us, at half-past six, even though it was barely daylight. We had only been back in bed for about two hours before it was time to get up. And Bonefinger was there too, moving silently about the house as usual, for all the world as though this was just any other morning and he hadn't been out by the yew-tree avenue half the night, burying someone.

Nick put his knife down on his plate with a slight clatter, and suddenly the old servant was at his elbow, as if he'd descended from the ceiling or melted out of a wall.

Of course, we didn't dare say a word to anyone about the night's adventure, but I couldn't resist glancing down at

Bonefinger's boots and leggings, as though he might have been so careless as to walk about in the same mud-streaked clothes he'd been wearing in the middle of the night. He hadn't, of course. He was as pristine and servile as ever; and his inscrutable, reptilian face betrayed no mark of exhaustion, discomfort, nervousness, or any other expression which might have hinted at the effort he'd expended in his grisly night's work. After he'd lifted our greasy breakfast plates onto the oak sideboard, he returned to stand by the table, and cleared his throat with three or four short, exaggeratedly polite coughs, as he always did when he was about to speak to us.

"Sir Septimus," he ventured, "wishes to see you both this morning, at eight."

I shot Nick a glance. He was looking studiedly at Bonefinger, avoiding my gaze for fear of giving something away.

"Have we done something wrong?" Nick asked him.

Bonefinger's face showed no surprise at the question, but offered no reassurance. "I am not privileged to have been made a party to the matter of Sir Septimus's request, Master Nick," his mouth said.

For the next hour, various uncomfortable possibilities crossed our minds as we returned to our rooms and prepared ourselves. Sir Septimus Wellynghame Cloy was a man every bit as pompous and tedious as his name. Ever since we had arrived, he had avoided us as much as he possibly could. His wife had died seven years ago, and they had never had children themselves, so he had little idea of how to speak to us, let alone look after us or behave with affection towards us. He had spent most of his life, and made a lot of money, out in India. No one ever said quite what it was he and his family did there in order to make their fortune; but whatever else Sir Septimus had been in India, he had been a collector. The house was piled high with objects and trophies he'd brought back: the stuffed and mounted heads of creatures he had shot; beautiful soapstone statues of tranquil-faced gods; delicately-carved Indian boxes and furniture, and ornate silk quilts which retained an exotic, slightly spicy smell. The big library and the sitting-rooms were decked out with oriental wall-coverings and richly-coloured rugs; and filled with countless ornaments, like ivory elephants and sandalwood tigers and brass camels.

But, being the seventh son – which was what the name Septimus meant – he had lived in the shadow of his elder siblings, all of them brothers, who had all been more important than he. Now that he was in his seventies, and widowed, he had returned to England to occupy this sprawling, ill-maintained family pile, which he seemed to do resentfully and with little residual enjoyment of life. His wife had been our mother's father's cousin – a bit like a great-aunt, though of course we had never met her – and a more approachable man might have found it in himself to let us call him "Uncle", now that we'd been discovered in the chaotic streets of London and brought into his care in the dusty twilight of his life. But Sir Septimus was not an approachable man, and "Sir Septimus" was all we were permitted to call him. The last thing he had expected, in his final, quiet, settled years in the country, was that two long-lost orphan children would be foisted upon him out of the blue. He didn't ask to see us regularly and, whenever he had done so, it had always been a bit uncomfortable, like going before a magistrate.

I felt sure this morning's summons was going to turn out to have something to do with the events of last night. Perhaps he'd seen us sneaking out, or sneaking back in. Perhaps Bonefinger had noticed us after all, and had complained about us following him, even though we believed we'd remained completely hidden. Or perhaps a gamekeeper, or a villager, had complained about Lash catching birds or rabbits. The sudden thought that it might be Lash who was in trouble, rather than the two of us, made me more nervous than ever.

So when Bonefinger escorted us up the echoing stairs of the central tower and into Sir Septimus's presence, my heart was pounding in my chest. We never entered the tower, or the rooms behind it, unless we were summoned by Sir Septimus to do so. They were his domain, and out of bounds to us; and they were dark, and chilly, and unwelcoming, like our uncle himself.

He was sitting at his desk in the wide window of his study, with the pale light of the autumn morning behind him. Standing to his right was Melibee, dressed completely in black as usual, like a silent raven. For the first few moments Sir Septimus didn't look up, pretending to be absorbed in a heavy ledger which was open on the desk in front of him. As we drew closer to the table he closed the book with a thud which sent a cloud of dust billowing into the air around him, and raised his heavy-lidded eyes in our direction for the first time.

"In observance of your request, Sir Septimus," pronounced Bonefinger obsequiously, "I have brought Miss Imogen, and Master Dominic, to see you."

Sir Septimus was about to say something in response, but Melibee suddenly began to cough as the dust reached his throat.

Sir Septimus sat waiting for silence; but Melibee's cough was proving persistent, and every time Sir Septimus opened his mouth to speak, there was another sudden outburst of spluttering from behind him.

"Sorry, Sir Septimus, sorry," croaked Melibee, holding his fist to his lips.

Sir Septimus paused for another few seconds, in case Melibee should cough again; but he seemed to have finished. Our relative glanced briefly from one to another of us, and then to Bonefinger, who was standing between us.

"Thank youm, Bonefingermmm," he murmured, with his habit of hardly opening his mouth when he spoke. And, with a curious gesture like an animal tamer giving a signal to the beasts in his charge, he gave two short sideways flicks of his forefingers, and both servants moved wordlessly away, and out of the room.

There was a resonating silence before Sir Septimus spoke. I wanted to cough too, but I fought to stop myself. Eventually he opened his mouth.

"Miss Imogennnn," he groaned, "and Master Dominic." It might have been my imagination, but whenever he pronounced my full name – which he always did, never once calling me Mog, or Nick Nick for that matter – he seemed to do so with a slight wince, as though the very name were somehow painful to him. "Bonefinger may have hinted, mat the reason behind my calling for youm."

It took us a few seconds to realise it was supposed to be a question. Nick was quicker than I was.

"No, Sir Septimus," he replied. "In fact," he added pointedly, "Bonefinger said he didn't know."

"Nonetheless," Sir Septimus continued, ignoring the dig at his servant's honesty, "I expect you have an ideam."

This was a question too.

"No, sir," Nick said. Sir Septimus glanced at me. I shook my head.

Sir Septimus opened his mouth again, but seemed to deliberate for a long time before finally deciding how to frame the words.

"Last eveninggg," he said – and my heart leaped into my throat – "mafter this study was closed up, and I had retired, mmm, someone came in here." He was watching our faces carefully. "My know this," he continued, "because some papers, mmm, and other itemmms, were . . . disturbed."

I could sense that Nick was about to speak: and suddenly I desperately wished we'd agreed our story in advance. I prayed he wasn't going to let on that we'd seen Bonefinger prowling around in the middle of the night. Something told me it would get us into far more trouble than if we said nothing.

"Does either of youm, know anything about how these things came to be, mmmmoved around?"

"Certainly not," said Nick. "We took our supper as usual, and went to bed, and slept all night long. We're not allowed in the tower, Sir Septimus. We didn't come anywhere near it last night, did we, Mog?"

I needn't have worried, and I almost sighed with relief as I said, "No. Not once. Not even anywhere close. At all."

He was looking at us through half-closed eyes; his eyebrows were so heavy, and the skin of his face so grey and weary, that fully opening his eyes always seemed to cause him as much unwelcome effort as fully opening his mouth.

"My need to know," he went on, "whether you saw anything, that might have seemed odd . . . or anyone in the house or the grounds with whom you were, munfamiliarm."

"Not at all," replied Nick earnestly, looking straight at Sir Septimus. "Has anything been damaged, sir? Or – taken?" I couldn't resist a tiny smile of admiration. If nothing else, growing up among the criminals of London had made Nick a brilliant liar.

"My don't believe anything to be . . . damaged," said Sir Septimus slowly, "but you might take a look at this." He moved the ledger in front of him aside, and pushed an open book across the desk. It was an ancient and dilapidated old volume with a gilt binding, and it was open at a page filled with dense and tiny lettering. Nick and I craned our necks to look at it. It was like a Bible, with the text in two columns; the paper extremely thin in order to fit a huge number of pages into the book. Much of it seemed to be in foreign languages; but as we looked more closely, we could see a passage which had been underscored in dark brown ink.

"I can't see what it says," I said.

Wordlessly, Sir Septimus moved it closer to us. Now the tiny print became clearer; but, although we could now read it, we couldn't really make much sense of it.

Of this be sure, it read, *that the Master of Kniveacres shall be cut off at threescore ten and seven, and that this shall come when the Devil resides here.*

"Is it a riddle?" Nick asked.

"It's like something – mystical," I said. "Like, witchcraft, or something."

"Witchcraft," muttered Sir Septimus through clenched teeth. "Mmmmm . . . witchcraft."

Nick was trying to see what the book was. "It looks very old," he said. "Is it a kind of prophecy?"

Sir Septimus couldn't bring himself to say any more; he was staring at us, trying, I suppose, to gauge our reaction to what we saw.

"What's that?" Nick asked, pointing at a long parchment envelope on the desk next to the old book, with two bright red ribbons trailing from its edges, which must have been used to tie it closed.

Sir Septimus lifted it from the desk. "This was left here, toom," he growled. Inside the envelope was a sheet of paper, crisp and creamy in texture, which he slid out onto the table. Both the envelope and the paper had something written on them, in small untidy characters, in the same red-brown ink that had been used to underline the words in the book.

"This paper is not . . . my take it . . . familiar to youm."

He should have been able to see from our expressions that it wasn't. But the writing on it was. As he pushed it over the desk towards us, I felt my skin prickle, with a mixture of excitement and horror. I was so amazed I couldn't move, or speak. I think my mouth may have dropped open.

The envelope simply read, SIR SEPTIMUS CLOY, in a shaky hand. But the paper inside bore a line of characters far more remarkable, far more astonishing than anything either of us could have imagined. A small row of letters in a foreign language, written so as to hang down under the line instead of standing up above it.

इम्यता

Whether Sir Septimus thought it odd that we were so utterly dumbstruck by the writing, I don't know: but we were, both of us. And it was because we had both seen this before, several times; and it was etched on our souls, as almost no other word, in any language, could be.

The silence was overwhelming, enveloping. I suddenly felt tremendously light-headed. It was as though the whole room, the pieces of paper, Sir Septimus himself, his desk and his chair, were a figment of my imagination; as though any moment now I would wake up, and find myself in bed again, with Lash nuzzling at my face and Nick bringing me to my senses, telling me off for disturbing him. It seemed like a lifetime before the silence was finally broken.

"Do youm . . . know what this says?" Sir Septimus ventured, at last, pulling the sheet of paper back towards him and folding it up again.

We simply stared at him, unable to speak.

"It says 'Damyata'," he said. "It's the name of someone I never thought I would hear of, nor wanted to hear of, again. And nowm," he continued, his voice becoming more animated and angry than either of us had ever heard it, "now that *you two* are in my house, mmmm here it is, left in my study in the night, mand *you two* denying it was you who left it. Well then, who did? Mmmm? *Who did?*"

He hadn't raised his voice from its usual murmur, but there was a guttural edge to it now, and he was trembling. He had worked himself up into a quiet, quaking rage. Nick and I just stood there, looking at him; it was hard to know what was more astonishing, the fact of seeing the letters spelling Damyata's name, or the violence of the reaction they had provoked in Sir Septimus.

After a few moments Nick piped up: "We're telling the truth, Sir Septimus. It wasn't us."

"It wasn't!" I joined in, shaking my head.

The fire of rage in his eyes died to a kind of steely shine, and he became calmer. He sank back in his chair, and regarded us fixedly as we stood before him.

"You won't confess," he murmured. "My never expected, mmmm that you would." He leaned forward again. "But I don't appreciate pranks like this," he said, "and you will learn it."

He didn't appear to have given any signal, and yet we were suddenly aware that Melibee and Bonefinger were both hovering a few feet behind us, one to either side. Sir Septimus looked up and nodded shortly, as if to signal that he had finished with us, and we found ourselves escorted from the study by Melibee, the tips of his fingers making light contact with our shoulder-blades to usher us gently out.

Bonefinger remained behind.

For several minutes, we simply couldn't speak. Melibee led us wordlessly through the passageways behind the tower, and out into the first-floor corridor of the east wing which led to our rooms. Melibee was a much milder soul than Bonefinger, slightly older to judge from his appearance and his movements, and inclined to treat us better than almost any of the other servants in the house. He was all but completely blind, and found his way among the rooms and corridors of the castle by touch and by habit. He could move quickly, but at intervals he would reach out his spread fingers to reassure himself that the landmarks of the house, by which he found his way around, were where he expected them to be. Occasionally we had fun at his expense, but we had found that his hearing, and perhaps his sense of smell too, were so acute that he was usually remarkably well aware of his surroundings, and it was hard to fool him. Nick had a habit of referring to him as "Melibeem", because of the way Sir Septimus pronounced his name.

An immense and magnificent stuffed tiger crouched against the wall of the passageway, its bony haunches up, its head down, its forelimbs stretched out before it, its lips pulled back by the taxidermist into an eternal, but eternally impotent, snarl. Here, after his outstretched hand made gentle contact with the coarse fur of the tiger's spine, Melibee stopped, and asked us gently if we were quite well enough for him to leave us alone. We found some breath with which to utter a brief word of thanks to him, and, with a polite nod, he melted back into the passage to the tower, to attend Sir Septimus again.

"Were we dreaming?" were Nick's first words. "You are here, aren't you? This *is* actually happening?"

I was thinking exactly the same thing. In that study, with the sunlight behind Sir Septimus, and those extraordinary pieces of paper suddenly appearing, and his rising but strangely contained anger, there had been an air of unreality, even of something otherworldly. But this corridor was cold, and I could touch Nick's hand, and I could run my fingers up the rigid lifeless back of the tiger; and we had both been in there, and heard and seen the same things, incredible though they were.

Damyata. It meant nothing, in English at least; and the curly little characters would have been dismissed by most people as insignificant. But Sir Septimus knew what they meant, as did we – and Sir Septimus *knew* that we knew.

"Where did it come from?" I asked. I was trembling.

"I don't know."

"Did Bonefinger put it there? Is that what he was doing in the study last night?"

"If it *was* Bonefinger," said Nick quietly. "You didn't actually see who was in there, did you?"

"No, but if – if it wasn't Bonefinger . . ."

Last summer, someone called Damyata had appeared in London, apparently on a ship from Calcutta, and had spent many days following and trying to make contact with us. We had never met him properly, or spoken to him; but he had left strange little notes for us, too, and we had become gradually more certain that he must have something important to tell us. When I met Nick, and we began to realise that we were brother and sister, he showed me something belonging to our mother which he had kept among his possessions for the whole of his life. It was the last page of a letter she had written, just after we were born, in which she begged an unnamed friend to look after us once she was dead, and to ensure that we were provided for. And she, too, had mentioned the name Damyata, in the letter.

Nick and I had talked about Damyata many times since we'd met. Almost everything about him seemed utterly mysterious. We didn't know for certain who he was, or why he had been trying to reach us; where he had come from, or where he had gone; we couldn't even be sure whether he was alive or dead, and it sometimes seemed possible he had never actually existed at all. Everything about him seemed to be surrounded with a kind of magic, designed to bewilder and mystify us and everyone else who came into contact with him. But he meant something to our mother, and we knew instinctively that he must somehow mean something to us.

"I never believed he was dead," I said, "did you?"

Nick said nothing. We hadn't heard of him since we'd left London last winter, and I suppose we had both quietly decided we never would. But now, here was his name, on a letter plainly addressed to Sir Septimus Cloy, which had apparently been placed on his desk in the middle of the night. No message, no explanation; just the letters of his name, in the middle of a sheet of paper, folded twice, and tied inside an envelope – and two lines in an old book of gobbledegook, underlined and left open.

"What does it *mean*, Nick?" I said.

Nick shrugged. "Maybe it means," he said, "that Damyata's back."

CHAPTER 2
RIDDLES

"Stop yawning, Imogen, and concentrate," snapped Miss Thynne. "And stop *scratching*."

"Sorry," I said, drawing my hand up quickly from my ankle. The lacerations the brambles had left on my ankle the night before had turned to a crisscross pattern of itchy scars, which it was almost impossible to leave alone. It was the afternoon, and we were sitting at a large table in a corner of the library, where our governess, Miss Thynne, was attending to our geographical education. Sir Septimus hadn't gone to great lengths to care for our physical well-being since we had arrived under his roof, but he had at least engaged a governess who supervised our everyday needs and taught us daily lessons. This had taken some getting used to. Neither Nick nor I had ever been taught lessons, back in London, when I worked six days a week for Mr Cramplock the printer, and Nick worked for the bosun on board ship and in the crowded, smelly docks of the Thames. A year ago, if you could have seen us, you'd have observed two ragged children, black from head to toe most of the time, completely at home in the filthy throng of the

London streets. This life of governesses and panelled libraries was a different one altogether, and to be honest there were times when we simply weren't in the mood to pay attention to Miss Thynne's lessons.

This afternoon, concentrating on her teaching was proving particularly difficult, with the events of last night and the astonishing revelation in Sir Septimus's study constantly whirling in our heads. There were suddenly a hundred questions to which we needed answers, a hundred places we'd rather have been than in this stifling library. Shafts of autumn sunlight were coming in through the mullioned windows and picking up the millions of specks of dust which hung, gently sinking, in the still air of the enormous room. Several times already this afternoon, I'd awoken from a reverie to find I hadn't been paying the slightest attention to anything Miss Thynne had said for about the last five minutes.

She was well-named, we had always thought: a brisk, fragile, well-mannered woman of about forty, very fair in complexion, with fine bones and a pretty face beginning to be pinched by age. She always wore dresses with long sleeves ending in lace cuffs, but sometimes I couldn't help staring at her impossibly thin wrists and wondering at the twig-like arms which the sleeves of her dress must conceal. I couldn't remember ever having touched her, but I was sure that, if I did, it would feel like holding an object made of glass, and I'd have to be careful not to break her. She was polite to us, but not friendly; without malice, but really without a trace of humour either. Nick had immediately pronounced her dull, and now that we had known her for six months or more, he hadn't changed his mind. He spoke of her rather disparagingly, and when she wasn't there he almost always called her "Miss Thing". Maddeningly, though, he found it effortlessly easy to tell her what she wanted to hear, even when he didn't seem to me to be concentrating on the lesson at all; and he often won her praise for doing as he was told. For my part, I couldn't help feeling she was a kind-hearted woman who somehow seemed to have been made very sad by something. But, compared to Nick, I think she found me difficult.

"Madras," she was continuing. "I want you to point out its position on the map." She looked at me expectantly.

"Sorry," I said again, "did you mean me? Sorry."

Lazily, almost without looking, Nick reached over and put the point of his pencil on the large outline of India, which was drawn on a big sheet of paper spread out in front of us.

"Yes," said Miss Thynne rather primly. "Good, Dominic."

"*I knew*," I protested.

"Well, we can't wait all day for you," she countered. "I don't know what you've been doing, Imogen, but you quite plainly haven't had enough sleep. I shall be making special arrangements to send you to bed long before suppertime this evening." She reached for something on the chair beside her, and a quizzical expression crossed her face. "Have you moved my bag?" she asked; we both stared at her, blankly, by way of denial. She stood up. "I've left something in my room, which I must retrieve," she said. "Excuse me for a minute. Please mark the other large towns on the map while I am gone."

"Creep," I hissed at Nick after the door had closed behind her.

"You make it too obvious," he shrugged. "She wasn't asking you to do anything difficult."

"She was asking me to stay awake," I said grumpily, "and I'm finding that hard in here, with all this dust drifting about."

"Listen," said Nick, "I'm going to try and find out what she knows about Sir Septimus in India. We might be able to get something out of her about Damyata. She'll just think we're showing an interest in the lesson."

"Or that we're being too nosy," I countered. "If we ask too many questions it's bound to get back to Sir Septimus."

"He can hardly expect us *not* to ask questions, after this morning," grunted Nick. He could see I was sceptical about involving Miss Thynne. "Well look, I'll do the talking," he said. "I won't give too much away."

I knew he wouldn't; and I *was* dying to know more about Sir Septimus's past. Something he had said this morning – about Damyata being a name he never wanted to hear again – had intrigued us both. What had his involvement been with Damyata? Had they been enemies, and was that why Damyata had returned – if indeed he had – to settle some old score?

Miss Thynne was back in the room in no time, and was a little disapproving to find we hadn't carried out the task she had instructed us to. For a few minutes we applied ourselves quietly to the map, marking the positions of India's seaports and cities, while Miss Thynne walked about nearby looking at the spines of books.

"Have *you* been to India, Miss Thynne?" asked Nick, at length, still looking down at the marks his pen was making. I watched his face, trying to guess what he was going to ask next.

Miss Thynne turned. She looked a little surprised by the question, and I could have sworn her face went slightly pink; but after a brief hesitation she said, "Yes. Yes, I have."

"Have you been to Madras?" asked Nick.

"N-no," she said, still hesitant. She wasn't used to talking about herself – at least, not to us. I couldn't remember ever having had a conversation with her before about where she had been, or anything that had happened to her.

"Have you been to Calcutta?" he asked. I tried to suppress a smile and lowered my head to look at the map. Nick sounded completely innocent, the very model of a curious pupil.

"Yes," she replied. "I – I lived in Calcutta, for many years, and had my first job as a governess there, as it happens."

"Was that where you met Sir Septimus?" Nick asked.

She came back to stand by the table. She was beginning to recover her composure. "I think we should get on with the lesson, Dominic, and not be asking so many questions," she said. But then she must have thought her obstruction of his question a little unfair, because she added: "Sir Septimus employed me here because of a – a family connection. Now – perhaps you'd like to trace in the principal rivers."

We were both intrigued, and I could tell Nick was itching to ask her more; but we did as we were told for a few more minutes, and made some blue lines on the drawing, and I did some more scratching under the table. Eventually Nick could contain himself no longer.

"Do you know much about Sir Septimus's time in India, then, Miss Thynne?" he asked. "Was he there for most of his life?"

Miss Thynne was about to tell Nick not to ask so many questions again, when it must have occurred to her that feeding our curiosity might be a useful way of making some of our geography lesson mean something.

"I – believe he was," she said. "Although I don't know much about his family, I know that his father, and he and his brothers – especially some of his older brothers – were very important in India."

"Are they dead now, then? His brothers, I mean?" I asked.

"All six of them are, I understand," she said. "But the whole family has involved itself in the government of the country, and been highly respected. He is too advanced in years, now, to play any further useful role there himself."

"So he was in Calcutta for a lot of years, was he?" I thought about this for a while as I sat, absently making wavy marks around the edge of the map in the spaces which denoted the ocean.

"In the East India Company," Miss Thynne elaborated. "The marks of his position and the souvenirs of his life are all around, in this house, are they not?"

I was looking directly at Nick, rather than at Miss Thynne, as I asked the question I knew had been nagging at us both since this morning's interview with Sir Septimus.

"So, while he lived in Calcutta," I said, slowly, "did he know our mother Imogen?"

There was a sudden quiet, dry cough, and we all looked up. Bonefinger was standing there, dressed completely in black as usual. None of us had heard him come in. He coughed again, to signal that he was about to speak. And then he bowed.

Bonefinger's bow was surely one of the strangest mannerisms a human being ever exhibited: slow and obsequious, it involved not merely bending his head or the upper half of his body, but twisting himself into a posture which was almost impossible to sustain for more than a couple of seconds. It was as though he were a louse curling up, or a creature undergoing some sort of metamorphosis before standing up again. Nick had tried to imitate Bonefinger's bow on a couple of occasions, and both times he'd fallen over. The man must have been double-jointed.

"Miss Thynne," he said, standing up. "I am instructed to convey the news that Sir Septimus wishes your attendance upon him. He has certain – matters to discuss." It might have been my imagination, but I fancied that his gaze flicked momentarily towards both Nick and myself before he finished this latter sentence.

Miss Thynne went slightly red once again; and as she stood up, with her fingertips lightly touching the table, I could see that her hand was trembling.

"Excuse me, Imogen and Dominic," she said, quietly, and then cleared her throat. "We'll continue this tomorrow," she said, and moved towards the door, Bonefinger following her out of the room with his hint of a prance.

"What was all *that* about?" Nick asked in a low voice.

"I know – and she was nervous. Did you see? She was trembling."

"Sir Septimus is *furious* with us," Nick said, "and Miss Thing's supposed to make sure we don't get up to mischief. She's going to be in trouble."

I was very much afraid he was right.

"Bonefinger's timing's perfect, isn't it?" I observed. "We were just getting to the interesting bit."

"I know. He'd probably been listening for ages. Infuriating man!"

We got up from the table and stretched.

"Ohhhh, I'm exhausted," admitted Nick, yawning.

We left the maps and pencils laid out on the table, and I went to look out of the window, out onto the garden. There was no one to be seen outside; but the late afternoon sun was catching the oaks and horse chestnuts in the parkland beyond the garden and making their yellowing leaves shine like gold. I suddenly felt weary, and longed to be outside, to get some fresh air after the stuffiness of the library and the tedium of Miss Thynne's lesson.

"I'm going outside," I said. "There's more than an hour before tea. Miss Thing's not coming back this afternoon, is she? Too busy being told off by Sir Septimus for letting us run loose. Are you coming?"

If we were pleased to be outside and to feel the autumn air on our faces, Lash was ecstatic; he leaped around us, yelping, as we ran on the grass. Lash had been a city dog all his life, as much at home among the stink and bustle of London as the pair of us; but he had adapted to life in the country with apparent euphoria, barely able to contain his excitement at the new world of smells and games and open spaces afforded by the fields and woods and streams and wild animals. There was no one else around this afternoon as we played, but I couldn't help glancing up at the windows of the house from time to time. Once or twice I thought I could see a figure watching us from a window in the upper storey of the east wing, but when I looked up again, there was no sign of anyone. In any case, we had learned that we could never assume we weren't being watched. At Kniveacres there seemed to be eyes everywhere.

Our game of chase took us down the path towards the lake; and it wasn't long before Lash was sniffing at the ground, and running along in a sort of zigzag trajectory. At one point, he went over to investigate some bits of straw which were stuck in the tall grass and nettles at the edge of the path. He'd probably picked up a scent trail from last night. I called him; he stopped, and looked back at me briefly, then put his nose back to the ground and carried on, getting further and further ahead. I knew he was heading for the yew-tree avenue.

"Look where Lash is going," I said.

"Don't you want to go and have a look?" asked Nick.

"I don't know – I'm a bit scared of being seen."

"It doesn't look suspicious," Nick said confidently. "We're just out for a walk . . . aren't we?"

Nevertheless, my heart was beating fast by the time we got to the top of the row of yew trees, and the night's events came flooding back; all of a sudden, I could even taste the blackberries.

Lash was running between the trees, and within a few seconds he had homed in on a patch of ground behind one of them, close to the garden wall.

"Uh-oh," said Nick, as Lash began pawing the ground. "Don't let him dig it up."

We caught up with him; and, sure enough, it was the very place we'd seen Bonefinger digging last night. If you looked carefully you could see a large trench-shaped patch in the grass where the turf was uneven and freshly replaced. The ground was flat, but the way he'd stamped the turf down was quite crude and there were several deep heel-marks in the soil. I pulled Lash away – with some difficulty, because every time I tried he turned his head back determinedly to the disturbed patch of ground. I fixed his rope to his collar and held it short so he could no longer reach. He whimpered, and strained at the rope a time or two before giving in.

Nick was walking around the nearest yew tree, surveying the ground.

"It's not a bad job, is it?" he said. "It won't be many days before the weeds grow back and cover it up completely. Then you'd never know." Bonefinger had almost certainly assumed no one would pass by this obscure corner of the estate until all the evidence was covered up.

On his leash, Lash was sniffing at another patch of ground. Nick watched him thoughtfully.

"When he went to get the – whatever it was," Nick said, "he went this way, didn't he?"

"Yes," I said, remembering how Bonefinger had disappeared for several minutes before returning, dragging the awful bundle.

"Lash can probably smell his tracks," Nick said. "Why don't you let him off, and see where he goes?"

Nick was quite right. Lash picked up the scent leading away from the hole and, with his nose to the ground, he trotted into the thick woods around the far corner of the garden wall. As we followed him we could see occasional heavy boot-marks, similar to the ones around the patch of dug turf. Nick knelt down to look at them.

"You can see them well here," he said. "Look – they go in both directions. The earth must be especially soft here."

"They're very clear coming this way," I said.

Nick looked up at me. "Well, you know why that is." I looked at him blankly. "Because," he said patiently, "when he came back he was carrying something heavy. So his feet sank further in."

As Nick spoke, there was a sound from somewhere among the trees. I turned my head to listen.

"Did you hear that?"

"What?"

I couldn't hear it now. "It's probably nothing – I thought I heard something, a sort of tinkling."

"Maybe it was Lash. Where did he go?"

There was no sign of him. This was where the grounds of Kniveacres ended and the woods really began. As we pushed our way between the branches of the trees, we found that the ground fell away, into a kind of crater so thick with undergrowth and bramble thorns it was hard to see how anyone could make their way down there.

"Lash!" I shouted. "Come here!"

There was a rustling, and Lash's nose appeared out of the undergrowth. He had some bits of straw stuck to his whiskers, and I brushed them off as I took hold of his collar again.

"What did you find in there?" I asked him.

"A rabbit hole, I expect," Nick said. He bent down to talk to Lash. "Was it a rabbit you could smell? Or was it a badger?"

"I don't think he'd pick a fight with a badger," I said.

"Not unless he's as daft as he looks," Nick put in.

"Where do the footprints go?" I wondered, looking at the ground around us. As if in answer to my question, Lash began pulling me off to our left, between two tree trunks where the undergrowth seemed a bit less thick. He'd still got a scent in his nostrils, and his tail was flapping with excitement.

"Down here? Steady on then," I said, doing my best to hang on to his leash as I followed him down the steep muddy slope.

And then, suddenly, I felt the ground slipping away beneath me, and my legs were kicking in thin air; Lash's lead slipped from my grasp, and there was an enormous crash and crunch of twigs and branches as I fought and scrabbled at the mud and thorns to find something, anything, to hang on to.

"Owww!" I screeched.

I had come to a stop, but only because my foot was wedged behind a thick tree root. There was the sound of Lash's frantic barking and Nick came slithering down the slope towards me, as quickly as he could.

"Are you all right?"

"I don't know," I said through gritted teeth. I hardly dared speak in case the effort of it made me lose my balance.

"What happened?"

"I don't know."

It felt as though I were clinging to the edge of some kind of precipice, and I could see Nick was worried about coming closer in case he fell too. I tried to look down. Lash was watching from a few feet above my head, whimpering.

"Reach up and get hold of that big stone, just above your head," Nick said. "It's about – no, a bit higher up – well done."

My hands closed around a big rectangular stone embedded in

the ground, and I tugged it tentatively to see if it would bear my weight.

"Can you pull yourself up?" Nick asked. "I don't think I can get any closer without falling in."

I heaved myself upward, shaking my leg to free my ankle from the root; and as I slowly pulled myself out and stood up on the stone, Nick stepped down to join me on the edge, holding my arm to steady me as I stood up.

"That was close," I grumbled, gripping his coat.

For the first time, now, I could see where we were. I'd very nearly fallen down a well. There was a wide circular hole in the ground, dropping away into the darkness, further than the eye could see; and beneath our feet were dead thorny branches and rotten planks of wood which had been placed over the top, and which had completely given way beneath my weight. The stone we were standing on was one of many marking the half-buried rim of the well.

"I never even knew this was here," I said. "Ouch!"

"Have you hurt yourself?"

As I'd slipped down, clutching at the undergrowth, I'd torn big gashes along my forearm on the bramble thorns. Otherwise, I was fine; but if the strong root hadn't broken my fall I'd have plummeted all the way down the well, and one glance into the depths of the chasm told me that would have been the end of me. I reached for a loose stone with my foot, and kicked it down into the darkness; we waited for several seconds before a dull thud told us it had hit the bottom. It seemed likely it was forty, fifty, possibly even sixty feet deep. Gingerly, we helped one another back up the slope; Lash scampered around to meet us at the top, and I got down to hug him. We were both filthy.

From up here, we got a much better view of the well, especially because, as I'd fallen, I'd yanked away all the branches that were previously hiding it.

"It's *really* dangerous," said Nick, gazing down at it. "There should be a good strong cover on there, to stop people falling in." He walked around, frowning, to get a good look from several angles. We could now see that there was actually one very narrow path down to the well, which looked much safer and flatter, approaching from the direction of the woods; but anyone losing their balance on this slope didn't stand a chance.

"I don't suppose it's been used for years," I said. "There are some planks down there, look – but they've just rotted away."

"You've got some bits of them still stuck to you." Nick was inspecting my clothes now, and brushing at them here and there with the back of his hand to knock the mud off.

"Thanks," I said, pushing him away, "but I can do that myself." I shivered. "Let's go back. It must be almost time for tea. And I need to get cleaned up."

Lash ran ahead of us again as we walked, quickly, back to the yew-tree avenue and towards the house. Its ancient roofs, dominated by its central stack of seven chimneys, loomed between the trees as we drew nearer, and it struck me with particular force this afternoon how unfriendly it looked; a forbidding dark slab, etched against the pale gold of the autumn sky.

"Are you all right?" Nick asked again, as we walked.

"I'm fine," I said. "Just a bit shaken."

"You need to clean up those cuts," he said.

"I'll do it as soon as we get back. Do you think we should tell someone about the well? How dangerous it is?"

"I don't," Nick said quietly. He stopped, and looked around him. Ahead of us, the big dark windows of the Hall glared down at us. "I don't think we should say anything," he said. "For one thing, we don't want anyone knowing we were nosing around near the yew-tree walk. And for another . . ." He hesitated.

"What?"

"I don't know," he said. "I've got a feeling that well wasn't just overgrown. That wasn't new growth that was hiding it, it was old dead thorns and branches and planks that looked as if they'd been chucked over it. I think it was deliberately hidden, Mog. As if . . . someone *wanted* us to fall in. Do you know what I mean?"

There was half an hour, as it turned out, before tea; and when I'd rinsed the blood from my stinging cuts, and scrubbed the mud from my face and hands, and changed my clothes, I went to find Nick in the library. He was sitting in one corner of a huge wine-coloured velvet sofa, with sides so high they came up above the head of almost anyone who chose to sit in it; and, because it was positioned with its back to the rest of the room, you could curl up in it and remain completely hidden. We used to spend a great deal of our time hanging around in the library, looking at Sir Septimus's books, or just talking; in a house with very little provision for children, it was by far the most comfortable and interesting room. It ran the entire width of the house, with windows looking out onto the gravelled courtyard and woods at one end, and onto the lawns and park at the other.

Almost every available square inch of wall space was taken up
with bookshelves, except for the occasional gap where there was
a mirror, or a dark and stern portrait of some Cloy ancestor or
other, mounted on the wall. Small stuffed animals stood on the
shelves: a mongoose here, a fierce-looking cat there; and there
were carvings of creatures in the ornate oak supports and lintels
of the bookshelves too – bees and bats and snakes.

Nick had gathered a little pile of books on the sofa beside
him. The one he was looking at when I came in was a great big,
heavy, leather-bound volume, embossed on the front with the
Cloy coat of arms. It was a history of the castle, and of the surrounding area and its buildings; and as he flicked through its
stiff pages I could see it contained a lot of enormous fold-out
maps and plans of the house and its grounds. I sat down on a
tall library stool, looking down at him as he read, occasionally
kicking the side of the sofa with my foot. There were so many
books in here it would have taken us a lifetime to have even a
cursory look at them all, let alone read them; but in the few
months we'd lived here we had found some favourites to which
we returned again and again. Sir Septimus's collection didn't
include a great many books written with children in mind, but
we found plenty to interest us in the heavy tomes full of mythol-
ogy, history, poetry, and descriptions of foreign places –
especially if there were maps or pictures in them.

"This is amazing!" Nick exclaimed. "Look."

I hadn't been taking much notice until I saw him unfolding
the pages so they spread right across his knees and onto the
cushion beside him. I jumped off the stool and went to sit next
to him so I could see the book the right way up.

"*The Kniveacres Estate and its Environs*," read Nick, "*being a Chronicle and Architectural Description of Kniveacres Hall and all associated Buildings.*"

My finger traced the line of Roman numerals below the title, indicating when the book had been printed. "*MDCCXIX*," I read. "Seventeen – er – seventeen hundred and nineteen? Is that right? It's more than a hundred years old then."

"I don't suppose too much has changed since," said Nick, turning over the densely-printed pages. "Look here – there are all sorts of drawings. The ground floor plan . . . the great hall . . . and you can see how it was at all kinds of different dates."

There were, indeed, pages and pages of plates, each with a sheet of thin tissue-like paper to protect it, showing the appearance of the house at various dates; and progressive plans of the layout, beginning in 1350, when it consisted of little more than the great hall and a few anterooms. As we turned over the pages the ground plan expanded, with new rooms apparently being added every century or so, until it took on the shape we knew. It wasn't just the house that was depicted in the minutest detail, but the grounds, the surrounding buildings such as the stables and the summerhouse; even the church, and the buildings of the village.

"Let's have a look at the maps of the grounds," I said, intrigued. "Do you think they'll show the well?"

He gasped. "They must do!"

As Nick leafed through the ancient book, hunting for the right page, some sheets of loose paper slithered out from between the leaves and landed on the floor at my feet.

"Hang on," I said, reaching down to pick them up.

It was actually a paper-bound booklet, little more than a pamphlet, I suppose, about half the size of the big leather book but inscribed with the same Cloy coat of arms on the front page. Its pages seemed thin and fragile, and I opened them gingerly.

"*A Supplement and Addendum to the Chronicle and Architectural Description of Kniveacres Hall and Environs,*" I read aloud, "*taking Account of Alterations made by the present Icumbent* – I think that should say 'Incumbent' – *and New Information not previously made Available to the Compilers.* And look at this!" I jabbed an excited finger at the line of tiny characters along the bottom of the title page. "*Printed by H.H. Cramplock by St John's Gate, Clerkenwell.*"

"Well I never," said Nick, intrigued. "Is that your Mr Cramplock?"

I had spent five years of my life working at Mr Cramplock's printing shop in London, and I was familiar enough with his initials. "He's W.H.," I said. "This was his father, old Mr Cramplock, who started the business."

"Did you ever know him?"

"No, he died years and years ago."

"But we're *miles* from London," said Nick. "I wonder how he came to print a book for the Cloy family, all the way up here?"

"Maybe there aren't many printers around here," I reasoned. "You might have to go as far as London to find someone who could do the job."

Nick inspected the pamphlet. "It's a poor effort compared to this big book here," he said. And he was right: the little booklet was made of cheaper, thinner paper, and seemed more fragile and yellowed with age than the bigger volume, despite not being especially old. The type was rather shakily set in places – and I'd already found a glaring misprint on the first page, which suggested someone had been a bit slapdash with the job in the first place. Maybe it had been given to a previous printer's devil, one of my own predecessors, who wasn't very experienced or careful. Cramplock's had been a busy printing shop, but we concentrated more on posters and handbills and newspapers than on elaborate printed books, and I knew from the Clerkenwell gossip that we were always at the cheaper end of the trade.

"Maybe the Cloys fell on hard times," I guessed. "Once upon a time they could have afforded to get all their books handtooled and bound in leather, but by the time they had this done, they didn't have so much money to throw around."

"It's meant to be read alongside the big book," Nick said, as he studied the pamphlet. "Look here – *Notes to page 48. Notes to ground plan on page 60.* You have to look up the original description each time."

I craned my neck to read the words.

"They seem rather *odd* notes," I said.

Some of the pages in the *Addendum* seemed quite straightforward. There was a large fold-out plan of the house showing all the things that had altered since the original book was printed: rooms whose use had changed, doorways which had been bricked up, walls which had been erected or demolished. There were lists of alterations to the allocation and decoration of servants' quarters, bedrooms and store-rooms described as having been "*ordered by Lady Cloy after 1800*". There was even a whole page showing how the lake had been reshaped. Other entries, however, seemed more like riddles.

"What does this mean, do you think?" I said to Nick. "*Supposing the Sakantala portrait to be 17th century, the frames of this and its neighbour appear to have been transposed. One might look into these.*"

"Then again, one might not," said Nick, laughing. "What about this one: *In this room, you would do well to observe the peacock, as the observe may be true?*"

"The *obverse*," I said. "The *obverse* may be true. It means the opposite, doesn't it?"

"Which peacock?" Nick asked. "Have you seen a peacock in the house?"

I thought hard. There were probably hundreds of animals around the house, either shot and stuffed, or depicted in paintings or tapestries; but neither of us could remember seeing a peacock anywhere. I was starting to think the little book wasn't as interesting as it had appeared at first.

"*Notes to page 66,*" Nick read aloud. "*A further intriguing connection has been latterly discovered between the buildings of the village and the Hall. Seek out the Letherskin grave in the east wall of St Moribunda's church, where the eye will find the secret.*"

He continued flicking through, absorbed.

"So – what about the well?" I asked, suddenly remembering what we'd been looking for before we got distracted.

Nick didn't answer. Something else had caught his eye. "Hang on, look at this," he said. "What do you suppose this means?"

He handed the little book up to me.

"Which bit?" I asked, peering at it.

"There – that line at the bottom of the page, where it's open."

"*For the story behind the hangings,*" I read, "*refer to the first floor plan on pages 168–9.*"

"That sounds a bit spooky, doesn't it?" He reached for the big book again. "You know, Mog – this could be really useful. All those bits of the house we're not allowed near – they're all in here, layouts and descriptions and everything. I bet no one would notice if we kept it for a bit."

"Take it away, you mean?" I asked.

"Just for a while, to give us time to look at it properly. No one will miss it. Sir Septimus barely ever comes in here." He flicked over the pages again. "Now then," he said, "the *well* . . ."

No sooner had he said this than there was a cough from behind us. We both sat up instantly, and our heads popped up above the back of the sofa like rabbits peeping from a warren. Bonefinger again! How long had he been in the room? Had he been standing there listening to every word of our conversation?

"I hesitate to interrupt your studious enquiries," he said, in his pedantic voice. "I am sure Sir Septimus would be encouraged to learn of your – diligence, and initiative. But I am instructed to escort you to tea."

He stood there, silently, waiting for us. His eyes regarded us balefully, without blinking. He could do this for such a long time that I sometimes suspected he didn't have eyelids at all. There was no way we could take the big leather book out of the room now without his noticing. *Curse* the man!

Nick shot me an agonised look, and as he remained seated in the big sofa I stood up and made great play of carrying several smaller books back to the shelf where we'd found them. By the time I'd replaced them, Nick was by my side.

"*If* you would be so good," Bonefinger said mincingly, and extended his thin arm, in a gesture of exaggerated politeness, towards the door.

We went through ahead of him; but when we reached the door of the small dining-room where tea was always laid, we both stood aside to let him go first. And as soon as Bonefinger's back was turned, Nick pulled aside the corner of his waistcoat to give me a brief glimpse of the *Supplement and Addendum to the Chronicle and Architectural Description of Kniveacres Hall and Environs*, which he'd tucked inside it as he left the library.

It felt like a victory; and perhaps Bonefinger wondered, as he watched us, why we kept smiling at one another all through tea.

CHAPTER 3
THE GARGOYLE

When we returned to the library after tea, the big book of plans and maps of the house had disappeared. It was neither on the sofa where we had left it, nor on the shelf where it was supposed to be; and we concluded with a grim inevitability that we were unlikely to see it again. Bonefinger had heard quite enough of our conversation to be aware that we were getting much too curious for his liking. Even having taken the *Addendum* from under his nose turned out to be of limited use; because as we pored over it some more before going to bed, we realised it made little sense, in most places, without being able to refer back to the original maps and descriptions in the big book. Nevertheless, we'd had our warning, and were determined not to let this book out of our possession even for five minutes. Nick took it to bed with him, to make absolutely sure it didn't go missing.

The weather in the night was much calmer, but I still slept terribly, haunted by the pursuit of the night before, by the accident at the edge of the well, and by Damyata's name on the letter. Several times I woke up to what I thought was the sound of sobbing again; but it was very distant, and Lash was curled up at my feet emitting a kind of wheezy snore, so it was impossible to be sure. I got up a couple of times to look out of the window; but tonight there were no lights flickering in Sir Septimus's study, no shadowy figures to be seen in the courtyard. About an hour before dawn, completely exhausted, I finally dropped off, and slept so soundly for the rest of the night that I didn't even hear the breakfast bell, and had to be shaken awake by Nick, who had come in, already fully dressed, to see if I was all right.

Although it was Wednesday, and we were supposed to have lessons morning and afternoon, it turned out that Miss Thynne was not feeling well enough to teach us; so we looked forward with mounting excitement to a full day's exploring in the fresh air. Soon after breakfast, in the damp of the morning, we set off through the castle grounds towards the woods and the track that led to the village.

Lash was off the leash, chasing birds and small creatures which darted away the moment they sensed his approach. He kept running ahead, then stopping and standing still, staring back at us expectantly for a few seconds as though waiting for an instruction, before scampering crazily off again in pursuit of something else. The ground was damp, and when we trod on rotten old pieces of wood that were strewn around the forest floor, they disintegrated with a slight squelch under our feet, rather than cracking noisily as they would if they'd been dry. This was still a new kind of landscape for us, and I don't mind admitting I found it scary sometimes. In the city, where I'd grown up, there may have been people you didn't trust, people who meant you harm, people whose only interest was in selling you something, and people who were, quite frankly, mad; but at least there were *people*. Here, you could spend several hours out of doors and hardly meet a soul. The narrow, crowded streets of London in which I'd been so at home had been replaced by wide open spaces, the only things resembling streets being the muddy tracks which crisscrossed the country several miles apart, often winding among woods in which you could turn around twice and be completely lost, unable to tell one tree from another.

It was a relief when the trees began to thin out and we started to be able to see, between them, the gold stone of the village buildings.

The village, if you could somehow have seen it from high above, would probably have looked a bit like an eye, with a broad oval green in the centre and a slightly crooked, concave arc of low buildings above and below. The church sat at the eastern corner of the eye, with a mill marking the westernmost end. The main road passed through the village – not through the middle of the green, but curving slightly towards the northern side before swinging southward past the church. Roughly in the middle of the northern row of buildings, like a stye on the eyelid of the village, was the old coaching inn, its stables and outbuildings sprawling around it. The wood came close to the village buildings all along the north side, and to the south were fields tended by the tenant farmers of the Kniveacres Estate.

The track through the wood approached the village from the east, taking you through a little iron gate right into the churchyard. Thus, before you encountered any of the village's living

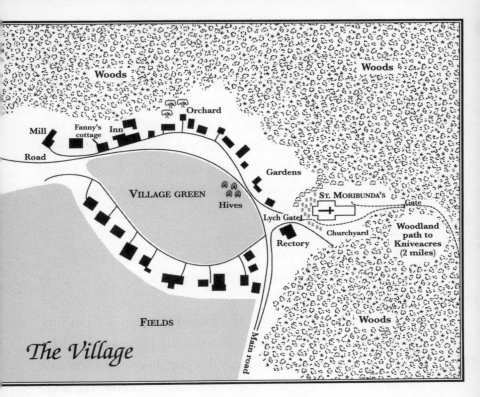

The Village

inhabitants, you had to walk past all its dead ones. Headstones
stood, squeezed close together in the tiny churchyard, in row
after row leading up to the church door. Some of the stones were
so old they were leaning over alarmingly, their engraved names
overgrown with moss and worn away by the weather. Here and
there you could make out a name, or a date: "Elijah Clench",
"Tobias Wodewose", 'Joshua Muchness, also his Beloved Wife
Hepzibah", "Departed this Life the 26th day of January 1681".
As we walked rapidly up the path between the headstones, Nick
put a hand out to hold me back.

"Wait a minute," he said in a whisper.

"What is it?"

"Sssh."

He'd seen a figure ahead of us, near the doorway of the little church. He ducked behind a large, flat gravestone, and pulled me after him.

"Lash," I hissed, "come here!"

The big mossy stone shielded our view of the doorway; but peeping around the edges, we could clearly see someone standing in the porch, deliberating, then reaching out to open the big oak door. It was Bonefinger.

"What's *he* doing here?" I said. "Honestly, wherever we go, he shows up too!"

"He could say the same about us," Nick said.

"He's probably seen us already," I grumbled, "you know what he's like. He'll just think we're following him."

"Which we would never dream of doing," said Nick sarcastically. I was about to say something, but stopped myself and just stuck my tongue out at him instead. "Anyway," he said, peering round the gravestone again, "he's gone inside."

I put Lash on the lead, and we emerged from our hiding place and walked on up the path towards the church. It was a strange, ancient, crooked building, with a very tall stone spire which stood high above the trees and which appeared straight from some directions and weirdly bent from others. Its honey-coloured walls had high stained-glass windows narrowing to sharp points at the top, and rows and rows of carvings of faces, crouching animals, and what looked like trailing plants around the windows and the doorway.

From above the porch, a gargoyle grimaced down at us, shaped like an elongated wolf's head showing its teeth, with a heavy snout, and two sharp stone ridges behind its head which might have been meant to suggest bony canine shoulders or possibly wings like a bat. It was a strangely unwelcoming face to have above the door to a church. Maybe it was designed to make you remember the enemies who lay in wait in the woods outside, and to make you scurry thankfully into the sanctuary of the church and the protection of God.

Nick was about to walk past the door, and carry on up the path to the oak lych-gate which led out onto the village green.

"Don't you want to know what he's up to in there?" I whispered.

He sighed, and shook his head at me slowly, in a gesture half of denial and half of despair.

"All right, hold Lash," I said. "I'll go in on my own."

Carefully, trying not to make a sound, I turned the big iron ring on the door to open the heavy latch. Although the door was huge and ancient, it swung open easily and silently.

It took a few seconds for my eyes to adjust to the low light in the little church; its narrow windows were filled with dark stained glass, so that the sunlight coming through was rather like light filtered through a container of red wine. Seen from the inside, the church was even more peculiar; at first it made you feel a bit dizzy. None of the walls was quite at right-angles to any other, and the ceiling was so high and so dark that, when you looked up, it was almost impossible to see the roof. At the far end of the plain nave, with its rows of dark pews, was a carved oak screen with some short choir-stalls behind it, a threadbare red carpet, and an altar. A few candles flickered on a low table and on tall stands either side of the altar screen, sending an eerie glow up the stone walls and, if anything, making the shadowy corners seem even darker by contrast. I stood still, taking in the scene before me, and listening. It was completely silent. The place was empty. There was nowhere for anyone to hide, except in the tiny vestry to one side, separated off from the nave by a curtain.

I moved quietly across the ancient flagstones, many of which were engraved, like the headstones outside, with the barely-legible names of long-dead villagers, now worn almost smooth by the feet of their descendants, coming in here every week of their lives. Putting my head close to the curtain, I listened; and, after a few moments, tentatively pulled it aside.

The vestry was empty too. There was a low chair, and a small bookcase with a dozen or so copies of a prayer book stacked upon it, and nothing else. A step led down to another small door in the east wall of the church. Had he gone out this way? Why come in at all, just to go out again straight away?

I was relieved that I hadn't encountered Bonefinger; but I still didn't quite believe he wasn't hiding here somewhere – crouched beneath a pew, perhaps, or up above my head – and I continued to move around completely silently, not daring even to cough.

There were sculptures and engravings all around the inside of the church, as well as outside. Little caricatures of monkeys, bears, musicians, craftsmen, acrobats and contortionists topped off every pillar, all of them seeming to watch me from above as I moved around the empty church. On the wall, a few feet above my head, was the Cloy family tombstone.

Here Lie the Mortal Remains, it began,
of BARNABAS EZEKIEL CLOY, and of his Beloved Wife ELIZABETH,
respected Master and Lady of Kniveacres Hall in this Parish.
Also of their Son, LANCELOT ARBUTHNOT CLOY, and of LYDIA JANE,
his cherished Wife who Passed from this Life the 4th day of October 1750 in
deliverance of their Seventh Child.

All of these words were carved out of the stone in the same style, evidently at the time the monument was first erected. Further names had been added down the years, at various intervals; but the stone had been quite small to begin with, and the successive names had had to be chiselled in smaller and smaller letters each time in order to fit them underneath. Above the words was a relief of a man's face, with sad eyes and what appeared to be a tangle of branches or leaves growing around his head like a beard. The branches coiled all around the top of the tombstone, and if you looked closely in the dim light you could see that they disappeared into the corners of his mouth, as though the whole mass of foliage was growing and unfurling from inside him. Behind his head the coils rose in two slender columns, which swelled outward and then tapered again at the tips, arching slightly towards one another. I think they were meant to be orchids; but to me they looked just like the heads of two cobras, flicking their tongues out.

I paced along the pews, looking down each row in case someone was hiding there; but when I reached the back of the church and there was no trace of anyone, I began to be more confident that Bonefinger really wasn't here. I was about to leave when a name on another memorial caught my eye. On the back wall of the church there was another large tombstone, shaped like an open book, with a carved skeleton standing to one side, holding it open and pointing a grim finger at the lettering on the stone pages. This one was mostly in Latin, with abbreviations I didn't fully understand. It began:

IN MEMORIAM
IOHANNVS LETHERSKIN
ob. 12. die Maij AD 1691
Aetat. suae 69

The names of other family members had been added; and below them, engraved in stark black characters right across the bottom of the double-page of the stone book, was what appeared to be a Latin motto.

SCURRA CAELI REX MORTIUM

But it was the name which caught my eye today. Last night, hadn't we read something in the little *Addendum* about seeking out the Letherskin grave to find something secret? Nick had brought it with him, so once I was outside again I'd check to remind myself just what the grave was supposed to show. We'd probably have to decipher all the Latin before it made a scrap of sense.

As I turned from the macabre memorial and started to make my way back towards the door, there was a sudden shout, and an enormous crash from outside, followed by a cacophony of barking from Lash.

"What on earth?" I said to myself, and I flung myself at the door, yanking it open by its big iron ring, and rushed out into the porch.

Nick was standing with his arms outstretched either side of him, staring down at something on the ground near his feet. Lash was still barking.

"What happened?" I asked, running out to him.

He didn't say anything; but he hardly needed to. When I looked down, I saw instantly what had happened. The gargoyle above the door with the snarling wolf's face, had broken completely away from the fabric of the church and come crashing down, a fall of twenty feet or so, missing Nick's head by inches. It lay on its side in the grass; one eye glaring up at us, its pointed nose glistening with mud, having gouged a huge chunk out of the ground where it fell. I hardly dared look up, in case there were any other bits of masonry on their way down after it; but as I stepped well back to gaze up at the spire I could clearly see the empty plinth where the gargoyle had been mounted.

"Were you standing right there?" I asked.

"Right here," said Nick. "We hadn't moved since you went in. There was no warning. I just felt it whistle past my ear."

I stared at the monstrous piece of stone lying on the ground. "It would have killed you if it had hit you," I said, gravely.

"I know."

I pushed it with my foot; but it was so heavy I couldn't move it.

"Are you all right? It didn't catch you at all, as it fell?"

"No. I'd just turned this way, actually, to pull Lash back from the door. If I'd stayed where I was, I'd have been right underneath it."

As we took in the horror of the situation, someone came around the pathway from the other side of the church. It was Bonefinger. When he saw us he increased his pace. Lash gave a low growl; I pulled his rope tighter to make it clear he wasn't to move.

"I heard a cry of alarm," said Bonefinger, coming closer, his gaze flitting from one to the other of us. "Is someone – injured?"

"No, thankfully not," I said, with genuine relief. For a few seconds I was almost – not quite, but almost – glad to see him.

"This gargoyle toppled off the platform up there," said Nick.

"And you were standing beneath?" gasped Bonefinger. "Master Dominic, goodness me, what a fortunate – what a very fortunate – escape, to be sure." He looked up at the empty plinth, and then followed the route down to the gargoyle, as though trying to recreate the incident in his head. "But how very dangerous," he continued. "There is hardly a breath of wind. For the gargoyle to fall in such conditions it must have been very loose indeed. An accident waiting to happen. Goodness me!"

"I hope there are no other loose ones up there," I said, glancing up again at the other animal faces leering out from the ancient stonework.

"I will alert the parish authorities," continued Bonefinger, "and make the strongest case for the fabric of the church to be looked at, as a matter of the utmost urgency. They must ensure there can be no repetition of such an incident. Such a terribly near thing! One can hardly bear to . . . Master Dominic, goodness me. But are you sure you are quite uninjured?"

"It's a miracle," admitted Nick, looking straight at Bonefinger, "but it missed me. Yes."

I nudged Nick to suggest we should move on. For all his

gushing words, it was hard to detect any real sympathy in Bonefinger's response. I didn't want him hanging around us any longer; we had come out to get away from him, after all.

"May I – escort you back to the Hall?" Bonefinger asked, waving a skinny arm in the vague direction from which we'd recently come.

Nick looked at me. "No," he said, "we're all right, thanks. Really. We were just out for a walk. We'll carry on, and make our own way back later."

"As you wish," said Bonefinger politely. "Just so long as you are not too . . . shaken."

"We'll be fine," I assured him; and we left him contorting himself in one of his low bows, and looking after us with his customary opaque expression.

"You know, there's no way that was an accident," Nick said after we had cleared the churchyard and were making our way along the north side of the village green. "Gargoyles don't just fall off the side of a church like that for no reason. What was he doing in there when you went inside?"

"He wasn't there," I said. "The place was completely empty. He must have gone straight out the other door."

"I'm going back to explore, some time," Nick said. "I bet he was up on the platform. I bet *he* pushed that stone."

"Why would he do that?" I asked, genuinely astonished.

"Who knows? But didn't you hear what he said?" He imitated Bonefinger's mincing voice. "'*And you were standing beneath, Master Dominic? Oh goodness me!*' If he wasn't there, how did he know it was just me standing underneath? It might have been both of us, or just you."

I thought about this. He was quite right. Neither of us had told Bonefinger anything about who was standing where when the gargoyle fell.

"Well, maybe he did see you, from a distance," I said. "It doesn't mean he went up there and *pushed* it." We had never exactly hit it off with Bonefinger, and it was true that he had been behaving increasingly strangely in the last few days – but I couldn't seriously bring myself to believe he would deliberately try to injure one of us. "In any case," I said, "how could he have climbed all that way up to the platform without our noticing, and get down again so quickly? It was only a few seconds before he came rushing up to see if we were all right."

Nick grunted. "He didn't seem too concerned," he said. "His mouth may have been saying the right things, but his eyes weren't, as usual."

I fervently hoped he was wrong, but Nick wasn't usually the type to believe the worst of people without good reason, and his suspicions made me feel distinctly uncomfortable. The strange nocturnal burial; Sir Septimus's fury and the reappearance of Damyata's writing; the incident at the well – and now this. There was no logical pattern to it, but *something* strange was going on.

"I wonder if anyone in the village has seen anything?" I said.

I let Lash run off the leash and he trotted over the village green with his nose to the grass, no doubt picking up all kinds of exciting scent trails. There were a few people moving about in the village this morning, working in their gardens or running errands between the cottages, and when they saw us, from a distance, they nearly all stopped what they were doing to watch us.

Since we'd come to live here, we'd made the acquaintance of several of the villagers, and some were more friendly towards us than others. Most of them still regarded us with suspicion, or at the very least with curiosity, and we had become very much accustomed to being stared at. Our belonging to the big house was an obstacle, for some of them; even though many of the villagers earned their living from the Kniveacres Estate, they seemed reluctant to associate themselves too closely with children from the Hall. Also, having come from London, we found them hard to understand; they didn't speak like the people we were used to, and we must have appeared quite stupid to them. Many times they had asked us questions and we simply couldn't reply, or gave some answer so wide of the mark that they laughed in scorn. It was hard to persuade some of them that we weren't just being rude, or superior.

But there was a further reason for their suspicion, and it had taken a few weeks for it to dawn on us. Nick had been the first to put it into words, but it had been nagging away at me too, without my quite realising it. Nick and I *looked* different. Where the villagers' complexions were pale and pasty, our skins were brown, even more so than usual after a summer of running and exploring under the open skies of the country. Our faces were a different shape from theirs, too, somehow sharper and narrower. It had never occurred to us that we were different. Back in London, people came in all shapes and sizes and colours; but here all the children in the village had broad, rather pudgy faces, which grew even broader, like full moons, when they laughed. And the grown-ups' faces, though not all plump, shared a kind of plainness. Nick said they were "like potatoes", which made me laugh – but it wasn't far from the truth. And every time we met them, I noticed it still more, and quickly realised we must have seemed quite unusual, suddenly appearing in their midst, without warning, nearly fully-grown.

We had even heard them gossip about the Devil having black hair and dark skin.

There was a cluster of beehives at the edge of the village green, not too far from the church, and the bees were drowsily drifting to and from the hives in the early autumn sunlight. As we walked past the nearest cottage gate, we saw a man we knew as Mr Greywether, heaving an enormous pumpkin up his garden path. A large, jovial man, with very few teeth – which didn't help when it came to working out what he was talking about – he stopped when he saw us, and nodded in greeting.

"Hello!" called Nick. "What are you doing?"

He put the pumpkin down, and came to the gate to talk to us.

"Fine mornin' to be out," he said. "You two black boys takin' the air?"

A lot of the people here in the country made just the same assumption people in London had made – that Nick and I were both boys. When I worked in the printing shop I used to have to pretend to be a boy, so I could earn a wage – and I spent the whole time terrified of someone finding out I was actually a girl, in case I was thrown out. I suppose it suited me, too, because I'd never been a very girly girl and I felt quite happy doing most of the things that boys did. Now, of course, I didn't have to pretend; but even though I was letting my hair grow a bit, it was no surprise that people who didn't really know us took us for brothers. And, because it was usually too complicated to explain, we still allowed people to believe it.

"What are you doing?" Nick repeated.

"'Sa beauty, that," he replied. He still hadn't got anywhere near answering Nick's question.

"Are you going to cook it?" I asked him.

"Too good to cook," he said, "with the guys coming."

I didn't understand. "You could make lots of soup," I said.

"No," he laughed. "It's the guys. No time to be wastin' the best one of the year, putt'n 'er in a pot, now is it?"

"Has it been a good harvest?" Nick asked, surveying the garden with its neatly-organised squares and rows of vegetables. Mr Greywether laughed. "Not sure I can remember better," he said through his broken teeth. "Turnups size of my 'ead. Cabbages too big to lift. Parsumps!" He went over to a nearby row of tall fern-like foliage, knelt, and eased one of the plants up out of the soft soil with practised fingers. A long white parsnip appeared, surely measuring the best part of a foot from the base of the green shoot down to the spindly point. He brought it to us, brushing the earth off it as he came. "A baby," he grunted. "'Ad parsumps the length o' my arm, just two days past."

"Mr Greywether," I said, "have there been any strangers in the village lately? That you know of?"

"Now there's a question," he said. At first we thought he wasn't going to answer it, because he wandered away, back over to his vegetable patch, and picked up a large fork which was standing up between some beanstalks. But he came back towards the gate, holding the fork. "I 'eard old Fanny Nisbet say sommat," he said.

"Some strangers, or one stranger, don't know what it was she said aright. But you ask old Fanny if you wants to know."

"Thank you very much," I said. "Lash! Lash, come here!"

Fanny Nisbet lived in the next cottage but one, a tiny but well-kept house right beside the inn. A withered, timid soul, she had been kinder to us since we arrived than most of the other villagers, and had quite often foisted biscuits or ripe fruit upon us in abundance when we passed by, believing us both to be too thin, and pronouncing it a "crying shame" that we weren't more wholesomely fed in the castle. Her cottage had no garden at the front, but made up for it at the back, where there was an extensive orchard stretching right back to the edge of the wood. Today, as we went round to the back of her cottage to look for her, we could see no sign of her tiny, nervous form in the garden; but we were greeted at the back door by her son, Lamb.

"Is your mother in?" Nick asked him.

Lamb didn't speak much. He had been born with a hare-lip so that, instead of having a top lip, his mouth and nostrils were parts of a single opening, which permanently exposed his upper row of teeth. Not having lips in the usual way, he wasn't able to speak clearly. We'd been frightened of him at first, because of his appearance; and other people in the village, especially the children, were routinely horrible to him. One of the reasons his mother behaved so nervously was perhaps because she was afraid of what others thought of her for having brought him into the world. But we'd quickly realised he was a gentle creature and quite well suited to his name. It may just have been a pet-name, but Mrs Nisbet, who cared for him very much indeed, never called him by any other that we were aware of.

Lamb turned and went back inside the little cottage; a couple of seconds later we heard a woman's voice, and Fanny Nisbet emerged into the daylight, tiny and bird-like in her stained apron. When she saw us, she began to twitter.

"Lamb," she said, "why didn't you tell me it was the children from the Hall, dear me, and look at me all grubby. My dears, I'm so pleased to see you, and on such a lovely day, but look at me, I'm not fit to be seen. Stay there, my dears," she said, pulling her apron over her head and rolling it up rapidly, "and I'll take this off, at least, so I look a bit more presentable, and in just a moment you two and we two can go and find some apples, there are more than ever this year."

She came out, and looked from one to the other of us, and continued to twitter in her softly lilting voice. "How nice to see you, and fancy Lamb not telling me it was you, and I didn't see you coming either. Come down the garden, my dears, you look as though you could do with something to feed you up, you know it's wicked, the way they half starve you over at Kniveacres, and here we are with more apples than we can throw at dogs." At this point Lash gave a sneeze, and she looked down, and gabbled apologetically, "Oh, not you, my dear, don't take it personally, it's just an expression, goodness the poor dog must wonder what kind of a person he's come to see. It's only Fanny letting her tongue run away with her, don't you be taking any notice," she said to Lash. "Come on, Lamb, don't be shy, you know Mog and Nick, come and help us. Now, how are you both, and how are things over at the Hall? I spoke to Mrs Fundle, you know, her boy looks after the horses there, and what does she say every time I ask her? 'No news is good news,

Mrs Nisbet,' she says, and bless me if she doesn't say that every single time. But one of these days there's going to be news, and then I expect it will not be so good. Still, last time there was news, it was that you two had come, and that was good news, wasn't it, in its way?"

During this monologue both Nick and I had opened our mouths several times, preparing to answer one of her questions, or simply to try and get a word in, but had been forced to close them again for fear of looking stupid or letting a fly in. At last, I managed to butt in.

"We wondered if you might be able to help us," I said, quickly, before she had a chance to start talking again.

"We really came round to ask you something," Nick added.

She looked slightly flustered. "Well," she said, "I don't know if I'll be able to tell you what you want to know, but I'll try, of course. Now look at these trees, have you ever seen trees more laden? Help yourselves, and tell me what's on your minds."

"Mr Greywether said," I began, "that you might know something about a stranger in the village, or something." I was a bit wary, and I kept looking at Nick for encouragement. How much ought we to tell Mrs Nisbet? "You see, we – there's been – we think someone came to Kniveacres recently, who wasn't invited."

"Sir Septimus thinks there was an intruder," Nick put in.

"Dear me," said Fanny Nisbet, looking from one to the other of us, "an intruder at Kniveacres? And you wondered if anyone here had seen a stranger, or someone suspicious, or anyone asking questions, or any clues, or anything like that?"

"That's exactly what we wondered," I said.

"Well, I'd have said no," she said, "normally, this time of year, everyone's busy, getting in their provender and getting ready for the guys, and we don't see a soul. Only, it's funny you should ask what you asked, because one or two people have woken in the night this week to find their animals disturbed by something, and they've gone out thinking it was the fox, but there's been no sign and no smell. And people have heard doors banging, and seen lights, in the barns where they know there were no lights when they went to bed. Superstition, you'd call it, if you heard it, but more people have said it than just one. And the latest is, last night I think it would be, old Sloughter Cripps – you know old Sloughter? – he was in the churchyard, last thing in the evening, I heard, when he heard someone singing. And he thought it must be someone who had taken a drop too many, cider you know, or the hops – it happens, it happens. And he went around the back of the church, to investigate, and the singing moved around to the front, and he went around to the front again, and now he thought it was inside, and he went inside, and the singing moved outside, and all the time it never stopped, but he never saw a soul. And—"

"What sort of singing?" I asked her.

"Ooh, I don't know," she replied, "sort of a strange singing, he said, not like the choir, not like a familiar song. One person on their own. Strange, unearthly singing, he called it."

"And what happened then?" Nick asked.

She laughed nervously. "Not sure anything happened," she said, "to speak of. He heard it, and he came away again, and he told a few people about it. And now there's been an intruder at the Hall, you say? Well, Sir Septimus had better watch out, hadn't he, if this is really the Devil himself come to live at Kniveacres after all these years! You know the old story, don't you? Heh, heh, heh," she cackled – though I didn't think I detected much genuine amusement in her face. "Of course," she went on, "it's not unknown for Mr Cripps to take a drop himself, and there are some think he was hearing things that weren't there, and have made so bold as to say so to his face. But they'd be braver than I am, contradicting a man like that."

I smiled. Sloughter Cripps was probably the one person in the village we would have been most reluctant to call on: a huge man with a reputation for a short temper, who had made us feel very unwelcome indeed on our first encounter a few months ago, and had never softened. The story went that he had been a champion wrestler, in his youth, and had travelled England as a strong man with a fair, taking on all comers. He could still break a wall-stone in half with his bare hands, people said. There was something rather pleasing about the picture Mrs Nisbet had just painted, of him in his cups, blundering round the church-yard in the dark, confounded by a mysterious singing voice that refused to stay still.

"We were at the church this morning," Nick said, slowly, "and something strange happened. I was standing outside, minding my business, waiting for Mog, and suddenly one of the gargoyles fell. From high up, above the porch, almost onto my head. If you go you'll see it, still on the ground where it fell. It could have been a terrible accident."

Mrs Nisbet's face went a little whiter. "Dear me," she said, "you poor boy, a gargoyle, just falling like that? With you underneath? And you not hurt? Well you look fine. But what a shock!

But those gargoyles must have been there for centuries, fancy one just deciding to fall, on a day like – was it today, did you say? Just this morning? For no reason?"

"Mrs Nisbet," I said, "nobody has died in the village in the last few days, have they?"

Her face went whiter still. "Died? No. No one's died, that I know of. Did someone tell you someone had died? You're scaring me now, Mog, that you are."

"No," Nick interrupted, "we must have misheard something somebody said. You've told us some very interesting things, Mrs Nisbet, thank you very much. And these apples look delicious."

"There are far more than you can carry in your pockets," she said. "Let me give you a box, and you can carry it between you, can't you? Come and help me get it for them, Lamb."

Lamb was kneeling in the grass, playing with Lash, who was rolling on his back and pretending to bite the boy's rapidly-moving hands.

"Get up now and stop tormenting the poor dog," Mrs Nisbet said to him.

"He's all right," I said, "Lash is enjoying it." But when he saw his mother going inside, the boy gave Lash a valedictory tickle, then stood up and followed her.

"What do you think of all that?" Nick asked.

"I don't know," I said. "It's not very conclusive, is it?"

"Well, do you want to try and talk to some more people?"

"No, I think they'd clam up. You know what they're like."

He nodded. "You're probably right," he said. "We've already frightened poor Fanny, and we hardly told her anything, did we? We mustn't go around making any more people suspicious."

I was relieved. For a moment I was afraid he'd been about to suggest we conduct house-to-house inquiries, and I wasn't sure that even my curiosity was sufficient to justify that.

"I don't think I'm very keen to confront Sloughter Cripps," I said.

"Certainly not!" Nick laughed.

Mrs Nisbet emerged from the house again with a strong wooden box, and Lamb followed. We allowed her to fill it with apples for us, I persuaded Lash to keep his nose out of it, and we had taken our leave, when we found Lamb walking round with us to the front of the house.

"It's very kind of you," I said to him. "We'll enjoy these, won't we, Nick?"

Lamb stood looking at us, silently, at the edge of the village green, as though reluctant to let us go.

"Well – we're going to head back to the Hall now, I think," I said.

Just as we turned to go he gave a little grunt, and extended his arm towards us. At first I thought he wanted to shake our hands; but then I noticed he was holding something out.

"What's this?" I said. "For us?"

I reached out, and took it from him. It was a tiny oval box, made of silver; a bit tarnished, but beautiful, and with ornate patterns woven into its circumference with silver thread. In the centre of its lid, it bore a small, delicate, curled representation of a snake.

I stared down at it in my palm.

"Nick," I said softly, "Nick, look at this."

I looked up. Lamb was already limping back towards the cottage.

"Lamb!" I called. "Lamb, come back! Where did you find this?"

He turned, and pointed at us. "Yours," he said in his indistinct voice.

"Yes," I said, "but – Lamb, we can't just take this. Where did you get it?"

He pointed over to the corner of the village green, and made an inverted "V" by pressing his fingertips together and tilting his hands away from one another to form a steeple.

"The church," said Nick, staring at him, "he means the church."

And before we could ask Lamb any more questions, he was gone.

CHAPTER 4
WHAT THE THUNDER SAID

The wind was getting up again, and it felt as though a storm might be imminent by the time we got back through the woods to Kniveacres. It was lunchtime; but first we went to my room to put the box of apples in the big oak wardrobe, and to hide the little silver tin away somewhere secure. Nick helped me pull my bed away from the wall so I could slide open the heavy drawer in the base which normally remained hidden from view. Nick had discovered it by accident one day, when he'd dropped something behind the bed and reached down to retrieve it; and now we stored all our most important possessions there. Since we'd known one another we'd become used to sharing almost everything: my belongings had also become Nick's, and vice versa. Even though we each had our own bedroom, we often left the adjoining door between them standing open during the day, and treated the rooms more like one big one than two smaller ones; so most of the time it didn't really matter whose things were in which room.

Among the other treasures in the secret drawer, gathered during the course of our lives together and apart, were two identical silver bangles which our mother had given us when we were babies. We couldn't resist comparing the decoration on the tin with that on the bangles, and we found there were striking similarities in the design and the delicacy of the silverwork. They might have been made by the same hand, or at the very least in the same place.

We were mesmerised by the little silver tin, and, although it was quite empty, it spoke to us with as clear a voice as if it had opened its lid, and poured out a thousand words. It thrilled us, and radiated a mingled promise of adventure and comfort, so that our hands seemed almost to glow warm as we held it.

"I'm going to hide this in here as well," said Nick, placing the flimsy *Addendum* in the drawer on top of some other pieces of paper. "I don't fancy carrying it around all the time, but if we leave it lying about we'll lose it. I don't trust Bonefinger not to come in here and snoop around."

I nodded my assent. The drawer was the safest place by far. We couldn't be completely sure no one else knew about it, but nothing we'd placed in there had disappeared, in the whole time we'd lived here. As well as the bangles, the drawer was the place where we kept our mother's letter – or at least, the fragment of it which Nick had guarded throughout his childhood, in which she'd pleaded with an unidentified recipient to look after us after her death. There were some little books Mr Cramplock had given me when I left London, as good luck tokens, which I'd helped to print, and which would remind me of my life as a printer's devil. There was a silver collar for Lash, and a silver bookmark for Nick, which were gifts from our friend Mr

Spintwice, the jeweller, and which we considered far too precious to use.

"And look, do you remember this?" said Nick, holding up a little square piece of paper he'd found in the drawer.

We'd brought this from London too. It had been left for us to find last year, soon after we had met, when we had no idea what it meant; and when we were persuaded it spelled something terrible and frightening.

दम्यता

The very same letters which had struck such a thunderclap into the heart of Sir Septimus this week. The name he never wanted to hear, and about which we were becoming increasingly excited. The name our mother's letter had said might never be traced.

Damyata. We knew, almost for certain, that he had tracked us down. It was more and more clear to us that Damyata *had* been here, at Kniveacres Hall, on Monday night; and that he had been prowling around the village, looking for information, or just looking for somewhere to sleep without arousing suspicion. And Fanny's story of Sloughter Cripps's encounter with the mysterious singer in the dark churchyard was beginning to sound like more than just the figment of a drunkard's imagination.

"He'll try and contact us, won't he?" said Nick. "He's put the wind up Sir Septimus, and he's been nosing around the village. He must know we're here. It's only a matter of time."

We pushed the bed back into place and closed the door of my

room behind us, leaving Lash sitting resignedly in his basket, and ran through the echoing corridor to the sparsely furnished little room which had been designated as our dining-room. We were slightly late for lunch, now, and our adventure in the village had given us a keen appetite. If we weren't there at the appointed time, the kitchen staff sometimes used to keep our food warm for us, if they were in the right kind of mood; and to get it sent up we had to ring the bell beside the dumb-waiter in the panelling of the wall. Within a minute or so it would appear, on the metal tray which moved up and down a shaft on pulleys between the kitchen and the rooms above. Miss Thynne sometimes ate with us; but there was no sign today that she had eaten here, and all three of the places laid at the table were undisturbed. Evidently she was still poorly.

"Ring the bell, then," said Nick, "it must be ready by now."

I took hold of the ivory bell-handle, and pulled, setting off a tinny sound somewhere far below. Almost immediately, there were muffled clatters from the dumb-waiter, as someone in the kitchen two floors beneath our feet opened the doors and prepared to place the plates on the tray to send up to us.

As we waited, Miss Thynne came in, quietly, and nodded a greeting before sitting down. Nobody said anything for a while, but I watched her as she settled herself at the table. Her face was white, almost like a corpse, and she looked, if possible, less substantial and more fragile than ever.

"We thought you were ill, Miss Thynne," I said at length, "we didn't expect you."

"I'm – a little better," she said, hesitantly. "I . . . haven't seen you for a day or so, and I have a few things I need to speak to you about." She picked up a napkin and nervously dabbed it at the corner of her mouth, even though she had no food in front of her. I thought it best not to inquire, just now, what "few things" she might have in mind.

"It's on its way up," I said, as a low grinding noise began behind the panelling, suggesting that the dumb-waiter had begun its ascent.

"I'm starving," Nick said. "We've been to the village. We thought – at least, someone told us, you . . ."

Miss Thynne smiled, in a rather watery way. "I wasn't able to teach you this morning," she said. "Don't worry, I haven't been waiting for you in the library." Her voice was unusually quiet, even for her.

The grinding noise behind the panelling stopped, and there was an alarming clunk and a shudder, which made the doors to the hatch rattle on their hinges.

"Is it here?" Miss Thynne asked.

"That's not the noise it usually makes," said Nick with a frown. "Has it got stuck, Mog?"

I pulled open the doors of the hatch and looked inside. The food certainly hadn't arrived; I stared into a dark hole, with nothing to see but the cords of the dumb-waiter's pulley mechanism hanging taut on either side.

"Have a look down the hole, and see if you can see it," Nick suggested.

I did so; but it was too dark to see whether the dumb-waiter had got stuck, and how far down it might be. I rang the bell again, and when I listened at the open hatch I could hear raised voices echoing up from the kitchen, as though people down there had realised there was a problem and were debating what to do.

There were a couple more clunks, as someone tried to start the mechanism again, but nothing else. It wasn't moving.

I stuck my head into the hole again.

"It's no good, I can't see anything," I called out to Nick and Miss Thynne. "Someone will have to go down to the kitchen and tell them."

I was about to pull my head out again when there was a sudden breeze in my face, followed by a sharp squealing sound of metal against metal. I leaned back just in time as the dumb-waiter hurtled upward and stopped with a gigantic crash right before my eyes, the bowls on its metal tray jolting from the impact, sending bright orange soup spilling out over the sides in all directions.

I gasped, and took a leap backwards.

"Mog!" Nick was by my side in no time. "That was a close one! Did you hear it coming?"

"I – sort of, felt it," I said. "There was a rush of wind."

The dumb-waiter consisted of a kind of iron box, with two shelves inside for the food. After decades of use, the mechanism was obviously becoming worn out. It was very heavy, and the top and bottom edges of the metal casing were jagged and battered. Moving at that speed up and down the shaft, it could have caused a serious injury to anyone who got their hands or any other part of themselves in the way.

"It could have taken your *head* off," said Nick, reaching up to the top of the hatch and running his thumb along the upper edge of the dumb-waiter.

"We must speak to someone about it," Miss Thynne was saying, looking on in alarm from the table. "Thank goodness you had the sense to step back, Mog. Are you sure you're all right?"

"I'm fine," I said. But I was happy to let Nick reach inside for the soup bowls, in case the dumb-waiter had any further unexpected tricks up its sleeve. I found I was trembling, as I sat down and lifted the spoon to my lips.

And who should come in at that moment but Bonefinger?

"I heard a cry," he said, in his mincing, theatrical way. "A commotion from the kitchen – and they tell me the dumb-waiter is misbehaving? I rushed up here as quickly as I could. I hope no one is hurt?"

"No, Mog missed out on being beheaded," Nick said drily, "but only by the skin of her teeth."

"Really? Miss Imogen, what a terrible thing!" cried Bonefinger. But his eyes betrayed no hint that he really thought it was terrible, at all. "It is clearly only a matter of chance that a *dreadful* accident has not occurred. I really think that, if the dumb-waiter is malfunctioning, you must remember to keep your head and hands well out of the way of the shaft and the hatch. The mechanism is cumbersome. It could be *very* dangerous. Very dangerous indeed." He turned to Miss Thynne. "You are not hurt yourself, Miss Thynne?" he fretted, and she reassured him with a small shake of the head. "Most important, Miss Thynne, to instil this lesson in your charges," he continued. "A dumb-waiter is not a device to be trifled with. Indeed no. In the meantime I will make strong representations to Sir Septimus to have it looked at, as a matter of urgency. Dear me." And he was gone, with a hasty bow and a swirl of his cloak.

"I'm going after him," muttered Nick. "Stay here. I'm going to see where he goes."

"I want to come," I said.

"Stay here," he repeated. "I want to be quiet, and quick. I won't be gone long."

"*Now* who's playing spies?" I nearly said. Instead, what I actually said was, "Be careful."

"Nick," came Miss Thynne's voice, "Nick, I don't think you should . . ." But her words trailed off, as Nick disappeared through the door and closed it quietly behind him, leaving his soup standing unfinished in its bowl on the table.

I pulled open the door, and went out onto the landing. Nick had disappeared; somewhere far below I could hear echoing footsteps on the stone stairs. I knew that Nick was an expert at stalking, that he'd never allow himself to be seen; and I realised he was right, that if I followed him I'd only be putting us both in more danger.

I went back into the dining-room where Miss Thynne was still sitting at the table, looking pale, behind the soup bowls.

"He'll be all right," I said.

"He doesn't know what he might get himself into," said Miss Thynne quietly. "That was very nearly a terrible accident. Who knows what might happen at any moment – to any of us?"

I looked at her, intrigued. She was trying very hard, I realised, not to cry.

"Nobody was hurt, Miss Thynne," I reassured her.

She looked up at me, pressing her lips tightly together. There were quite clearly tears in her eyes, which she made a brave effort to blink away.

"Sorry, Imogen," she said. "I was – that is, I . . ."

I sat down at the table with her. "Is something wrong?" I asked her.

"It's nothing," she said, trying to smile.

"We didn't mean to get you into trouble," I said. "If it's because of us, we – I . . ."

She reached out a skinny hand and placed it on mine, on the table, to quieten me. "No," she said, "it's nothing like that. You haven't done anything wrong."

"Sir Septimus thinks we have," I said.

She looked around, her hand still clutching mine, and lowered her head slightly as though she thought it might make her less audible. In a quiet voice she said, "I just want you to be careful, Imogen. You and Dominic."

"What do you mean?" I wasn't used to this sort of kindness from Miss Thynne; she had certainly never held my hand before.

She smiled again, but her eyes were still watery. "Just be careful," she repeated.

I was spooning up the last of my soup when there was a gentle click at the door, and Nick slipped into the room. Miss Thynne stood up.

"There's something you've got to come and see," he said to me in a low voice.

"Excuse me, children," said Miss Thynne. "I'm going to my room. But I'd like to see you for lessons this afternoon, in ten minutes."

She gave me a long, significant look before she picked up her bag from the chair, and left the room.

"We haven't got long," Nick said when she'd gone. "Was she all right? She looked a bit – strange."

"Something's going on," I said. "She seems very concerned about us. I'm sure Sir Septimus has said something to her."

"Come and look, quickly," Nick said. "I followed Bonefinger. But he disappeared into thin air."

"He's always doing that," I said.

"No, but Mog, I followed him into his tiny little room," said Nick, "and he just wasn't there. There isn't any other door, or anywhere he could have hidden. He just vanished."

Trying to be quiet, we crept down the long stone staircase which led towards the kitchens. As we neared the ground floor, Nick turned to me and put his finger to his lips. We could hear the clattering of pans and occasional voices from behind the kitchen door, which was slightly open. I followed him along the passageway until we came to the door of the little butler's pantry which Bonefinger used as a kind of office, just beyond the kitchen on the opposite side.

"He came in here," he whispered.

Nick pushed open the door to let me look inside. The room was empty. He held out a hand, to signal me to go in. He followed me in and closed the door.

"He came in here," he said again. "I followed him. I watched him come in, then a few seconds later I put my head round the door. I was going to pretend to ask him something, just some nonsense. But Mog, he wasn't here! He had disappeared! But there's nowhere for him to go, is there?"

The room was about six feet square. If I had stood in the middle and taken a single step in any direction, I'd have been able to reach out and touch the wall in front of me. There was a desk against one wall, with a chair behind it; a few shelves with books and bottles on; and a small low cupboard which was slightly open. A coat was hanging on a hook on the back of the door. Above the desk was a little wooden rack, with a series of hooks and a line of keys hanging on them. In the opposite corner there were three wooden steps, which led up to a blank stone wall.

"What are they for?" I asked.

"I don't know. But they don't go anywhere. You can't walk through a stone wall."

I took two tentative steps up, and the big cold wall was up against my face. I ran my hand over the stones.

"You see?" said Nick. "There's no hidden door there. It doesn't go anywhere. They're just steps, for no reason. Once upon a time I suppose it was the start of a proper staircase to somewhere, but then someone built this wall, and blocked it off. You can't get through."

I pushed at the big flat stones of the wall. Nick was quite right, there was no possible way through. These stones hadn't moved for years. There was no secret door, no window, and no other way out of the room. I looked up.

"Maybe there's a trap door in the ceiling."

But the ceiling was far too high to reach from the top step, and there were no hand- or footholds in the wall. Only a spider, or a lizard, could have climbed it. Nor was there any evidence, in the ceiling above our heads, of any trap door. I was as baffled as Nick was.

"He must have slipped out, somehow, before you went in," I suggested.

"Mog, I watched the door *all the time.*"

I looked around again, and pulled aside the coat hanging on the back of the door. "Maybe he hid here, behind the door, until you were in the room, and then nipped out behind your back." But we could both see that the room was too small for anyone to hide in, even for a moment. The coat wasn't big enough to conceal a person standing behind it. You simply couldn't be in here without being seen. If what Nick said was true, either Bonefinger had become as thin as paper and slipped through a crack in the stonework, or else he'd evaporated. There were no other explanations.

"Well, I don't know," I said. "Look, let's get out of here before Bonefinger comes back. We've got to go and see Miss Thynne anyway."

We slipped past the kitchen, and back up the stairs towards the library. The afternoon sky had grown thunderously dark, and there was so little light coming in through the big windows that, when we first peered around the door, it was hard to see whether there was anyone in the huge room. As we ventured in, it became clear there was nobody here; and we went to sit on the big sofa to wait for Miss Thynne.

"I'm a bit surprised Miss Thing wants to teach us," said Nick. "She didn't look very well at all, at lunch."

"She's very worried about something," I said. "She kept telling me to be careful. She was very – well, she was different, somehow. More friendly. But *scared* of something."

"Scared of Sir Septimus, I expect," Nick said. There was a sudden quizzical noise from his stomach. "Sorry," he said, "I didn't get a chance to eat my lunch."

"Go back and get something."

"It's too late now, it'll have been cleared away." He picked up a book which was sitting on the sofa beside him. "Did you get this out?" he asked. "I thought we put all the books away last night."

"So did I," I said, "but Bonefinger's been in here, remember? Taking away the big book of maps and plans. Maybe he's been looking at it."

The book Nick had picked up was bound – like the one we'd been looking at yesterday – in dark leather, with the Cloy coat of arms embossed on the front. It was a bit smaller; but as Nick opened it up we could see that this book, too, was full of drawings and diagrams.

"*An Inventory*," Nick read, turning to the title page, "*and Catalogue of Objects and Documents in the Possession of the Cloy Family, and which are kept at Charnock House, St John's Square, Clerkenwell, in the City of London.*"

"And which are kept *where?*"

I grabbed the book from Nick, and stared at the title page in disbelief. "Charnock House, St John's Square, Clerkenwell," I parroted.

"That's what it says," said Nick.

"But Nick, don't you *see?* Don't you know where that is?"

"Charnock House," said Nick, his brows furrowed as he tried to remember. "I don't—"

"It's next door to Mr Cramplock's," I explained. "It's the house next door, Nick!"

When I had worked at Mr Cramplock's printing shop, the big old house next door had been a source of fascination and fear: a once-grand town house, its windows blackened by fire and abandoned years before, always dark and silent, presenting its forbidding face to the street and seeming to stare at me with its burnt-out, sightless eyes, every time I went past. And, around the time I met Nick, we had had the strangest of adventures in there. Creeping inside one evening on my own, I had found its walls and floors completely intact, as it must have been before the fire ever happened. And yet, a day or two later when I took Nick inside to show him, the floors and walls had all disappeared and it was just an empty shell, wrecked by fire as it had always been. Trapped inside the ruin, we had had a terrifying encounter with criminals who were trying to kill each other. I had never been able to explain what had really happened in the house, and until this moment I had not the slightest idea it had any connection with a family so closely related to my own.

Nick was poring over the book. "There's loads of stuff in here," he said. "Pictures of precious things – look, goblets and plates and carvings, and I don't know what. And lists of things. Pages and pages of lists – descriptions of paintings, and jewellery." He looked up at me. "Do you mean to say," he said, "that the Cloys owned that house all the time? And you didn't know?"

"I had no idea," I said.

"Didn't Mr Cramplock ever mention it?"

"No. Never. But maybe he didn't know either."

"I think he probably did." Nick held the book open at the title page, and ran the palm of his hand up the middle of the open spread so the pages wouldn't flip over. He handed it out to me, solemnly.

I stared at it. At the bottom of the page, beneath another little engraving of the Cloy coat of arms, was the unmistakeable legend:

Printed by H.H. Cramplock by St John's Gate, Clerkenwell.

Just as I was taking this in, we heard the door click open, and we both sat bolt upright in alarm; but we relaxed as we saw Miss Thynne come in and close the door quietly behind her.

"It's dark in here," she said, and went around the library lighting lamps, including one over on the table where we were to work. "What a dreadful afternoon it is, all of a sudden." She came close to where we were sitting. "Have you found something interesting?" she asked.

"Not really," said Nick, trying to close the book casually. But I took it from him, and he was so surprised he didn't try to stop me.

"Actually, I think we have," I said.

I took the book over to the table and laid it down in the lamplight. Miss Thynne came and looked over my shoulder.

"This is a catalogue of the Cloy family's possessions, kept at Charnock House in Clerkenwell," I said. "Do you know where that is, Miss Thynne?"

She hesitated. "I – have a rough idea," she said quietly.

"I used to live next door to Charnock House," I said. "Right next door, in the very shop where this book was printed. In fact, I lived there until the day we came here. And all the time I had no idea who it belonged to."

"How extraordinary," said Miss Thynne, faintly.

"Look at all this," I said, leafing through the pages, showing her the long lists of paintings, the drawings of silverware and treasures and sculpted figures and valuable objects by the score. "All this stuff must have been worth a fortune," I said. "But where is it now? The house was burned down. Years and years ago. So were all these precious things lost?"

There was no reply. I continued leafing through the book, on the desk in front of me. Suddenly a drawing on one of the pages made me stop.

It depicted a figurine, a small sculpture in pale wood or bone, of a person standing on one leg in a kind of dance, with six arms held out at various graceful angles, the whole thing framed by a slender arc like a kind of halo. Sculpted with an almost impossible delicacy, it was hard to tell whether the figure was male or female; but it was utterly beautiful. And I'd seen it before. Very recently indeed.

And, as my gaze travelled around the room, I found myself looking at the very same six-armed figurine, standing on a bookshelf ten or twelve feet away. A little white god, turning slightly yellow in places, about a foot tall. Contemplating me from its shelf with an expression somewhere between tranquillity and amusement. I looked down at the book, and back at the ivory statue. They were identical.

"That's it," I said, "over there. Isn't it?"

"The Lord Shiva," said Miss Thynne quietly. "Yes, it looks like it."

"So are all these other things in the book here too, somewhere? Were they rescued, and brought to Kniveacres? What happened?"

Miss Thynne couldn't help looking around the library before she spoke.

"I don't know the whole story," she said. "Charnock House was the Cloy family's London home, years ago, certainly. Sir Septimus had lately returned from India when it burned down, and I vaguely remember people talking of the disaster."

"You knew the Cloys back then?" I asked.

"Yes," she said. She looked around again, nervously. "It was only about ten years ago," she said. "My family has had connections with the Cloys for a very long time. Just as—" She bit her lip.

"Yes?" I encouraged her.

There was a pause while she gathered herself. "Just as yours has," she continued, slowly.

Nick was still sitting watching us from the sofa. I don't think he had believed me when I told him that something about Miss Thynne had changed; but when he heard her say this he stood up, in quiet excitement.

I turned over another page. This time the picture which met my eye was of another statuette, again of an Indian god: a seated figure with the head and trunk of an elephant, apparently made of gold or bronze, with a dark jewel set in the centre of its forehead like a single enormous eye.

"Of *course*," I said.

"Is that one here somewhere as well?" Miss Thynne asked.

"I don't know." I gazed at her pale face in the lamplight. It was now almost completely dark outside, even though it was only just after two, and the thunderclouds were low and massive over Kniveacres. "Miss Thynne," I said, in a low voice, "Sir Septimus knew our mother, didn't he?"

"Yes," she said.

"She didn't like him, though, did she?" I continued, not taking my eyes off her face.

"No," said the governess eventually. "No, Imogen, she didn't. Not at all."

Nick came over, quietly, and stood beside me at the edge of the table. Our voices were so low now that no one could have heard us even a few feet away; but Miss Thynne was still nervously casting glances around the library in case anyone should appear unexpectedly.

"Have you ever heard the name Damyata?" Nick asked.

She looked straight at us; first into Nick's eyes, then into mine. There was another long silence.

"Let me read you something," she said; and she got up and walked over to a shelf, close to the statue of the six-armed dancer, taking down a tall old book which she flicked through as she came back towards the table.

"It's from a book of ancient stories from India," she said, holding the big book open with some difficulty at the right page. "Here we are. There were three kinds of being in creation. They were the Manavas, or people; the Asuras, or demons; and the Devas, or gods. All of these three were discontent, and wished to ask the Lord Creator how to achieve their desires. So, in a great crowd, they gathered to demand advice, and in reply Prajapati the Creator uttered only the huge and terrible sound of a clap of thunder. DA! Then he closed his eyes and returned to contemplation, saying not a word more.

"The crowd returned to their homes in the earth, the underworld, and heaven, to consider what the word of the Lord Creator meant. The Manavas – the people – considered that

'DA' must be the beginning of the word '*Datta*', which means 'give'. We must be more giving, and share more of our world with our fellow creatures, they decided; and they agreed to endeavour to live by this. The Asuras, or demons, thought that, by 'DA', the Lord Creator must have meant to utter the word '*Dayadhvam*', which means 'be merciful'. We must show more mercy and compassion to those in our power, they decided; and this became a rule by which they were to live. Last, the Devas or gods decided that by 'DA' the Lord Creator intended the word '*Damyata*', which means 'be self-controlled'. 'To attain our desires we must control our excessive pride and indulgence, and exercise restraint in all things,' they decided; and this became their guidance for a happy existence.

"But it is as hard for gods and demons to live by the Lord's rules as it is for humans. So frequently the thunder has to sound its reminder – 'DA!' – of the lessons all beings must remember."

We were completely silent as she read this; even when she got to the word "Damyata" and I felt the hairs on the back of my neck standing up, I looked at Nick and he was just gazing at her, saying nothing. There was a sudden momentary flicker of light at the big library windows, and, a few seconds later, the unmistakeable rumble of thunder.

"How much do you know about Damyata?" I asked. "I mean, the person?"

"You must know," she said, "that that name is forbidden from being uttered in this house. If anyone heard us talking about him . . ."

"I know," I said, "but Miss Thynne, we think he has been here. In the last few days."

Miss Thynne stared out of the window at the black sky, and at the flecks of rain starting to appear on the big panes. "So that is what Sir Septimus meant," she said to herself. Then something caught her eye through the window; she stood, watching the garden silently for a few moments, and then turned and came back to the table.

"Bonefinger is outside," she said, "under the trees. Don't look out of the window. Sit down and concentrate on what's on the table. He can see us up here in the lighted window, and he must think you are being taught your lessons as usual."

I picked up a pencil, and looked down at the desk, turning the pencil over and over in my fingers as my mind worked to understand what was happening.

"Miss Thynne," I said, "we've met Damyata before. Last summer, he came to London."

"Not only that," added Nick, "he went to the Cloys' house, didn't he? Next door to where you lived in Clerkenwell."

"He was hiding out there for a bit," I said. "We didn't have a clue who he was. We thought he was just a strange man, who kept a snake, and who kept chasing us around. We had no idea he had any connection with our mother. But maybe he went to Charnock House thinking he'd find Sir Septimus, instead of which he found it in ruins. Maybe he was waiting there in case Sir Septimus came back at some point."

"Or maybe," said Nick, "*maybe*, he was looking for some precious object he thought would be there. Something in the book, which was burned up in the fire?"

"Or something that's here now!" I exclaimed.

"Keep your voices down," said Miss Thynne, nervously. She

reached for the book of the Cloy family treasures, and started to look through it, searching for something. After she had turned over thirty or forty pages, she found what she was looking for and she passed the book silently across the table to us.

It was a picture of a comb — made of silver, delicately patterned, and apparently very similar in style to the box Lamb had given us that very morning, and to the bangles which Nick and I had been given by our mother and which we kept in our box of treasures.

"Is this here somewhere?" Nick asked.

"Read the description," said Miss Thynne.

Beneath the drawing were a few lines of small print.

Item 5.12 A silver filigree hair-comb, of Indian origin, date unknown. Entered the family's possession 1814. Fine engravings of feathers and birds' heads as part of design. Tarnishing on inner surface. Characters engraved, approx $1/4''$ high, reading:

इम्यता

"Damyata," I said. I looked up at Miss Thynne. "That's what it says."

"We'd know it anywhere," put in Nick.

"Do you know where it is?" I asked.

"No," said Miss Thynne, "but I know *what* it is. It was a love token, given to your mother by the man whose name is inscribed upon it. It came into Sir Septimus's possession after she died."

"Damyata gave this to our mother?" I stared at the drawing.

Things were starting to fall into place. "He was in love with her?"

"Yes," said Miss Thynne, "and she with him. She had to leave him behind, and come home – it was all a terrible scandal, and a most awful tragedy. Because, after you two were born, she – died. As you know."

I did know; but suddenly, I knew a whole lot more besides. I was thinking about the letter my mother had written, just before she died, the last page of which we now kept in our secret drawer of treasures, along with the bangles. We both knew more or less the whole thing by heart. And seeing this love-gift, and hearing what Miss Thynne said about Damyata, made part of the letter resonate in my mind – and a meaning emerged which I had never even realised was there.

"What was it our mother called us in the letter, Nick?" I asked, trying to remember the exact phrase. "The warm little souls . . .?"

"The warm and desperate little souls," quoted Nick, "to whom my transgression gave life."

"That's it, isn't it?" I said, looking at Miss Thynne.

"I don't – really know the letter you're talking about," she said hesitantly, "but . . ."

"But that's it," I persisted, "that's the point. 'My transgression'. *That's* what it means." Miss Thynne was smiling at me now, as if she could follow my innermost thoughts, and was affirming them. As for Nick, it was clear he hadn't yet quite understood.

"Do you mean that Damyata has come here to get this comb back?" he asked.

103

I obviously wasn't explaining myself very well.

"Imogen loved Damyata," I said to Nick. "They were in love. That's what the comb means. But she had to come home. There was a scandal. She had done a terrible thing. Don't you *see*? It all makes sense now, and there's no wonder he's come back to find us."

Nick was silent.

"Nick, he's our *father*," I said. "Damyata is our father." I looked at Miss Thynne. "Isn't he?"

She nodded, and there were tears in her eyes again. I clutched the edge of the table. My heart was thumping, and I felt very peculiar: almost dizzy with excitement. We had known for a long time that Damyata was somehow significant in our lives; but how could we have realised how significant, until now? It was suddenly as clear as daylight. It wasn't some precious object Damyata was trying to find at Kniveacres; and it wasn't a precious object he'd been trying to find in London last summer. It was two precious objects – the two most precious objects he could imagine. Us.

I remembered how much time we had spent running away from him, and I felt overwhelming remorse that we hadn't understood at that time, mingled with a tingle of excitement that he had returned.

We sat listening to the noise of the rain on the glass, as it all sank in. For thirteen years, I had believed I was an orphan; that my mother was dead, and that my father was unknown, or also dead, or untraceable, or all three. Now, suddenly, I knew not only who my father was, but that he was very much alive. "And now he has come to this house," I said. "He left his name on a sheet of paper, addressed to Sir Septimus, in his study the other night. Sir Septimus was furious. He thought we had done it as a prank."

"But it really *was* Damyata," said Nick to Miss Thynne. "He's been in the village too. One of the villagers found a little silver box in the churchyard, which he must have dropped."

"Sir Septimus wasn't furious," Miss Thynne said, "he was frightened. He still is. He's terrified out of his wits."

"There was the prophecy," Nick remembered. "Do you know about the prophecy, Miss Thynne? How did it go, Mog?"

"Damyata underlined some words in an ancient book," I explained, "and left it with the paper he signed. Something about the Master of Kniveacres being cut down."

"At threescore, ten and seven," said Nick.

Miss Thynne was staring at the darkness outside again. There was another loud rumble of thunder.

"That does sound – horribly familiar," she said. "There has been talk of a prophecy ever since I was a child. A curse, some call it. There are people who think the whole family is cursed. Most of Sir Septimus's brothers have met horrible deaths. His eldest brother was crushed to death, in India, when an elephant sat on his tent. The next oldest was buried alive while supervising drainage work not far away from there, and two others were lost at sea. The children in the family are often born sickly, or have dreadful accidents. And there's this thing about something happening to the Master of Kniveacres, when he is seventy-seven years old, and when the Devil comes to live here." She shuddered, and looked back at us. "The people in the village believe it," she said, "but I think, to the family themselves, it's always been a bit of a joke. Until now."

Something made her suddenly stiffen and fall silent; and above the noise of the rain I, too, thought I heard voices outside the library door. She picked up the books we'd been looking at, and walked over to the shelves, where she slid them carefully back into their places. Before she came back to the table she stood by the door, listening.

"It's too dangerous," she said when she returned. "Open your books and look at your lesson. Not another word."

"But, Miss Thynne," I whispered. I was desperate, now, to find out every single thing she knew; but there were still so many questions I wanted to ask that it was impossible to know where to start.

Glancing at the door, Nick picked up his pencil and opened his book, as he'd been told to. Looking down at the page, he asked her one final question, in a voice so low as to be almost a whisper.

"Why did you tell us all that?"

She put her finger on her lips in a sudden governess-ish gesture of reproach, and a flash of the old Miss Thynne was back.

"Because someone has to help you," she said. "Now – not another word. Do you understand?"

The storm continued late into the night. Kniveacres was lashed with unrelenting rain and buffeted by wind as we lay in our beds; and the noise, along with the tumult of the day's events and discoveries whirling in my head, made it very difficult indeed to sleep soundly. When I did fall asleep, for short bursts, I found myself having vivid and disturbing dreams. I dreamed that I was standing at the library windows, in complete darkness, looking out over the gardens, and that I could plainly see Damyata standing in the middle of a gravel path, his domed brown head and prominent nose illuminated in occasional flashes by the lightning, his cloak whipped and flung around him by the wind as he stood. It was so vivid that, even after I'd woken up, I felt quite sure that I really had just been to the library in my night-clothes, and I got up to look out of my own window, to see if there was any further sign of him.

The next time I fell asleep, I was running along a cold stone corridor somewhere in the castle, in pursuit of a dreadful wailing and crying sound I could hear from nearby. I opened doors to the left and right of me, finding nothing but empty rooms. I began to sense that the corridor was endless; I had looked in thirty, maybe even forty rooms, finding nothing, and still the corridor stretched on ahead of me, with no end in sight, and still the wailing continued to echo from somewhere further along. Ultimately, I found myself looking at a door which was neither to my left nor to my right, but directly ahead; and I knew this was where the crying was coming from. I seized the handle, and walked inside; and kneeling on the ground, in the far corner of the room, was a woman in a nightdress, her head in her hands, sobbing.

Tentatively, I stepped forward, and as I came up behind the crying figure I reached out to place a hand on her shoulder. She turned and looked up, and she had a pale and beautiful face which, for all its tear-marks and clinging stray hairs, I recognised from hundreds of dreams I had had throughout my life.

"Mother," I said. "Mother, what's the matter?"

And my mother, whose face I had never seen in my entire

living memory except in dreams, mouthed silent words as she sobbed, and the tears ran down her lovely cheeks, and I held both her hands, and begged her to tell me why she was crying. And, however urgently she tried to make me understand her words, through the sobbing, I couldn't hear what she said. Tears poured from her eyes, and made big wet patches all over the front of my night-clothes, as I tried to calm her, and tell her she was all right.

When I woke up, I had been sweating so much that my nightshirt was damp, and clinging to me. Again I got out of bed, taking deep breaths, shaken by my dream and anxious to wake myself up properly; and with the sweat still damp on my body I was soon shivering uncontrollably. Hearing me stir, Lash got up and started to lick my hands, and I sat down on the bed and hugged him, and talked to him in a quiet voice about the dreams I'd had. He had a knack of lifting his head to lick my face at precisely the points in my story where I needed the most comfort, and he made me feel much better.

But I was wide awake now, and still feeling unsettled; and, despite the cold, I stood up again, and went over to the adjoining door which connected my room with Nick's. I listened, but could hear nothing except the constant drumming of the rain. After a few seconds I turned the handle and went through.

The room was empty. Nick's bedsheets were flung back, but he wasn't there. All his clothes sat draped over the back of a chair, his shoes left at untidy angles on the floor by the bed. As I looked around the room I realised the door was ajar: perhaps he had only gone out a moment ago.

Lash had followed me into the room. Holding on to his

collar, I tiptoed out into the corridor and looked over the balcony, down the stairwell; then upwards. There was another floor above us, where some of the servants had their rooms, including Miss Thynne. I could hear nothing either from above or below.

Then, from along the passage behind me, I heard a sudden strange noise: the long, eerie creak of a door slowly opening, and what sounded like the jingling of tiny bells. I had heard it somewhere before. It seemed distant, but quite distinct.

"Nick?" I whispered. "Is that you?"

Shivering as my bare feet moved along the flagstones, I followed the passageway as far as I could, with Lash padding quietly at my heel, surprised and pleased to be on such an unexpected nocturnal expedition. The passage opened out at the end into a kind of small circular room, where there was now a heavy oak door in front of us. This was where the noise seemed to have come from. I worked out we must be in the far corner of the east wing; the room behind this door would look out over the gardens and the parkland at the front of the house. My heart in my mouth as I remembered my dream, I reached out my hand until it rested in the middle of the door, and pushed. It swung open away from me, with the same low creak I had heard a minute ago.

By the window at the far side of the room was Nick; and he seemed to be leaning out of it.

As I went silently up to him I realised he was speaking to someone.

What on earth was going on? Who could he be talking to, outside the window, at this time of night? I felt a shiver of fear;

and coming right up behind him I heard him calling: "Where have you gone? Are you there?"

"Nick," I said, "Nick, it's me. Who's there? Who are you talking to?"

He jumped in surprise; and his sudden movement scared me so much I found myself crying out and clutching him. He stared into my face for several seconds, as though unable to understand what I might be doing there.

"What are you doing?" I asked him in a whisper.

"Where is she?" he asked.

"Where's who?"

"She was just here. A minute ago. I came over to . . . and . . ."

He stopped talking. Lash started licking his hands, and there was a long silence as he gradually came to his senses.

"Nick," I said, "what's happening? *Who* was here?"

"I – must have been dreaming," he said eventually. "What are you doing here?"

"I came to find you," I said. "I found your bed empty, and I heard you opening the door. Into here. Were you sleep-walking?"

"I don't know." He took a few steps round the room, trying to get his bearings. "Where are we?"

"We're in the room at the far end of the first-floor passage."

"I don't think I've ever been in here before."

"Neither have I. Nick, what were you doing? Can you remember who you were talking to?"

"It was just a dream," he said. "I was in a corridor, trying to find someone. I could hear a person crying, and I kept opening doors to look for them, but every room I looked into was empty.

Until I came to one door at the end of the corridor, and inside I found a woman sobbing, who turned round when I went up to her, and somehow I knew it was Imogen. Our mother."

I felt my skin crawling. "Nick," I said, "we've just had exactly the same dream, at the same time. That's exactly what— But – but how did you end up in here?"

"I'm not sure. I suppose I must have walked about in my sleep. I was trying to talk to her, and she was crying, and I got down on my knees so I could hear what she was saying. And then I realised she wasn't here, and I thought she must have gone through the window."

"You must have half woken up," I said, "and thought you were still in the dream."

He shivered. "It's cold," he said.

"The window's open," I said. "Did you hear anything she was saying? Our mother? In the dream?"

"Couldn't make out a word," he replied. "She was terribly upset about something, but I just couldn't hear her."

"Neither could I," I said, biting my lip. "And yet I could hear her crying all the way down that long corridor."

I went to the window to pull the sash down and close it; but it seemed to be stuck. The wind was howling through the open window into the room. To get a better grip on the heavy sash, I put my knee on the stone sill.

"Aaagh!" I cried; and there was a simultaneous scraping sound as the sill suddenly gave way beneath my weight. I had to clutch at the window sash to steady myself; and as I did so, the entire stone lintel toppled outwards and tumbled, twenty-five or thirty feet, down to the ground below.

I hung there, my fingers around the window-frame, until Nick leaped forward and helped me in.

"What happened then?" he cried.

"I don't know, it just gave way. I didn't even put my whole weight on it, I was just leaning on it to get into a better position."

"Are you all right?"

"I think so."

We stared out into the dark, where the sill lay far below us. We'd both heard the thud as it hit the ground. If I'd been a split-second slower reaching up for the sash, I'd have been down there with it.

"Come on," said Nick, "let's go."

"We can't just leave the window like this!"

"What else are we supposed to do? You're not suggesting we go out in the dark and drag the sill back up the stairs, are you? It's enormous, Mog, we'd never be able to carry it."

"But – it's just sitting there, and there's this great big hole up here. It will be obvious in the morning what happened."

"Well we can worry about it in the morning, then," Nick said. "It's *freezing*, Mog. I want to get back to bed before anyone comes down to find out what's happening. And if we're in trouble in the morning, well we'll just tell the truth. We were in here because we – heard a noise. And the window was already open."

"Was it?"

"I think it must have been. I don't remember opening it. Come *on*."

Reluctantly, I went with him, back down the passage towards the bedrooms. There didn't seem to be anyone else stirring;

perhaps we'd got away without our noisy adventure having woken anyone else.

"How strange, that we should both dream exactly the same thing," he said, once we were back in his room.

"I don't like it. I think it's a bit spooky," I said. "Especially with you wandering around in your sleep. Have you ever done that before?"

"Not that I can remember."

"Why not lock the door in case you try and get out again?"

He thought the idea was funny, of locking himself into his bedroom to stop himself sleepwalking; so he did it, and I went back to my bed to warm myself up, with Lash helping no end by curling up on top of my feet on the bedcovers. I was asleep in no time.

But there wasn't much left of the night, by now; and it can only have been a couple of hours later when I woke to find the grey light of morning pressing at the window, and the most dreadful screaming coming from the staircase outside the bedroom.

I leaped out of bed, and rushed into the passageway. I couldn't see anyone, but I could hear a commotion going on upstairs, on the floor immediately above: the sound of feet rushing backwards and forwards, and voices shouting at one another. I couldn't believe the discovery of the fallen lintel could cause this much fuss; but I felt slightly sick with fear at what was going to be said. Within a few seconds I could hear a scrabbling at Nick's bedroom door as he tried to unlock it; and there he was beside me.

"What's going on?" he asked. "Surely all this can't be because of—"

"I don't think so. They're all upstairs. Come on."

The wailing continued; but this was unmistakeably real, not like the ethereal wailing I thought I'd heard through the howling wind the other night. When we reached the upper floor we could tell that the noise was coming from Miss Thynne's bedroom, which was just along the passageway from the top of the stairs. The door was slightly ajar. Judith, one of the housemaids, intercepted us on the landing, looking ashen-faced; and she held out a hand.

"No you don't," she said. "Stay out of there, that's no place for children."

"What's happened?" I asked her.

"Who's that crying?" Nick asked. "That's not Miss Thynne's voice."

I felt the light touch of a hand on my shoulder-blade, and when I turned I saw Melibee standing there.

"Master Dominic," he said, "Miss Imogen, Judith is quite right. You must come away."

"What's happened?" Nick asked again.

"Take the children *away*," Judith was shouting, above the hubbub.

Melibee was feeling his way along the passageway by running the fingertips of one hand along the top of the balustrade; and he chivvied us to go ahead of him. But before we had a chance to move, the door of Miss Thynne's room swung wide open and a younger maid came out, in a distraught state, still whimpering, tightly clutching two large pillows.

"I was just checking she was awake," the girl was sobbing, "she always likes me to go in and say a word, first thing. I've never seen – I've never . . ." And she became incoherent with crying, again. Judith ran back towards her from the top of the stairs, pushing past us and trying to close the door; but it was too late to stop us seeing exactly what had caused the commotion.

Miss Thynne's room, for the most part, was immaculately tidy, the bed made, the photographs and hairbrushes on her small dressing table neatly arranged. But, while one of the heavy red curtains was tied back, the other was hanging loosely across the big window of her room, blocking out the dawn light. And the curtain wasn't the only thing hanging there. Suspended from the curtain rail, framed in the window with the rope normally used to tie back the curtain noosed tightly around her neck, was Miss Thynne. Her head hung limp and her feet dangled ten or twelve inches off the ground. Melibee may have urged us forward to the stairwell, and Judith may have pulled the door shut as quickly as she was physically able to; but we didn't need a word of explanation from anyone, now.

Miss Thynne had clearly been dead for several hours.

CHAPTER 5
SUSPICIONS

We were almost completely silent as we walked through the woods, lost in our own thoughts. Lash knew something was wrong: at first he tried to bring us sticks to throw, but he soon sensed we weren't in the mood, and he stayed close to us, without running ahead. The atmosphere of shock and confusion in the house had continued; and, without anyone actually saying so, we knew it was best if we made ourselves scarce today. Amid all the chaos, nobody had mentioned the damaged window; and any worries we might have had about getting into trouble for that had been diminished by events a thousand times more terrible.

"You liked her, didn't you?" said Nick, after we'd been walking for a long time.

"She was starting to be our friend," I said. And I felt acutely — more so than Nick did, I suspected — the force of her words yesterday afternoon: "Someone has to help you." There weren't actually many people doing that, and Kniveacres had started to feel like a dangerous place to be. "She'd just got round to trusting us enough to tell us things," I said. "And there was lots I still wanted to ask her. Hundreds and hundreds of things."

"Yesterday afternoon," said Nick, slowly, thinking it through as he spoke, "didn't you think it was strange how she was suddenly on our side? How she changed? Once we were in the library, she told us all sorts of things – but she's never done that before, she's always told us to stop asking so many questions. It was as though she *knew* something was going to happen to her. Like she realised there were some things she'd better say before it was too late."

"She'd fallen out with Sir Septimus," I said. "That was what changed. She suddenly wanted to help us because she realised what an old ogre he is." We came to a gigantic old oak tree, which we always used as a landmark to guide us in the right direction through the forest. "You know," I added – I had been thinking about this in the night, before any of this morning's terrible events had unfolded – "she was about the same age as our mother."

Nick fell silent again. He was more used to death than I was, I realised. He had grown up among violent people, many of them sailors, who lived a grim life at sea and a vicious life on shore between voyages. People around him must have died violent or unpleasant deaths quite regularly. The bosun, the man he had always taken for his father, used to beat him on the slightest pretext and treat him with general rough contempt; and the dreadful Mrs Muggerage was, if anything, even worse. To cap it all, the bosun had been killed last summer in a fight, his body thrown into the Thames. It was all routine as far as Nick was concerned; and yet he was plainly shocked by this morning's discovery, having thought, no doubt, that he'd left all that violence and death behind him.

Something had been bothering him before we left the house, and he had made a point of moving my bed and fishing in the drawer for the *Addendum* we had secreted away from the library. Within seconds he'd found the words he was looking for – which I had completely forgotten, until he showed them to me again. *For the story behind the hangings, refer to the first floor plan on pages 168–9.*

Was this what it meant? Had "the hangings" started again? Or might this be some kind of prophecy – like the one in the other old book Damyata had left open for Sir Septimus to find? Unfortunately the *Addendum* didn't seem to provide much more information or anything that could be construed as a further clue. Nevertheless, Nick had put it in his pocket and brought it with him.

We were nearing the village, and I had just made out the golden stone of the church through the trees for the first time, when I felt a sharp pain on the side of my neck.

"Ouch!" I cried. "What was that?"

"What was what?"

"Something hit me – or bit me." I lifted my hand to my neck, and found a rough graze just under my ear.

"Are you bleeding? Let's have a look."

Lash gave a sudden bark. There was a sharp crack as something hit Nick's coat.

"What's happening?"

"Someone's throwing things at us."

There was a crunching sound from somewhere among the trees behind us; a few seconds later another missile hit Nick, this time above his eye.

"Argh!" He bent down and picked up the object that had hit him. It was a piece of white gravel, the size of a broad bean.

"Who's there?" he called. There was more rustling, and the cracking of twigs, but no one showed themselves. Lash began to bark now, continuously. "There they are," Nick said.

Through the trees we could see two children, probably a bit younger than ourselves, running away. We didn't bother chasing them. Lash's barking had scared them off.

"They must have had a catapult," said Nick, rubbing his head. "Are you all right?"

"Yes, it's nothing."

"Two of the village kids. Thought it was a good joke, I suppose. Little horrors."

"They've gone round the back of the church," I said. "I don't suppose we'll meet them again."

We walked up the path through the churchyard. Someone had taken the fallen gargoyle away, but hadn't yet put it back where it belonged. Kicking at the grass near where he'd been standing the other day, Nick could see dents in the earth where the gargoyle had hit the ground.

"This is where it fell," he said. "Where do you suppose they've taken it?" He looked around, to see if someone might have propped it up against the church wall; but it wasn't there, and it wasn't in the porch. "Didn't you say yesterday morning you were looking at a tombstone we'd read something about?" he recalled, reaching inside his pocket for the flimsy little *Addendum*. "While I was standing out here almost getting crushed to death? Shall we have another look, now that we've got this with us?"

"I'll show you where it is," I said.

As we pushed open the heavy oak door, we could see that the little church was as empty and silent as it had been the previous day. There weren't even any candles flickering on the tall stands. The shadows in the corners were profound, and the silence so intense it was a bit like stepping out of the world altogether.

"I wonder whereabouts Lamb found that silver box," Nick whispered, looking around. "We don't know whether he meant inside or outside, do we?"

"He wouldn't be so careless as to drop something else," I said.

"It's not a question of being careless," replied Nick, looking carefully between the pews as he walked down the aisle. "He probably *meant* someone to find it. Don't you think?"

But there was nothing to be seen on the floor of the church, and I beckoned Nick over to the gravestone which I'd been inspecting yesterday, with its sick-looking skeleton and its Latin inscriptions.

"Letherskin," read Nick, "yes, that was the name, wasn't it?" He turned over the pages of the *Addendum*, looking for the right place. "There's not really enough light to see properly," he said. "Can you remember what it said?"

"Something about, if you want to know more, look at the Letherskin grave," I said, not very helpfully.

"Got it," Nick said, squinting at the pages, and reading aloud with difficulty. "*A further intriguing connection has been lately – latterly – discovered between the buildings of the village and the Hall. Seek out the Letherskin grave in the –* the what? *– the east wall of St Moribunda's church, where the eye will find the secret.* Erm – that's all it says."

"Well, I'm afraid my eye's not finding any secrets," I said. "It's all in Latin. SCURRA CAELI REX MORTIUM. Doesn't help me much, that."

"No," muttered Nick, "me neither."

"I wish I'd asked Miss Thynne," I said.

There was a long silence. We both stared at the tombstone, but it was a few minutes before we could get Miss Thynne's image out of our heads and concentrate on what secrets it could possibly conceal. "Is there a skeleton at Kniveacres, at all?" I asked.

Nick was looking up at the fleshless hand with which the skeleton was turning the page of the big carved book. "There's a bone-finger," he said.

"Very funny," I said. "Surely that's not the secret – is it?"

He laughed. "Shouldn't think so," he said. "But I wish we knew what the Latin meant. I *bet* that's it."

I looked around the church. "Well, this isn't getting us very far," I said.

"Let's go, then," said Nick. But something occurred to him, and he started looking closely at the walls near the door.

"What are you doing?"

"I wondered if I could find a doorway, or a staircase, or some-thing – some way Bonefinger might have been able to get up the tower to dislodge that gargoyle."

"You're obsessed with that gargoyle," I said.

"It nearly killed me!" he squeaked, indignantly. "If *you'd* been standing under it you'd be quite interested in how it got pushed off, too."

But there was no door to be found, and no stairs – just the

ancient stone walls and the high dark space of the tower, rising far above our heads; and I persuaded Nick back out into the soft autumn light. Lash had sat down in the porch to wait for us, and he was pleased to be off again.

"So where shall we go?" I wondered. We'd come out for a walk, but without any clear intention of what we were going to do; all we were concerned about was not being in the Hall. Nick may have been about to offer a suggestion when, just as we approached the lych-gate out onto the village green, he stopped in his tracks.

"What's *that*?"

I gasped. Clinging to the gate, with its head sticking up over the top, was a figure – which, for a few seconds, I thought must be a real person. Until I realised it was an effigy: a stuffed manikin, like a scarecrow.

We went up to it. It had been tied by the neck and ankles to the wooden gate, and consequently hung there in a saggy posture, with its arms limply by its sides and its belly protruding forward. Lash sniffed at it, fascinated. It was really just a few old clothes, stuffed with straw to imitate a human figure, with a head made of a cracked old plant-pot onto which someone had drawn eyes and a mouth in charcoal, and put a woollen hat tightly on top.

"What a *very* odd thing," I said.

"Look over there," said Nick, pointing, "there's another one."

Sitting by a wall under an overhanging horse-chestnut tree was another effigy, slumped just like a drunken man asleep, with its arm hooked around an empty glass cider-flagon. It was dressed like a huntsman, in riding breeches, long black boots and a tweed jacket. Again, straw spilled from the end of the jacket sleeves, betraying what the figure was really made of; and, going closer, we could see that its head was a muslin grain-bag, stuffed and squashed to form a sphere, with cloth patches sewn on to represent eyes, a nose and a mouth.

"These weren't here yesterday, were they?" I said.

"No," said Nick, "they're a bit weird, aren't they?"

"What do you suppose they're *for*?" I wondered.

"There's someone coming," Nick said. "It looks like Mrs Gossage. Maybe we should ask her."

Scuttling along by the wall of the churchyard, from the direction of Mr Greywether's cottage where we'd been yesterday, was the small, bonneted figure of Amelia Gossage – a brisk, sharp-tongued woman with a face as round and purple as a turnip, who was a good friend of Fanny Nisbet and with whom we'd had many conversations in the months we'd lived here. She gave her opinions readily, and had struck us at first as a bit fierce; but we'd become used to her manner. Today, though, she was looking troubled; and when she saw us she quickened her pace noticeably, as though she was anxious not to speak to us.

"Good morning, Mrs Gossage," called Nick.

She shot us a glare from under her bonnet; but, unless she turned right round and walked back the way she had come, she had no choice but to come along the path towards us.

"It's not a good morning," she said as she approached, "and you've no business calling it that to my face. You won't find a welcome here so you'd be better off getting yourselves back to Kniveacres." And she continued on her way.

"Mrs Gossage," Nick called after her, "what do you mean, we

won't find a welcome?"

She slowed, and seemed to be thinking about whether or not to say any more. In the event she turned around and, standing a few feet away, she more or less spat at us: "After what happened, you expect people to be pleased to see you?" Her lips curled in scorn and fury as she spoke. "Justina Thynne was a good woman. Good, really good – do either of you know what that means? She had more goodness in her little finger than any Cloy ever had in their whole body and soul. She didn't deserve any of this and nor did her family. No good ever came of anyone who got themselves involved with Cloys. It's a shame you two ever came to Kniveacres, and a shame you're not going away again this very day!" She turned to go; but one further thing occurred to her, and she looked back at us. "But you listen to me," she said, "our celebrations will be going ahead, you can be sure of that. You can't take *that* away from us!" And, rage boiling in her round little face, she wheeled around and carried on up the path away from us, walking faster than ever.

"I don't understand," I said to Nick, feeling a bit shaken. "What are *we* supposed to have done wrong?"

"I don't know." Nick was watching some children on the green outside the nearest cottage: five of them, all different ages. They had seen us, and had started to jeer. "Maybe we had better go back," said Nick in a low voice. The biggest of the children, a boy about our age, solidly built with a pudgy, hostile face, went over to a wooden box near the cottage wall, and picked some things out of it. They were crab-apples and plums. As we stood, not sure where to go, the boy began to throw the fruit at us. Three or four hard little apples sailed towards us, and one of them hit Nick's arm, surprisingly hard. The other smaller children joined in, laughing now.

"Stop that," shouted Nick, picking up an apple and flinging it back.

"Don't," I said to him. "Ignore them."

Lash was barking at them, and the two or three youngest children were looking at him uncertainly; but the eldest boy was plainly not afraid of him, and as Lash started to venture towards the group of children a well-aimed apple hit him, with a sharp thud, on his flank.

"Lash!" I shouted. "Come back here! Here!"

The children were all throwing the fruit now, and quite a lot of it was hitting us, mainly that thrown by the eldest boy. I took hold of Lash's collar; he was still barking, but he was confused by the falling missiles, not sure whether to chase them or dodge them.

"De-vils," one of them taunted; and the others took up the chant, until in no time they were screaming at us, running forward to fling the fruit before retreating back to the box to get more. An under-ripe plum caught me smack in the middle of my cheek. We were doing our best to shield ourselves with our arms; but wherever the hard little fruits hit home, they hurt, and they were splitting as they hit us and making a sticky mess of our clothes.

"De-vils, de-vils, de-vils!" The children were getting bolder, and coming closer before taking aim. They had backed us against the wall of the churchyard. Fruit smashed around our heads on the stones of the wall, and fell around our feet. The wooden box now empty, they started to gather up fallen conkers – both in and out of their spiky casings – and throw those instead.

"Let's try and get to the gate," I said to Nick. "We've got to go back." Still under attack, we moved back towards the lych-gate where the stuffed scarecrow was hanging. I was still holding on to Lash, afraid that he'd be hurt; and when I next looked back at the children I could see that the large boy was now clutching not a conker or an apple, but a stone the size of a big potato.

"No!" I shouted at him. "No, stop it now! That's enough!"

"Quick," said Nick, "they won't listen. Just run."

"That's enough! That's enough!" Suddenly another voice broke through the shouts of the children; the jeering died away and the missiles stopped coming. Fanny Nisbet was in the midst of them, pushing them aside, slapping the conkers out of the little ones' hands. She was no bigger than the eldest of the boys, but she instantly made sheepish infants of them all. "Go home!" she snapped. "Go on, get back home, all of you!" They began to slouch away, resentfully; and she came over the grass towards us with a face full of concern. Lash barked at her in recognition, and as she got closer I let him go and greet her.

"Come on," she said, putting her hand reassuringly on Lash's furry head, "come quickly, and get cleaned up." She marched with us over the green, in a straight line to her cottage: it was only half a minute's walk, but we spent the whole time looking around warily, in case we were about to encounter someone else who was going to throw things or shout inexplicable curses at us. And there did seem to be people standing around, watching us, from outside a few of the cottages – until we realised they were just more scarecrows, mounted on wooden posts in people's gardens or propped against walls, at various points around the green. As we neared Fanny's cottage we could see one looking out over Mr Greywether's garden wall: it had been arranged in an old wooden bathchair, its legs covered up with a blanket, like a watchful old man, with a huge grinning head made from the gigantic pumpkin we'd watched him carrying around yesterday.

Fanny ushered us inside, and there was Lamb, sitting on a bench in the stone-flagged parlour. He stood up, in his awkward way, when he saw us.

"Ngao," he said.

"Hello, Lamb," I replied.

Fanny closed the door, and stood there for a few moments, ashen-faced. "What a terrible day," she said, shaking her head. "What a terrible, terrible day it is."

"What's going on, Mrs Nisbet?" Nick asked.

"If only I knew," she said. "It's a terrible, terrible day. To think of that poor young woman, just like that, and with no explanation. That's the terrible thing, you see, my dears, that no one can explain it, and when there are no explanations people turn to suspicions and – and supersititions." She came up to us, and touched us both on the arm. "But are you all right? Did they hurt you?"

"We're fine," I said, "it was just – unexpected."

"Terribly frightening, I should think," she said, going to the stone sink and picking up a cloth, "the other children turning on you like that, whatever next?" She began dabbing at our clothes with the cloth; then seemed to change her mind. "If you take these coats off, I'll rub them clean," she said. "Put them down there. I'll do that in a minute. First we must – oh, I don't know what we must do, what a terrible day. I'm all at sixes and sevens." She was visibly trembling as she sat down, and motioned to us to do the same. Lash went from person to person, licking their fingers; I made him sit down at my feet.

"You must tell me how it really was," she said. "Did you see her, the poor thing? When were you last with her? Oh, it's all so hard to believe."

We told her about how upset Miss Thynne had been in recent days, and about our conversation with her yesterday afternoon, and how changed she had seemed. And we went through what we had seen this morning: the commotion and wailing upstairs, and the dreadful glimpse of her through the open door. All the time, Fanny reacted by sighing and pulling faces suggesting ever-mounting anguish and compassion.

"She was well known," said Fanny, rocking backwards and forwards. "People knew her since she was a little child. She went away, as a girl, to India, and she's had postings as a governess here and there, but she came back often, and her family belongs here. There have been Thynnes at the Red House for as long as anyone remembers. They're good people."

"But Mrs Nisbet," said Nick, "why is everyone so angry with *us*?"

"It's just their way," she said. "Things changed at Kniveacres when you two came. There's been a lot of gossip about you. Suddenly Miss Thynne was engaged there to look after you, and now this happens. I suppose people think that you're . . . to blame. That you must have made her life hard." She looked nervously from one to the other of us. "And they remember . . ."

She hesitated, now, her flow suddenly inhibited.

"They remember what, Mrs Nisbet?" I inquired.

"It's a lot of nonsense," she said, going slightly white, "but after all that's happened . . . well, people are talking about the curse, again. Now then. How silly it all is. But people will be people."

The shrieks of the children on the green echoed in my head. "Do you mean, about the Devil coming to live at Kniveacres?" I asked.

Nick snorted with disbelief. "And they think *we're* the devils?"

"Ever since you came," she said, "they've – now, I shouldn't be saying this."

"I was a *printer's* devil," I said. "Is it because of that? It's not like a *real* devil. Didn't they realise? Is that why they thought—?"

"It's not that," she cut in. "But you arrived, from outside, just all of a sudden, one day you weren't here and the next day you were, and nobody quite knew why, and everyone was suddenly talking about you. And ever since you came, they've said things about you. The pair of you. About your hair, and eyes, and the way you both look just the same. Can't tell them apart, people say. Devil's children are like that, they say. The one soul, in two bodies. Can be in two places at once. Not natural."

She was parroting the things she had heard, but her discomfort was obvious, and when I looked at Nick I could see he was thinking the same thing.

"Mrs Nisbet, you don't believe all this, do you?" I asked gently. "You can't possibly believe it, can you?"

"We're twins," said Nick. "Of *course* we look alike."

"Well now," said Fanny, looking a bit scared, "maybe people here haven't had twins, not for a lot of years. Maybe people don't know what they're like, or why such children should come and live among us. And why people should start hearing strange things, and why the children's governess should just hang herself at Kniveacres with no explanation."

I was starting to feel frightened. It sounded a little bit as though Fanny was going to turn on us too: having started out being kind, she was sitting here talking herself into believing the same nonsense as Mrs Gossage, and apparently everyone else.

"Mrs Nisbet," said Nick, "we're only trying to understand, like everyone else. We're frightened too. We don't know what's going on, or why this has happened, any more than anyone in the village does."

"We need you to help us," I said. "You and Lamb, you've been so kind. We feel as though we're running out of people we can trust."

"Mrs Nisbet," continued Nick, "has this happened before? Have there been hangings at Kniveacres before, which people remember?"

She looked at us, her face still white.

"I'm not sure I know what you mean," she said.

"It's just that – we found a book, in the library at the Hall," Nick elaborated, "which said something about 'the story behind the hangings'."

"Well, I don't know what that would be," she said. "As far as I know there haven't been – at least, I never heard of it."

"And so why do they say bad things always happen to people

who get mixed up with the Cloys?" persisted Nick. "Mrs Gossage said that to us just this morning. What does she mean?"

"Oh, people tell all sorts of stories," she said. She was looking at Lamb, as though she wanted his eyes to tell her whether she should say anything.

"Like what?" Nick asked.

She was still hesitating; but maybe Lamb's eyes *had* signalled something, because after a few seconds she continued. "Well, now," she said, "I don't want to go telling too many tales because I don't know, aright, one way or the other. But there's a lot of talk, and there's always been a lot of talk, about – what they call the Cloys' 'reputation'."

"And what is their reputation?"

"That Sir Septimus, and his brothers, have – secrets in their past," she stumbled.

This was maddening. Was she going to tell us anything, or not?

"What sort of secrets, Mrs Nisbet?"

There were a few more seconds' silence. Then, suddenly, it was like the cork of a bottle popping. "That they can none of them leave young women alone, for one thing," she blurted. "And that the family money hasn't been made by what you'd call honest means – especially in India. And that they're known out there for their cruelty, cruelty that goes far beyond the way they treat any poor young wretch from the village who's caught with a rabbit over by Kniveacres at night, and heaven knows that's cruelty enough. And that their powerful friends have covered up for them, many times over. And that they're only out for themselves, and everyone else – including their honest servants – can go hang." She realised what she'd said, and brought her hand to her mouth in horror. "I meant – I didn't mean . . ."

"It's all right, Mrs Nisbet," I said. "We know what you meant, and we won't breathe a word of what you've said, to anyone. Will we, Nick?"

He shook his head. He'd been gazing at her, intently, as she spoke every word. "No," he said at length, "no, of course not."

"Well. There now," she said. "I'd best not say any more. I don't want to go telling tales."

I couldn't resist a slight smile at Nick.

"I think we'd better go," I said. "We've put you to enough trouble."

"You haven't," she began, "it's not . . ." But there was the glint of tears at the corners of her eyes now, and it was clear we'd only upset her if we stayed here any longer.

As we stood up and got ready to go, Lamb went through to the little sitting-room at the front of the house; and a few moments later he came back, with an urgent expression in his eyes. He grunted, and beckoned to us.

"Dear me, now, what else has Lamb been finding?" worrited Fanny, as we followed him through into the tiny, neat room. He was standing at the window: there was something outside he wanted us to look at. He gestured, and Nick drew back the lace curtain so we could peer out.

The window gave us a clear view out across the village green. Stalking towards us, from the direction of the church, was Bonefinger. Even if his clothes hadn't been so unmistakeable, his extraordinary walk gave him away.

"He must know we're here," I said, gripping the back of a

chair in fear. "He's come to find us."

But, between the lace curtains, we watched him walk right past the cottage, without so much as glancing at it.

"He's going straight past," I whispered, incredulous.

"He's heading for the inn," Nick said, with relief.

Sure enough, Bonefinger slowed as he reached the threshold of the inn next door. A low, broad-fronted building with leaded windows and an entrance porch supported by two huge oak beams, each the girth of an entire tree, it proclaimed its function with a dirty wooden sign which today was swinging gently in the breeze. "THE CLOY ARMS", it said, in faded black letters; and above this legend, the familiar shield-shaped coat of arms which was imprinted on so many of the books in the library, and on the cover of the little book Nick still had in his coat pocket. Because the buildings of the village curved around the green, the façade of the inn was tilted away from the front of Fanny's cottage at a slight angle; and from this front window we could see Bonefinger in the big entrance porch, where he proceeded to stamp his feet, hard and repeatedly, to rid his boots of the mud they'd picked up on the woodland track.

"You be careful of that man," said Fanny.

"Is he well known in the village?" I asked.

"Well enough known, but not well liked," she replied. "Wouldn't trust him an inch. Does all the Cloys' dirty work, and always has – and he still thinks he can fool people by smiling and fawning and being ever so charming. Well, nobody's daft enough to be fooled. He's got a nerve, showing his face in the village this morning. I suppose he's come to meet the mail-coach. There, look," she said, peering out, "he's gone inside now. You keep out of his way, and get back to the Hall as quickly as you can."

"Thank you for coming to help us, Mrs Nisbet," said Nick solemnly. "And thank you for making us so welcome, Lamb." He held out a hand.

Uncertain at first, Lamb reached out and took Nick's hand. Nick's grip tightened slightly, and while the poor boy's face was hardly capable of anything you could call a smile, there was a sudden warmth in his eyes.

"What are all these scarecrows for?" I asked, as Fanny led us to the back door.

"The guys?" she said, surprised. "You don't know about the guys? Oh, that's an old tradition. Ancient, they say. Every house makes a guy, around the equinox. They draw off the evil spirits."

"Like Guy Fawkes night?" I said. "But it's not November."

"No. It's – well, I don't know where it comes from, but it just happens, here, in the country. Always has, far as I know." She looked a bit flustered at having to explain. "All the evil spirits go into the guys. That way they leave us alone, for another year. It's a ceremonial. Lamb has made ours – but you haven't put it out yet, have you, Lamb? Needs a few finishing touches, I think. But he's very proud of it, bless the boy."

She remembered our coats. "Oh dear, and look, I haven't cleaned them for you," she said. "Let me just give them a rub—"

"It really doesn't matter, Mrs Nisbet," said Nick, taking them from her, "they're not too bad. Look – these bits of apple just come off with a flick."

"We'd better go," I interjected, before Nick started demon-strating by flicking tiny chunks of apple all over Mrs Nisbet's parlour floor.

"Now you two will take care, won't you?" she said anxiously. "Get back home, quickly."

We took our leave. I fixed Lash's rope to his collar again to stop him running off; and as we rounded the corner of the cot-tage and came out onto the village green, I felt Nick take hold of my wrist.

"Wait," he murmured, pulling me back. "I'm not sure about this."

There wasn't much sign of life in the village – it was lunchtime, and most people had probably gone indoors to eat – but there were still the guys, ten or more of them, dotted around the village in their various strange postures. Even though we knew they weren't real, it was still hard to believe they weren't somehow watching us, acting as eyes and ears for their suspi-cious owners. As we hovered by the wall, deliberating, I caught sight of a massive, florid figure with a shock of white hair stand-ing up on top of his head, striding across the green towards the front door of the inn. It was Sloughter Cripps, the man Fanny Nisbet said had heard the singing in the churchyard the other night. His stride was purposeful, his fists clenched: if I hadn't known that was the way he always walked, I'd have sworn he was coming over to the inn to pick a fight with someone.

"He looked furious," said Nick, as Sloughter disappeared inside. "Did you see him? I wouldn't want to bump into *him* today."

"Do you think the coast's clear?" I asked nervously. We'd

certainly be very exposed if we just walked back across the green towards the church, and neither of us fancied a repeat performance from the village children, or any further tirades from the grown-ups.

Lash had pricked up his ears, and was standing staring into the distance; and before long we heard a rumbling from the far end of the village and realised what he'd been listening to. As we watched from the cover of the cottage wall, a big stagecoach came into view and trundled noisily up the road, its coachman shouting raucously to the horses and to alert the people in the village to their arrival. The handsome, shiny black and claret sides of the coach were flecked with mud, and the four big wheels sent spray flying up on either side as it veered off the main road and through the deep puddles on the track leading up towards the inn. There was a sudden flurry of activity next door, as people emerged from the inn to meet it. With loud cries of "Whoa, now, whoa!" the coachman pulled the horses up right outside the front door. There was a hubbub of voices, and a jingling of harnesses as the horses shook their heads, glad of the chance to rest. Someone stepped up to the coach to open the doors; men took hold of the bridles of the horses, and two or three boys came running with pails of water and bags of feed.

Now people began to emerge from houses nearby, some just to stand by their gates and watch the daily routine, others to walk over and greet the coach. The emerging passengers stood looking around them, greatly relieved to be able to stretch their limbs before stepping inside the inn for refreshment. There was a woman, dressed neatly in grey, with two tall young men of about fifteen who were presumably her sons. There were two or three local men, dressed roughly, who jumped down and began bantering with villagers who'd come over to talk. There was an uncertain-looking young man clutching a leather bag of the kind doctors carried, who cast a long glance around the entire landscape of the village before venturing towards the porch of the inn. And there were two gentlemen in long frock coats whose collars they turned up high against the chilly wind as they stepped down. They seemed to have a sense of purpose about them; we watched them conversing briefly with someone from the inn before nodding at one another and going inside.

"What do you think Bonefinger's up to?" I hissed. "He's obviously meeting someone from the coach, isn't he?"

Nick shrugged. "Maybe he's just come to pick up the mail, like Fanny said."

"I wouldn't be surprised if it was those two," I said, ignoring him.

The coachman, eager to follow his passengers indoors and enjoy the ale that was no doubt waiting on the counter for him, reached into his pocket and pulled out a handful of coins, which he counted into the palm of a tiny boy. As the coachman turned and slouched into the inn, the boy leaped onto the running-board of the coach and pulled himself with great agility up onto the roof, where he sat down among the pile of boxes and luggage, to guard it. Happy and self-conscious, he spent the next few minutes sticking his tongue out at his playmates standing on the road below.

"This is our chance," said Nick. "While everyone's distracted by the coach."

"Wait," I said. "I just want to go and have a quick look."

"Mog, come *on*," said Nick, "let's just make a break for it."

"Take Lash," I said, "I'll catch you up. I'll be half a minute. Everyone's gone in, they won't see me. I'll be all right. Honestly."

While Nick and Lash made their way back down the path, past the beehives, towards the church, I crept around behind the stagecoach and over to the side wall of the inn. Nobody noticed me as I pressed myself against the wall, and peered cautiously in through the tap-room window.

Coach passengers and villagers were milling around inside, calling for orders; and, irritatingly, at the precise moment I started to watch them, one rather large man came to stand with his back right up against the diamond-leaded pane, and suddenly all I could see through the glass was his fat backside. But, when he briefly moved aside, I could plainly see Bonefinger sitting at a table, right beside the inn's enormous inglenook, in which an open log fire was blazing. He was talking earnestly to someone: before I could see who it was, the large backside moved into view again, and I had to wait for another chance. I turned to take a quick look down the path just to make sure Nick and Lash hadn't got out of sight. Now, as the backside moved again, I got another glimpse of the scene inside the inn; and I could make out two other men opposite Bonefinger, their heads leaning in over the table so the three of them could whisper together. Sure enough, it was the two heavy-coated men who had got off the coach a few minutes earlier. They had beer and bread in front of them; and, as I watched, they all suddenly burst into laughter and raised their glasses in a gesture of hilarity. Through the glass I could hear them as they roared some indistinct toast or, possibly, oath, before quaffing copiously and grinning at one another. And now, moving once again to let someone inside squeeze past, the backside pressed itself against the window and obscured my view completely.

But I'd seen what I wanted to see; and I was about to turn and run, to catch up with Nick and Lash.

"Seen enough, 'ave yer?" came a voice. Startled, I looked up.

It was the little boy sitting on top of the coach, looking after the luggage.

"Thought no one could see yer, spyin'," commented the boy, looking triumphant. "Well I seen yer, and I'll get pennies for tellin'."

"You can tell who you like," I said.

"I will!" he shouted at my receding back, as I ran down the path. "Devil!"

I caught up with Nick as he was nearing the overhanging trees by the churchyard; he turned as he heard my footsteps.

"I was right," I said, breathlessly. "Bonefinger was – meeting those two men. They were – talking and laughing. They looked – thick as thieves. Finding something ever so funny."

"Did anyone see you?"

"Only a little boy. I don't think . . ."

My words died on my lips. I reached out instinctively to take Lash's rope.

"Don't think what?" asked Nick. Then he saw it too.

Right on the edge of the green, by the churchyard, someone had stood up a frame of wooden planks shaped like an upside-down L, to represent a gibbet. Hanging from it were two more guys – small ones, in tatty old children's clothes, with heads made of stuffed sacks. Black wool had been attached to the sacking to give both the figures a conspicuous clump of dark hair. A rope tied around the crosspiece held them both by the neck at its other end, so that their heads lolled grotesquely on their shoulders; their empty breeches dangled and flapped in the wind.

We stopped. The gibbet had been placed right opposite the lych-gate, so that it was the first thing anyone would see if they approached the village through the churchyard. It hadn't been here when we came through the gate this morning. Whoever had put it up must have done so while we were inside Fanny Nisbet's cottage. The child-scarecrows revolved, slowly, on their short rope, swinging round first in one direction, then back in the other. And only now that we were close to them could we see that, most chillingly of all, hanging in between them was another crude little figure: a collection of yellowing pillowcases and old rags, stuffed and twisted into the likeness of a scrawny dog.

"Nick," I said, terrified, gripping his arm, "they're *us*. Aren't they? They're supposed to be *us*."

CHAPTER 6

BONEFINGER TIGHTENS HIS GRIP

We made it back to the Hall without meeting anyone else; but we had never run so fast through those woods, nor stumbled over so many roots, nor slipped into so many muddy puddles. When we got home we were shaken, breathless and filthy, and Lash had turned from a honey-coloured lurcher into a sort of brownish-grey wolfhound. I didn't dare take him inside, and I tied him up under the kitchen windows, by the door at the bottom of the stairwell which we and the servants used as our entrance to the east wing.

To our astonishment, as we were climbing the stairs, we met Bonefinger coming down them.

"Miss Imogen, and Master Dominic," he said, nodding politely. His unblinking eyes flicked up and down, taking in the sight of us. "Your attire would suggest you have met with some accident, or else been somewhat reckless in your choice of pastime."

We couldn't reply. For one thing we hadn't got our breath back, and for another we were simply too astounded to see him, standing calmly on the stairs. The last time I'd seen him he'd been deep in conversation over a full jug of ale, by the fire at the Cloy Arms; and we'd run back as fast as our legs would carry us. How on *earth* had he got here before us?

"You'll wish to change," he observed, "and I must convey a request from Sir Septimus, that you both attend him in his study at four. He has certain items he wishes to communicate, arising partly, no doubt, from the distressing events of this morning." He looked from one to the other of us. "You'll excuse me," he said, "there are many arrangements to be made. Please do your best to avoid any – *disruption*." And he continued past us, down the stairs.

"What on *earth* is going on?" I squeaked, as soon as we'd got far enough up the stairs to be out of earshot. "How did he get here? Not a trace of mud on him, and not even out of breath!"

"I don't have a clue," said Nick, emphatically, shaking his head. "It can't – it wasn't – it can't have been somebody *else* we saw at the inn, can it?"

"You saw him with your own eyes," I said, "and so did I. There can't be two Bonefingers. Maybe he came on a horse?"

"He was on foot," Nick said. "We saw him."

"Well, maybe one of those men *lent* him a horse to get back on."

Nick shrugged. "I really don't know," he said. "I'm going to go and get changed."

He disappeared up the stairs; and I was about to go to my own room and change, when I decided to turn around and go back outside. I unhooked Lash's rope and we went for a walk, on our own. A minute or two on the stairs had persuaded me I wasn't ready to spend time inside the house: it was too

oppressive, and the memory of the terrible events of this morning – only a few yards further up the very same staircase – was
too fresh and raw. Four o'clock, when we'd been summoned to
see Sir Septimus, would be quite soon enough.

We played in the gardens, and ran down to the lake, and
walked in a huge circuit around the park. The storm had practically stripped every tree of its leaves, in a single day, and had
left the grounds strewn with fallen twigs and small branches.
There was no shortage of sticks to throw for Lash, and he
fought and scrabbled for them in the piles of leaves just like a
puppy.

My thoughts were spinning in my head, and I was trying to
get things into some sort of logical order. Miss Thynne, just as
she was turning out to be the best, if not the only, friend we had
inside Kniveacres Hall, had killed herself – or, at least, so it
appeared. Instead of helping us, the village was actively blaming
us for the tragedy – regarding her death as their loss, and our
fault. Bonefinger's behaviour was getting more and more sinister, and goodness only knew what Sir Septimus was about to tell
us to add to our troubles. I was starting to feel the fear of lone-
liness closing in, and I was more thankful with every passing
hour for Lash, and Nick. In my darkest days, as a little girl in the
orphanage in London, I had had no one. Nothing, but nothing,
could ever again approach the lonely terror of those years, and
I never wanted to experience anything like it again. As I grew
up, and found my feet in the city streets and learned a trade,
Lash had been my comfort. Now, I had Nick, who was so trust-
worthy, and who read my thoughts so effortlessly; even though
we'd only been together for such a tiny part of our lives, it

sometimes felt as though I'd grown up with him. I couldn't imagine life without him, now.

And somewhere out there, I reminded myself, was Damyata.

The mystery and possibility which that thought engendered sent a thrill running up my spine. To know that our father was close by – our *father* – I had to say it aloud to myself, and still I couldn't believe it, it sounded so strange and unfamiliar on my lips. Of course, he was still a distant and mysterious figure: someone we'd never properly met, and whom I still wasn't quite sure whether to be frightened of. But surely he must be on our side. For all the terrible and extraordinary things that had happened in the last few days, I couldn't stop thinking about the words Fanny Nisbet had uttered so bitterly this morning about Sir Septimus and his family. That, out in India, they had been notoriously cruel. That – how had she put it? – that they "couldn't leave young women alone". It made my flesh creep; but instinctively, I knew that Damyata knew all this, and that this was why he was such an enemy of Sir Septimus.

I felt a great deal better after our walk. An hour or so ago, when we got back from the village, Lash had been black with mud. Now, without having appeared to wash, he had become his golden-haired self again, as though the mere fresh air had been cleansing every trace of dirt from his coat as he ran. Even I didn't feel half as dirty as I had been, and the mud had dried sufficiently for me to be able to brush it easily off my hands and my clothes in light, harmless flakes. As we came back towards the courtyard, a sleek black carriage swept quietly away along the drive from the front of the house, pulled by a pair of elegant grey horses. I began to wonder what had been happening here while we were out this morning. I supposed there must have been a succession of carriages and visitors today: doctors, clergymen, undertakers, perhaps lawyers. I didn't know what time it was, but I sensed it must be nearing the time when we had to face Sir Septimus. I was dreading it; but I was very anxious not to be late.

I found Nick in the library, sitting looking at a book, at the table where we normally took our lessons. The sun was low in the sky, and a shiver ran through me as I remembered the last time we'd been in here, this time yesterday afternoon, with the storm raging outside and Miss Thynne in the mood of quiet indiscretion we had never seen before, and would never see again.

"I thought I'd wait in here," he said.

I couldn't sit down. I paced up and down beside the bookshelves. There were four clocks in the library: they varied in size from a tall grandfather clock beside the door, to a small jewelled carriage clock on a shelf at the far end; but they were all in agreement that there were less than ten minutes to go. Nick was silent. I didn't know what he'd been doing, or thinking, while I was out with Lash, and he didn't tell me; but I was willing to bet he was feeling just as much trepidation as I was, and just as much confusion and sheer exhaustion from the events of the last few days and nights.

"Did you find anything?" he asked.

"I wasn't looking for anything," I answered.

Outside the big windows, a gardener was raking up leaves. Even on a day like this, the sluggish mechanism of the Kniveacres routine ground on, and someone was devoting himself to trying to make the gardens look tidy. No matter what terrible events had unfolded indoors; they had no bearing on the gardener's tasks. The fallen leaves must be cleared: that was what he knew how to do, that was what he had been asked to do, so that was what he did. I found myself wondering whether this same gardener had had the task of clearing up the mess made by the falling lintel – about which, I was afraid, Sir Septimus would be having some stern words in a few minutes' time.

The door opened, and Melibee came in. At first he just stood at the open door, listening, saying nothing.

"You were not in your rooms," he said, after a few seconds. "I thought I would strike lucky if I tried the library." His keen ears had not only detected the sound of breathing, or slight movement, but had worked out that both of us were in here. "I believe Bonefinger told you that Sir Septimus has called for you."

We went with him, wordlessly, through the low-ceilinged passageways that led between the main part of the house and the tower. To get there he had to unlock two separate doors, and lock them behind us again. The floorboards creaked, and the corridors sloped at strange angles, until we emerged into the main stairwell of the tower and there was stone beneath our feet again. We were never allowed to come this way unaccompanied. When we got to the door of Sir Septimus's study, Melibee waited, and knocked. There was a gruff signal to enter.

Sir Septimus was again sitting at his desk, framed against the window in the late afternoon light. He looked tired, and troubled; and greyer than usual, if that was possible. "Thank youm, Melibeem," he said – and I heard Nick stifle a snort – "you may leave us." He sat, saying nothing, just looking at us, until Melibee had closed the door behind him. Then he spoke.

"It has been a – difficult dame," he said, hardly moving his lips as usual. "Things are – difficult. There is a lot of mm-idle talk, about what happened here last night, mand it is not easy to disabuse people of myths, once they start running." He waited, as though he expected us to say something; I was just about to open my mouth when he continued. "Bonefingerm, has reported alarming news," he went on, "that the villagers are in a violent mood. And that someone has erected, mm, meffigies of you two, on the green – hanging from a noose."

"It's true," I said in a low voice. "We saw them this morning."

"The villagers," he said, "are gentle people – mindividuallymm. But what they are capable of collectivelymm, is less certain. I hope you will understand meem, when I say I believe it is too dangerous, at present, for you to venture away from Kniveacres Hall. My wish you to remain here at all times. Is that clear?"

"May we go into the grounds and the park?" Nick asked.

"My see no harm," he muttered, "massuming you stay away from the woods, and never go beyond the park fences." He looked at us, expressionlessly. "My suppose I cannot confine youm, mindoors entirely."

There was a short silence. I glanced at Nick.

"That is all," said Sir Septimus. "But I do not wish to hear reports of your disobedience, mmm, or any nuisance caused on your part."

The door opened, without any apparent signal from Sir Septimus; and this time it was Bonefinger who came in. His gown flapped around his thin silk-stockinged legs, like the wings of a flying beetle.

"We are finished," grunted Sir Septimus shortly; and Bonefinger, looking at us, put his head on one side and gestured to the door with a slow, exaggerated unfurling of his arm.

"It could have been a whole lot worse," I said to Nick, after we'd got rid of Bonefinger and were sitting down with bread and jam in the dining-room. There was no cake for tea, because, in the grief and confusion of this morning, no one had made any; but we still didn't have much of an appetite anyway. "He didn't even *mention* the window. I thought he was being quite kind, actually, for him. He just doesn't want us to put ourselves in danger."

Nick swallowed a mouthful of bread. "He's got us where he wants us, though, hasn't he?" he said. "It's very convenient for him if we don't leave Kniveacres. No more gossip from the villagers. No more finding friends who can tell us things he'd prefer us not to hear."

"But the villagers *aren't* our friends," I said.

"Not today, maybe. But they'll come round. When they get over the shock, and find out a bit more. And anyway, what about Fanny?"

He was right, of course. It would suit Sir Septimus very nicely indeed if he could stop us from having any more contact with Fanny Nisbet. With no Miss Thynne, Fanny was more or less the only person left who might give us a straight answer to any of our questions.

"You don't imagine he doesn't *realise*," said Nick. "Bonefinger will have told him we've been spending time talking to Fanny. They'll have put two and two together."

"You think he saw us there?" I asked, worried.

"Maybe not, but he knew exactly where we were. Anyone in the village could have told him we'd gone inside with Fanny yesterday. And on Wednesday, for that matter."

"Who do you suppose those men were?" I asked. "In the Cloy Arms?"

"Who knows? Something to do with Sir Septimus's business affairs? We've no idea what they get up to, have we?"

Both Fanny and Miss Thynne had said things which made it obvious that Sir Septimus wasn't the most honest of men. There was no telling who he might be mixed up with – and Bonefinger evidently did plenty of his dirty work for him.

"Well, look," I said, "we can't *go* anywhere now, because Sir Septimus has forbidden it. And there's no one to teach us any lessons. So why don't we concentrate on watching Bonefinger really closely? Find out where he goes, and what he gets up to?"

"You'll have to be careful," said Nick. "He's got eyes in the back of his head, you know that. And in lots of other places besides."

"I might start tonight," I said. "I'd really love to have another look in that little pantry of his."

Nick stood up, and picked up his empty plate. "Well don't forget it's bath-night," he said.

I *had* forgotten; and it made my heart lift. Bath-night was the best thing that ever happened at Kniveacres. Huge pans and cauldrons of water were put on to boil in the kitchens from around the middle of the afternoon; and we were usually allowed to help with the process of bringing the water, in copper kettles and pewter jugs, to the oak-panelled bathroom on the ground floor, where we poured them into a huge porcelain bath-tub standing in the middle of the floor. Once we'd mixed hot and cold water in the tub, to the point where it was only *just* cool enough to avoid scalding ourselves, we took it in turns to wallow up to our necks in the water for ten luxurious minutes each. According to the servants, Sir Septimus, and Lady Cloy when she was alive, had insisted on introducing to Kniveacres the bathing practices to which they'd been accustomed in India. That meant a room so full of steam the panelling glistened with droplets of condensed water; chunks of soap, like amber, sitting in a china dish on a pedestal by the bath; bottles of oil scented with sandalwood to soften and anoint the skin afterwards; and huge cotton towels, laundered each week, and folded and piled on top of a linen-chest in sixes. For a household which was oth-erwise run in such an austere manner, it was a wonderfully extravagant ritual, and the weekly anticipation of it helped us to put up with all kinds of other privations. For a few minutes, as I lay there with beads of sweat on my face, my entire body gently poaching in the soapy water, I almost forgot the shocks and fears of the past few days.

I was still glowing, sitting in the library in a clean cotton nightshirt and a warm wraparound shawl, when Nick joined me, his hair damp and clean from his bath. We spent the last hour or so of most of our days this way, reading by lamplight. Only, tonight, I didn't have a book open when Nick came in.

"You know, your hair's getting quite long," was the first thing he said. Then he came to sit beside me and placed the *Addendum* on the table in front of me.

"I thought we could have a proper look," he said.

"It's getting a bit battered," I remarked, watching him smoothing out the paper of the flimsy book. "Maybe you should stop carrying it round in your pocket all the time."

"What have you been doing?" he asked.

"Thinking," I said.

He put the book to one side, without opening it, and leaned on the table, his head propped up on his hand, looking at me. "Me too," he said.

"Does it make any more sense to you?" I asked. "Than it did last night? Or the night before?"

He gave a short, ironic laugh. "It's hard to say, isn't it?"

"Well, what do we know, so far?" I said. "We know that two people have died. One of them, Bonefinger buried in the grounds on Monday night. But we still haven't a clue who that was. The other was Miss Thynne, who hanged herself."

"Things have been getting gradually worse," observed Nick, "ever since we followed Bonefinger that night. Before then, things were all right, weren't they? I mean, the house has always been creepy, and Bonefinger's always been a really suspicious type – but since Monday it's all gone out of control."

"Sometimes," I said, "I can feel – it's probably silly to say it, but I feel a sense of evil. Do you know what I mean? There's something not right. Something's in this house, a kind of – I don't know, maybe the villagers are right, maybe it's a curse."

Nick nodded, slowly. "It's since Damyata came," he said. "Do you think it's anything to do with him?"

"I don't know. But it's as though there's an evil spirit at Kniveacres, trying to harm us. Remember what happened out at the well? And the dumb-waiter, and the business with the window last night."

"And don't forget the gargoyle," said Nick. "It's not just the house. Everywhere we go, scary things happen. And the guys on the gibbet."

"Did you hear what Fanny said?" I asked him. "About the guys? That they make them every year so the evil spirits will move into them, and leave the village alone. I thought that was really interesting. It's like another superstition, isn't it, that evil spirits can go and live in the guys, and stop bothering everyone else. But it doesn't seem to have worked this year, does it?"

"Not yet," said Nick grimly.

"Evil spirits, or whatever they are," I said, "they got Miss Thynne."

Nick looked at me, significantly. "Just a few hours after she talked to us about Damyata, whose name is forbidden from being mentioned in this house," he said. "You know, I've been wondering whether she really did hang herself, or if it was just made to look that way."

"You mean, she might have been *murdered*?" I said.

"Ssh! Keep your voice down," said Nick. "I wouldn't be too surprised," he continued. "Would you put it past Sir Septimus? Or Bonefinger? Think about the things that have been happening to us. All those close shaves. You said it yourself: the well. Then the gargoyle. Then the dumb-waiter. Now the window-sill."

"You don't think they were *deliberate*?" I said incredulously. "The window-sill collapsing? How could anyone make that happen on purpose? No one would even expect us to be in there."

"I just don't see how they can all have been accidents," muttered Nick.

"But – why would they want to *murder* Miss Thynne?" I asked, trying to follow Nick's train of thought.

"To stop her talking."

"So the other person – the one Bonefinger buried – might have been murdered too?"

"Perfectly likely," said Nick.

"I think we're getting ahead of ourselves," I said. "We know Sir Septimus is frightened. Miss Thynne said so, didn't she? And we know Damyata's been here, threatening him. But—"

"We know Damyata and Sir Septimus have been enemies for a long time," interrupted Nick. "There's obviously something in Sir Septimus's past in India which Damyata wants to avenge. Judging from what Mrs Nisbet said, there could be any number of things the Cloys did in India which might make people want vengeance. It looks as though they've got quite a lot to answer for."

"But we don't know that Sir Septimus has *killed* anybody."

"I suppose not," conceded Nick, reluctantly.

"But Damyata's definitely come after him, for something," I agreed. "I expect he was looking for him in London last year, and didn't find him."

"But he found us," said Nick. "And now he's back, and he's tracked Sir Septimus down this time. And now some really frightening things have started to happen."

"Nick, Damyata's not going to turn out to be evil after all, is he?" I said in despair. "I was starting to think . . ."

"I think there was plenty of evil already here," said Nick. "If he really has worked out that we're here, too, he'll want to help us – because – well, because we're . . ."

"His children," I said.

Despite himself, Nick laughed. "That's almost the hardest thing of all to take in."

"I really can't believe it, Nick," I said. "After all these years of thinking I had no parents, suddenly to find out who he is. It's like a dream. And yet, he's not here. He pops up in the night and leaves his signature on a bit of paper, and hides away in churchyards and leaves clues and tokens for people to find. And meanwhile all sorts of horrible things start happening, and people start dying. But I want to *talk* to him. Don't you? I want him to *explain*."

There was a pause. "Yes," said Nick quietly, "I do, too. And I'm sure he will, Mog. Why would he want to hide from us? He's just playing games with Sir Septimus at the moment. He can't just walk in here, can he?"

"No. You're right. He *will* come and find us, won't he? When he can."

"I'm absolutely sure of it," said Nick.

I reached for his hand, and squeezed it hard.

"I want to go to bed," said Nick. He stood up.

"We should put some lamps out," I said, yawning.

"Leave them. Take one with you, and leave the rest. Someone else will come in and put them out after we've gone."

We closed the library door behind us and padded down the long corridor, past the stuffed tiger, towards our bedrooms; but halfway there, Nick stopped.

"Just a minute," he said, "I'm going back for a second. I left something in the library."

"What?"

"The *Addendum*."

I grimaced. "You'd better go and get it."

"I know."

As soon as I'd opened the door of my room, Lash got up to greet me; I put the lamp down and sat down on the edge of the bed, my shawl still wrapped around me, to make a fuss of him. I think he was always a bit disappointed when I'd had a bath: for the first few hours the soap probably blotted out all the exciting smells and tastes he was used to finding on my fingers and wrists, and he gave me a few brief licks and then looked up at me, a bit crestfallen, as if to say: "Well *that's* not very interesting."

After a minute or so, there was a knock at the door.

"It's me!" came Nick's voice.

"Come in."

He practically burst through the door. "Mog," he gasped, "it's Bonefinger!"

"What's Bonefinger?"

"Mog, I went back to the library to get the book, and I met him coming out. He sort of – looked at me, you know how he does, and I said I'd left something inside. And he said he'd get it for me, what was it – well, I couldn't tell him, could I? He'd never have given it to me. So I said it didn't matter, it could wait until tomorrow."

"That's a blow," I said.

"But Mog . . ." He looked around him now, and pushed the bedroom door shut as a precaution. "He was looking at me – and his face said it all. If you'd seen him . . . Mog, he *heard* us! He must have been in there all the time. We never checked the big sofa, did we? But I bet he was sitting in it, listening to us, the whole time we were talking. What idiots we are, Mog! He heard *every word*!"

Sleep didn't come easily, that night.

Every creak of the ancient house, inside or outside my room, made me sit bolt upright. The wind was still high tonight, and, although I knew it was absurd, I could have sworn several times that, amid the incessant rush of the wind in the trees, I could hear Miss Thynne's voice again, calling for help. She was outside somewhere, calling my name; occasionally screaming, as though something unspeakable were happening to her. I fervently hoped Nick hadn't gone sleepwalking again to try and help her; and I buried my head under the pillow in an attempt to stop the noise.

Beneath the bedcovers, as I scrabbled to pull them tighter around myself, I felt a sudden odd sensation in my hand: lifting it and staring at it in the dark, against the faint moonlight of the window, I got a dreadful shock.

I had seven fingers.

I made a fist, squeezing my fingers in as tightly as I could as though to crush and destroy them; and then uncurled them again. Still, quite plainly, seven. I stared at my hand in horror, filled with sudden disgust, as though it were the foul hand of some other creature that had appeared at the end of my wrist. That was when I knew I'd finally fallen asleep; but I was so frightened by the dream that I woke up again instantly.

I needed to clear my head of the night's fears. As soon as dawn broke, which it did reluctantly, behind swathes of ash-grey cloud, I let myself and Lash out of the house, and we walked in the still-slightly-eerie half-light around Kniveacres, as lamps lit up the windows one by one. The east wing, where all the servants slept and worked, was soon alive with rectangles of orange light. Great blocks and chunks of the rest of the house remained dark, their walls towering blankly up towards crenellated rooflines, their big windows untroubled by light from inside for many years, perhaps even for a generation. These were the sections of the house into which Nick and I were forbidden from venturing. Nobody ever gave us a satisfactory answer as to why: whether they were decayed and unsafe, or whether they contained precious objects, or other secrets we weren't trusted to lay eyes on, was never explained.

I couldn't resist looking up at the façade of the east wing, to see if I could see evidence of the damage caused by the lintel crashing to the ground the night before last. The window had been closed, but there still seemed to be a patch of rough broken stonework beneath it, which no one had attempted to repair. There was no longer any trace of the big stone lying in the garden: someone had even raked over the earth beneath the window, to smooth it again.

There were voices in the stableyard, and Lash and I went around to watch as four or five boys and men scurried about, harnessing horses and wheeling out the smaller and faster of Sir Septimus's coaches. The mares huffed and snorted in the chilly morning air, the ringing of their shoes echoing off the high walls all around the yard. Lash had learned to be wary of the horses, but I think part of him still couldn't help believing that they were actually just very big dogs, liable to enjoy a game as much as he did; and he approached them a few times, with his belly near the ground as though he were stalking them, as they reared their fine heads and pawed the gravel while they waited.

"Who's the coach getting ready for?" I asked one of the stablehands.

"Sir Septimus, who else?" said the boy.

"Where's he going?"

But the boy just shrugged, and disappeared into the stable to fetch something else. Eventually the coach was taken around the front of the house, where it waited by the front door for three or four minutes. As Lash and I chased sticks in the gardens, conveniently close enough to see who got in, the slow and heavily-coated figure of Sir Septimus came deliberately down the steps, and was helped inside by the coachman, while Melibee stood to one side, fussing ineffectually.

The windows of the coach were too dark for me to be able to make out Sir Septimus's face as it passed by. Lash ran alongside as it picked up speed on the gravel, heading for the drive and, eventually, the main gateway to the road. I called him back; but he chased it for a long way before finally giving up and starting the long scamper back towards me, a little speck against the distant trees, his tongue hanging out.

I was getting the familiar sensation of being watched, and I tried to glance up at the windows of the Hall without making it obvious that I was looking. Sure enough, at one of the library windows there was a figure, gazing down on the carriage as it left, and at Lash as he chased it off – a figure I would have sworn was Bonefinger.

Melibee stood on the gravel until the carriage had receded so far into the distance that he could no longer hear the sound of the horses' hooves on the drive. Just as he was turning to go back inside, I called to him, to stop him.

"Where's Sir Septimus going?" I asked him.

"To London," came the reply. "I didn't realise you were out here, Miss Imogen, until I heard you calling the dog. Sir Septimus will spend the weekend in London to . . . settle some business – and expects to be back on Monday."

"Where will he stay in London?" I asked.

"I believe he has arrangements in Hanover Square," said Melibee. "Perhaps you know where that is, Miss Imogen, I sometimes forget that you know London so well. Sir Septimus stays at his Club, which I am told has new premises. He has been involved in the negotiations to secure them." As Melibee shuffled off towards the house, I grabbed hold of Lash's collar and pulled him round with me into the courtyard. He was panting. I knelt, and grabbed his muzzle to stop him licking my face.

"Now, listen, I'm going in for breakfast," I told him. "You sit here and wait for me. And no mischief. All right?" He sometimes came with me to the breakfast-room, even though he wasn't supposed to, and I fed him scraps from our table; but it was part of his routine to get his breakfast from the servants in the kitchen, and I knew if I tied him up out here, by the entrance to the kitchens, they'd make sure he was fed.

"Morning," I said, slipping into the breakfast-room where Nick was already pouring sluggish honey onto porridge. "Sir Septimus has gone to London. I've just watched his carriage leave."

Nick licked his spoon before replying. "Don't see how that

helps us," he said. "The servants will have been told to watch us."

"I just thought you might be interested," I said. "Is the porridge warm?"

He shrugged. We ate in silence. To be honest, I didn't feel much like talking either. I was tired; and after last night it had become clear that talking about anything significant was a risky occupation, however discreet we tried to be. This place was even making us afraid to speak to one another. It was tightening its grip.

"I'm going to get Lash," I said after a few minutes, putting my spoon down.

I scampered down the stairs to where I'd left him. If the servants had given him his breakfast it would have taken him about five seconds to wolf down; he'd be standing there now, his bushy blond eyebrows furrowed, anxiously looking for me.

He wasn't there.

Perhaps someone had taken him into the kitchen. I went in to find out, but there was no sign of him, and the two people who were in there busily washing vegetables for the day's meals denied having seen him.

I began to worry that I hadn't secured his rope properly, and that he'd run off. I went over to look in the stables, and around the side where the pumps stood from which they filled up the horses' water buckets, and where he often jumped around and played with the spurting water. When I couldn't find him there I went to the front of the house to see if I could see him on the lawn.

"Lash!" I called. I waited to see if he came skidding round the corner from somewhere. I called a few more times.

Perhaps he'd gone upstairs, and had found his way into my room.

But the door to my room was still locked, as I had left it; and when I went inside I found Lash's basket empty, and no trace of him on the bed, except for the big kidney-shaped indentation and the few traces of wiry hair he'd left at the bottom of the bed-spread from last night.

I ran down the stairs, jumping them three or four at a time in my haste to get back outside.

"Lash!" I called, panicking now. "Come *here*, boy!"

There was almost no one about, now; but in the yard I spot-ted the stable lad I'd talked to earlier. He'd heard me shouting.

I didn't have to tell him what I wanted. He pointed, saying nothing, in the direction of the courtyard gate.

And, almost immediately, striding through it in his flapping black cloak came Bonefinger – looking especially smug, I realised. My heart missed a beat.

"Have you seen my dog?" I asked him, abruptly, when he was still several yards away.

He came right up to me before replying.

"Ah, your *dog*, Miss Imogen," he wheedled, as though only just remembering. "I'm afraid I have had no choice but to lock him up."

"Well, could you unlock him," I said. "I'll look after him now. Thank you."

"I'm afraid not," he said, putting his head on one side and doing an impression of someone who was being as kind as he could reasonably be. "You see, Miss Imogen, I found the dog in the chicken shed. Someone had evidently been careless enough to leave him unsupervised, and, under those circumstances, Miss Imogen, a creature's true character will out. It is nature at work, after all. But if I had not appeared in time, untold damage would have been done, and untold expense caused. Sir Septimus would never allow such a mishap, if it could be avoided."

"He doesn't chase the chickens," I said, "he's scared of the cockerel."

"Be that as it may, Miss Imogen, that is where I found him," said Bonefinger, "and I would be neglecting my duty if I were to free him, only to have you turn your back and release him to pursue the self-same mischief a second time. You surely understand."

He beamed, and I swear I have never in my life wanted to launch my fist into someone's face so much as I did at that moment.

"Where is he?" I asked him through gritted teeth.

"I'm *really* not at liberty to say," he replied, and turned around.

"Just a minute." He stopped. "I want my dog back," I said. "What do I have to do?"

He turned his head, not the rest of his body at all, and it was like the motion of a grotesque giant grasshopper.

"I imagine," he said slowly, "you will be reunited with your dog, Miss Imogen, in due course. But I cannot take the risk, while Sir Septimus is absent. You will excuse me." And, before I could find my voice again through my rising, furious tears, he was gone.

CHAPTER 7

UNDERGROUND

I was going to find Lash. I didn't care how long it took, or whether I ate or slept in the meantime. If the vile Bonefinger wouldn't tell me where he was, I would find him myself.

Nick and I spent the morning hunting systematically in every corner of the grounds. Part of me knew, of course, that Bonefinger was too clever to appear from the very direction in which he'd just taken Lash. But we had to start somewhere, and the walk down to the lake led towards several places where it seemed likely someone might try to hide a dog: the boathouse, the summerhouse, the abandoned dairy, and any number of other neglected old outbuildings and sheds. There were even some dilapidated kennels, which we inspected; but not only was Lash quite obviously not there, they were so rotten and broken-down that it would only have taken a few seconds for a dog to scratch its way out. The only remotely useful things we found were some lamps in the summerhouse, one of which we took with us as we continued our hunt, in case we needed help seeing into the darker recesses of the outbuildings. We called his name, endless numbers of times, and listened for an answering bark, or even a whimper, in case his muzzle had been tied. There was nothing.

"There's only one bit of the garden where we haven't looked," said Nick, after a few hours.

"Where's that?" I was eager to make sure we'd explored every possibility before moving somewhere else. I couldn't bear to think of Lash being confined somewhere, unable to make us hear him. The longer our hunt went on, the more panic-stricken I was getting about finding him.

"It's not so much the garden, it's more a part of the wood," said Nick. "You know the place – where that old well is, the one you nearly fell into."

My heart missed a beat as I thought of Lash at the bottom of the well: barking for help, unheard, fifty feet down, or possibly hurt from his fall, and whimpering weakly in the near-darkness. Surely Bonefinger wouldn't be so wicked as to shove him down there?

Instead of risking sliding down the dangerous slope again, we approached the well from the other direction, where we'd seen a well-defined path snaking round from the woodland to the north. This path also took us past the mouth of a little cave, which we'd explored a few times before: it wasn't very deep, and it didn't seem likely that you could hide a dog there, but perhaps it was worth another look.

I clung to the stones at the rim of the well and to the roots of a nearby bush to steady myself, as I put my head right down into the chasm and called. Nick came up close behind, telling me to be careful, unsure whether he should try and hold on to me in case I fell. There was no sound from the bottom of the well, once the echo of my own voice had subsided. A faint occasional drip of water; otherwise nothing.

"What if he's *drowned*?" I wailed. "There's no telling how deep the water might be at the bottom. If he hurt himself as he fell, and didn't have the energy to swim, he'd just *drown*."

"He won't have drowned," said Nick – scornfully, rather than reassuringly, I thought. "There can't be that much water in there. There isn't even a splash when you throw something down. Is there?"

"No," I said, "but—"

"He's probably indoors," said Nick wearily. "Bonefinger will have got him locked up in the house somewhere – in some place that's out of bounds to us.

"Or in the woods," I said. "He could be somewhere in the woods, couldn't he? In a hut somewhere. There are loads of overgrown old barns he could have taken him to, or places the gamekeepers use. If he was way out in the woods somewhere, he could bark all he liked and we'd never hear him." We had been expressly forbidden from venturing into the woods, but I no longer cared two hoots for Sir Septimus's instructions. I squinted between the endless tree trunks, as though there was a chance I might catch a glimpse of Lash somewhere in the dim recesses of the forest. "I might start looking," I said.

"Mog, the woods go on for miles," said Nick. "Think about it. We don't *know* them, except the bits between here and the village. We'd just get lost."

"He didn't have time to take him far," I said with growing certainty. "I only left him for about ten minutes, while I had breakfast with you. He can't be far away. Come on, Nick, we might find him. Let's start in this direction."

"Just a minute," said Nick, "we haven't looked at the cave yet."

We'd always thought the cave was an intriguing thing to have in a garden. Little more than a gash, really, in a wall of rock at the fringe of the wood, it might have been a remnant of a little quarry from which stone had been cut to build part of the house. You had to clamber up from the path onto a big square stone to enter the cave in the first place: ahead of you was an opening only just wide enough for an adult to walk into, which went back ten or twelve feet before it became too narrow, and the ceiling too low, to squeeze any further.

Lash certainly wasn't in here. There were a few muddy marks on the stone floor of the cave which might have been made by someone's feet; but there was nothing to suggest anyone, or anything, had been in here recently.

"He's not here," I said, "let's go."

"Just a minute," said Nick, who had followed me in. Suddenly a pale orange light illuminated the rocky ceiling of the cave. He was holding up the lamp, so we could have a proper look around the dark narrow space for the first time. We'd never had a lamp with us whenever we'd been in here before.

"What's this?" He was reaching up to a kind of ledge at the level of his shoulder – and inspecting some long pieces of straw he'd picked up from the rock.

"This looks very fresh," he said. "We found some of this in the grass the other day, do you remember? Up along the path to the lake."

We hadn't thought anything of it at the time; but now Nick mentioned it, I remembered Lash getting some straw caught in his coat that afternoon too. There was a lot of straw in the stables – but why would there be any all the way out here in the cave, unless someone had brought it in on their boots?

"Help me up," said Nick, looking up. I held on to his ankles and pushed as he scrabbled up onto the ledge; and when I looked up he was standing upright, in a space we'd never been aware of before, high above the floor of the cave. "Mog, there's *loads* more of the cave up here," he said excitedly. His voice was echoing, as though it were suddenly booming around a much bigger cavity. "Come up and look," he said. "It goes all the way back here . . . goodness me!"

"What?"

He knelt, held out a hand, and pulled me up onto the ledge, and then helped me from there onto the next step up, so I was standing beside him in the high part of the cave. The lamp revealed a space not only high enough to stand up straight in, but so deep that we couldn't actually see the back of it. It seemed to disappear into a narrow, dark tunnel between walls of rock: we'd never imagined this was here when we'd been exploring the narrow entrance below.

"I wonder how far back it goes?" Nick said, holding the lamp up and trying to peer down the tunnel. "Careful, Mog, it might not be safe." Underfoot, however, the cave seemed solid, not even slippery, as I ventured tentatively forward into the narrow gap.

"Lash!" I called, into the chasm. There was a weird echo, not like a human voice, more like a long howl made by the wind, as though my words were resounding along the rocky walls for miles, and eventually coming back to us distorted beyond recognition. "Lash! Are you in there?"

The strange echoes swirled, and howled, and died away gradually.

"It's huge," Nick said slowly. "Isn't it?"

"You know, I think Lash might be down there," I said. "It would be just the kind of place Bonefinger would put him. He'd think we'd *never* find him in here." I put my hands on the rocky wall to make sure it seemed firm, not crumbly or loose. "Are you coming with me?"

Nick insisted that he go first, holding the lamp in front of him. In places the tunnel was so narrow that his body blocked out all the light: as I followed him it was impossible to see where I was going; I just kept going forward, a pace or two behind. Every so often we'd stop, to inspect the tunnel ahead of us and make sure it still looked safe, or to call Lash's name and listen for an answering bark among the strange echoes that swept back at us along the tunnel. There was no gradient to speak of, so we decided we must be walking more or less consistently ten feet or so below ground level; and although it was impossible to be certain about our bearings in here, the tunnel seemed to be taking us roughly in the direction of the village. It smelled damp, and our hands often came up dirty and wet as we felt our way along the walls. Here and there, the roots of trees penetrated the rocky roof – suggesting we were walking immediately under the forest.

Far from becoming narrower and harder to negotiate the further we went, the tunnel seemed to widen out; and before we had been following it for very long, we found we were standing in a little chamber forming a distinct three-way junction.

Another spur of the tunnel went off into the darkness to our left, while the main passageway continued straight ahead.

"Which way now?" pondered Nick.

I called down the tunnel to the left and then ahead of us, but as we stood waiting for the echoes to die, there was no distinguishable sound from either direction. If Lash was down here, it was anybody's guess where; and I fervently hoped we weren't going to come to more confusing forks and offshoots. For all we knew, it might be like a labyrinth down here; and neither of us relished the prospect of getting lost underground, with the oil reserve in our lamp diminishing.

But once we'd decided to carry on in a straight line, the tunnel presented us with no more options. The walls had been hewn from the bedrock, in the shape of a high arch of more or less consistent width. Here and there, brickwork had been used to shore up a rough patch of tunnel wall, or to give it shape. It was now abundantly clear that this passage beneath the forest wasn't a natural feature; and furthermore, it was in a very good state of repair, as though its upkeep had been quite recently attended to. Nick occasionally had to call back a warning about an uneven patch of floor, or a deep puddle we had to tread carefully around where water was leaking into the tunnel. In other places the tunnel became very narrow, perhaps where whoever constructed it had been unable to break through a particularly awkward lump of rock, and in one or two such places you had to turn sideways to squeeze between the walls for a few yards. But then, inevitably, it opened out and became easily passable again; and for much of the tunnel's length it was possible to walk quite rapidly, or even run, through it.

Our hearts beating from the exertion, we pushed on for what must have been twenty, twenty-five minutes, all the time marvelling more and more at the sheer length of the tunnel, and the effort and skill that must have gone into constructing it. What on earth was it *for*?

"Now then," said Nick, eventually; and he came to a stop. I clutched him and peered over his shoulder, as he lifted the lamp to illuminate another chamber, much bigger this time, with wooden boxes against the walls and some big round stones, or cannonballs or something, littered around the floor.

And, sitting with its back to us against a box a few feet away, was a human figure. We both gasped and I clawed at Nick's arm in terror, trying to grab hold of him for safety.

It didn't stir; nevertheless it took us a few seconds to realise it wasn't a real person, but another scarecrow.

It was dressed like a jester, or a harlequin, in garishly colourful patchwork clothes, with a cap falling over its face which, we could see as we got closer, had two peaks in it with little bells on the end. Straw poked out from beneath the cap to serve as hair, and the hands which protruded from the sleeves of its colourful coat were made of carefully-tied ears of wheat.

Nick ventured right up close, to take a better look at it. He put a hand on its shoulder to pull it into an upright position; and we both got the shock of our lives as its capped head tilted backwards towards us and we found ourselves staring into the sightless face of a human skull.

I screamed. In this confined space, my scream sounded incredibly loud, and scared us both even more. And now for the first time I began to take in the rest of the scene around us. We were in some kind of bone-chamber. The boxes which stood around the edge of the chamber were coffins, including the one against which the jester was sitting: its lid had been lifted off and propped up on the ground beside it, as though the jester had recently climbed out of it. There were old bones piled up in heaps against the walls, and now we realised that the large stone-like objects were not stones at all, but more skulls, strewn around the room – maybe twenty or thirty of them altogether, yellow or brown with age. My blood ran cold.

"Nick," I wailed, "where are we?"

"It's all right," he said in a low voice. "There's nothing alive in here."

Instantly, his words were contradicted, as he took a step forward and a huge rat heaved itself out of one of the boxes and ran along the line of the wall to take cover in the shadows behind us.

"Nick, let's go," I said. "I want to go back. Lash isn't here. We've made a mistake."

"Wait a minute."

Nick was holding up the lamp, turning around with it, inspecting the contents of the room carefully. The orange light ranged over the bone-piles, the open coffins, the skulls which stared at us from their random positions on the dirty stone floor.

"Nick, I don't want to be in here!"

"Look!" He took the lamp over to a corner of the room, ignoring me, and knelt down. The darkness seemed to envelop me, I felt a sudden cold draught from the tunnel behind, and the lamp in Nick's hand seemed to flicker as though it was becoming exhausted. I ran over to join him.

He'd found the gargoyle. The one which had fallen from the

church. Someone had laid it here, on the ground, in this room full of skulls and bones.

He reached out and ran his fingers over it, along its row of grinning, wolf-like teeth, over its sandstone haunches poised to spring, down its moss-flecked back to the rough, broken base where it had been wrenched from the church.

"You know, I think I know where we are," Nick said. He looked up at me. "This is a crypt. We must be right underneath the church."

The lamp flickered again. We were going to be without light very soon indeed.

"So how do we get out?" I wondered, looking around.

"Just a minute. Look at this." He'd found some strange indentations near the base of the gargoyle, where it had broken off. "Aren't these chisel marks?" he said. "Look, they go all the way round here. And they go down quite deep into the stone. I *knew* it, Mog. Someone chiselled this gargoyle off the church – or at least, they made it so loose it was easy to knock it off when we came by."

He seemed to be absolutely right. The narrow, regular indentations of a chisel or similar tool marked the base of the gargoyle on three sides. The stone exposed by the chisel marks was clean and pale, not weathered and discoloured like the rest – as though the marks had been made very recently. And they corroborated all of Nick's suspicions: for the first time I agreed the gargoyle's fall almost certainly hadn't been an accident.

He stood up. "Now then," he said, "where's the way out?"

It wasn't immediately obvious. If this was the crypt, it didn't appear to have steps leading up into the church, as you'd have expected. Neither could we make out any kind of wooden hatch or trap door in the ceiling as we held the lamp up, trying hard to keep it level to stop the light from dying.

"What's that?" I asked, noticing an iron ring, like the kind used for tethering horses, set into the wall. "You wouldn't tie up a horse down here, would you?"

"You're dead right." Excited, Nick started running over to the wall where the ring was; but as he did so he tripped, the lamp swung crazily in his hand, and the light went out altogether.

"Nick!" I screeched.

And at that very moment there was a grinding sound, followed by the sound of Nick gasping. The darkness was the most complete, impenetrable darkness I could remember in my entire life; but Nick spoke, to assure me he was still close by.

"I've got hold of the ring," he said. "I kind of – fell onto it, and when I grabbed it something happened. Did you hear?"

"Yes." I had been hoping it wasn't just the sound of the ring coming away from the wall completely. "Have you still got hold of it?"

"Yes. I'm going to try turning it."

There was another grinding sound, and I heard Nick gasping with effort. "It's – very – stiff!"

But the strain was paying off. Suddenly, above our heads, there was a chink of light. By turning the ring, Nick had opened a hidden trap door in the wall: two big stones were slowly moving apart. After a few turns, the gap between the stones was big enough for one of us to squeeze through. Using the iron ring as a foothold, Nick pulled himself up to the opening, and, once he was through, helped me up after him.

There were five or six steps leading up a little narrow tunnel, to another opening ahead of us which was where the daylight was coming from. As we got to the top of the steps we found a drop of about three feet on the other side; and when we'd jumped down, we were standing in the nave of the church. Nick held both my hands until I had climbed through the gap, then dusted himself off. We looked around, our eyes adjusting to the low, wine-coloured light coming through the stained glass.

"That was just in time," I said quietly, and surprised myself by finding a lump in my throat from the relief. I swallowed. "We couldn't have managed without light down there," I said, "I don't know what we'd have done."

"Felt our way back along the tunnel, I suppose," said Nick, shuddering at the thought of it.

We gazed back at the opening in the wall. It wasn't just two ordinary blank stones which had opened up. We were standing in front of the Letherskin memorial, and the tombstone had split apart at the seam of the big marble book, so that the whole carved scene was separated into two halves. On one side stood the skeleton, his bony hand now pointing directly at the entrance to the crypt. The family names and the Latin inscription on the stone pages of the book were split in two: one side of the Latin motto read "SCURRA CAELI", the other half "REX MORTIUM".

I was shaking. I went to sit down in a pew, with my back to the tunnel entrance. Nick was still peering at the tombstone, trying to work out how the mechanism worked, and how to close it again.

"I don't think I've ever been anywhere so *creepy*," I said. "All those skulls – and that jester thing – I don't mind if I never go down there again."

"I can't shut it," Nick said, grappling with the tombstone and trying to force the two halves back together. "There must be another iron ring or something, to make it easy to get in from this side."

He came and sat down beside me.

"Something else makes sense, though," he said, almost triumphantly. "Do you remember what the *Addendum* said? That part about the Letherskin grave?"

"Not precisely," I said, frowning. "Seek out the Letherskin grave, where—"

"I'll tell you what it said. I learned it off by heart. *A further intriguing connection has been latterly discovered between the buildings of the village and the Hall. Seek out the Letherskin grave in the east wall of St Moribunda's church, where the eye will find the secret.*"

"Very good," I said, still not sure what he was driving at.

"*An intriguing connection*," he said. "That's it. It means a tunnel. An actual *connection* between the Hall and the village."

"That's *very* clever," I said, as it sank in. "So all those notes in there we couldn't understand are probably all riddles, like that. Obvious when you already know what they mean, but mystifying to anyone else."

"Deliberately mystifying, maybe," said Nick. "Whoever wrote the *Addendum* was dropping hints, but didn't want everyone to know what they were writing about."

"And this is how Bonefinger manages to get backwards and forwards to the village so quickly, without a horse," I realised.

"Remember how he turned up back at the Hall yesterday so soon after we saw him in the Cloy Arms?"

"Without getting muddy!" exclaimed Nick. "Because he doesn't have to plodge through the mud, he just goes through the tunnel."

I had a sudden feeling of grim satisfaction. Kniveacres was beginning to give up some of its secrets. We had found persuasive evidence that the gargoyle accident wasn't an accident at all. And for the first time, I felt as though we were starting to get the measure of Bonefinger.

But he still had Lash.

"What are we going to do, then?" I wondered. "There's no way I'm going back through that tunnel. But we've got to go and look for Lash. I want to search the house."

"We can't leave the secret entrance gaping open like that," Nick said. "Come and help me try to close it. Then we'll go back through the wood."

We shoved and heaved at the stone memorial; we even tried standing on either side of it, both of us trying to push the halves together – but nothing moved.

"It's got to be easier than this," I said. "There must be another lever somewhere."

Nick ran his hands around the walls, and walked around looking at the flagstones of the church floor.

"It's not hidden somewhere over here, is it?" I wondered, inspecting the elaborate Cloy grave nearby, with its glum-looking face bedecked with greenery and the two carved rising cobras. Nick came over and helped me look, feeling around the bottom of the intricately carved stone.

"There are plenty of names on here, aren't there?" he said. "One, two, three . . . eight Cloys altogether, along with quite a few of their wives. They've all been squeezed in a bit."

"I know. It's quite hard to read their names, further down," I said. I started to read out the inscription, in a deep, sing-song voice, like a monk intoning a prayer or a plainchant.

Here Lie the Mortal Remains
of BARNABAS EZEKIEL CLOY, and of his Beloved Wife ELIZABETH,
respected Master and Lady of Kniveacres Hall in this Parish.
Also of their Son, LANCELOT ARBUTHNOT CLOY, and of LYDIA JANE,
his cherished Wife who Passed from this Life the 4th day of October 1750 in
deliverance of their Seventh Child.
Also of SIR HUBERT CLOY, d. at Howrah the 20th April 1771, and
MARGARET ESME, LADY CLOY, d. 1st January 1800. Also of
NICODEMUS MONTAGU CLOY, d. 10th May 1802. Also of . . .

"Shush a minute," said Nick, as my singing reverberated around the church. "This bit about the seventh child." He reached up and traced the lettering with his forefinger. "Sir Septimus is the seventh child, isn't he?" he said. "The seventh child of Sir Lancelot Arbuthnot Cloy and Lydia Jane his cherished wife. That's Sir Septimus. Isn't it?"

"I suppose it is," I said. "And all these names at the bottom must be all his brothers. Sir Hubert Cloy, Nicodemus Montagu Cloy, Augustus Incitatus Cloy, and so on – they all seem to have popped off one by one. So does that mean he's the only Cloy who's not actually here?"

"Because he's the only one still alive, you mean," said Nick.

"Yes, that makes sense. Do you remember what Miss Thing said, about them all dying horrible deaths? Sir Septimus was obviously born on the 4th of October 1750, and his mother died giving birth to him. It says so. That means he's . . . seventy-seven. Nearly seventy-eight. *Very* nearly seventy-eight, in fact. His birthday's next week."

"Well, happy birthday, Sir Septimus," I said, sarcastically. "What shall we buy him?"

Nick stared at me. "But Mog," he said, "remember the prophecy?"

"What does that have to do with buying him a birthday present?"

"No, you don't understand. His *birthday*, Mog. Don't you remember how it went? '*The Master of Kniveacres shall be cut off at threescore ten and seven.*' That's what it said. Threescore ten and seven is seventy-seven."

It was sinking in. "And that means—" I said.

"That means," interrupted Nick, "before next Friday."

I considered this for a moment, and laughed. "It's a lot of nonsense," I said.

"Maybe," said Nick, "but the villagers seem to believe it, and Damyata obviously wants Sir Septimus to believe it."

"Sir Septimus probably does believe it," I said. "Maybe that's why he's disappeared off to London." I went back to the opening in the tombstone nearby. "I'm cold," I said. "I wish we could work out how to close this. What did the *Addendum* say again?"

"*A further intriguing connection has been latterly discovered between the buildings of the village and the Hall. Seek out the*

Letherskin grave in the east wall of St Moribunda's church, where the eye will find the secret," quoted Nick, obligingly.

I gazed up at the skeleton as he spoke, and something occurred to me.

"Nick," I said, "can you come here? I think I need a leg-up."

With Nick's help, I climbed up and clung to the marble slab so my face was more or less on a level with that of the skeleton. Reaching up, I wormed two fingers into the skeleton's eye sockets. They disappeared into quite deep holes.

"Aha!" I said.

There was a sudden clunk.

"What did you do?" gasped Nick.

I jumped down. With a brief and surprisingly quiet scraping sound, the two halves of the Letherskin memorial moved together, and the gap through which we'd climbed disappeared completely.

"You've done it!" Nick said. "But how on earth did you work that out?"

I grinned at him. "It was just a hunch. I thought, if the bit about the intriguing connection is a riddle, maybe that last bit about the eye is a riddle too. And you know what? There's a little metal lever inside the eye-holes, which you can just reach with your fingers if you stick them in."

"*The eye will find the secret,*" groaned Nick. "How could we miss that? It's obvious what it means, isn't it?" He was thrilled that I'd worked it out, but also slightly jealous that he hadn't. "Let me have a go," he said. "Give me a leg-up."

I knelt, and helped him get a foothold on the tombstone; and sure enough, as he pushed his fingers right inside the skeleton's eye sockets, another clunk sounded from somewhere behind the wall, and the marble halves of the book fell apart as the stones swung on their hidden mechanism. He jumped clear as the stones moved.

"So that's how it's done," he said with satisfaction. "And it's so well hidden. If it weren't for that clue in the book, we'd *never* have found it."

"Close it again, then," I said; and I helped him up one more time, so he could reach for the little lever behind the skull, and the two halves of the memorial moved back together so neatly you would never have guessed there was a join.

I shivered. "Come on," I said. "I think we should go back to the house and look for Lash."

As we emerged into the daylight, we were greeted by two silent figures in the churchyard near the porch. More scarecrows. One of them was dressed like a clergyman, with a grubby white dog-collar, standing before the porch as though receiving his parishioners into the church. His hands were pressed together in an act of prayer, and his head had been made from a piece of wood with markings in the grain which bore a remarkable resemblance to a face, sagging in the most melancholy of expressions, with a large blackened knot suggesting a groaning, suffering mouth. As we walked around it, it really looked for all the world like a shabby and penitent vicar.

"Maybe people in the village have got a sense of humour after all," I murmured.

The other one, a little distance away among the gravestones, was even more remarkable. Rather than standing on the grass, it hovered a few feet off the ground: in fact a closer look revealed it was propped up with what appeared to be the supporting-pole of a washing-line, to create the effect of being suspended in mid-air. It was obviously supposed to be a female figure, in the act of lifting off on a hazel broomstick, like a witch. She was wearing a ragged old linen nightdress and a knitted shawl, which had been soaked in something to stiffen it and make it stand out behind her as though she were really flying. I went up to her. Under her woollen bonnet she had a strange, white, pock-marked little head – which, I realised as I got close, was a cauliflower. Her trajectory, with the handle of the broomstick pointing determinedly up in front of her, seemed to suggest she was actually flying out of one of the graves. The little headstone behind her was a memorial to a Mary Eldritch, "Wise Woman of this Parish", who had died about thirty years ago. I knew nothing at all about her, but I suddenly felt sorry for her. I wondered if it was another of the village traditions to caricature her as a witch by making a guy like this at her grave, every year since her death.

"Shall we have a look and see if the gibbet's still there?" Nick said.

"You go," I said. "I'm not sure I want to see it again."

Nick went to the lych-gate, while I studied the effigies; after he'd been there a few seconds he called:

"Mog! Come and look!"

I joined him at the gate. The gibbet was still there; and the black-headed guys representing the two of us were still hanging from it. But they had been joined by more figures, swinging from the cross-beam. Two guys with long black cloaks which were very similar to one another, except that one of them had impossibly thin black legs sticking out at the bottom; and another figure dressed like a country squire, with a grotesque pink tongue lolling out of his mouth like a real hanged man.

Bonefinger, Melibee, and Sir Septimus. The guys dangled, all in a row, like a mass execution. It was starting to feel less lonely up there.

As we looked around the village green, we could see that the number of guys on display had roughly doubled since yesterday. There were now very few houses which didn't have one sitting outside; and they seemed to be getting more and more colourful and imaginative. One of the cottages had its guy on the roof, clinging to the chimney with both arms, and looking down as though terrified of heights. Standing among the beehives was a man collecting honey, dressed like a beekeeper with a wide-brimmed hat and bulky gloves, and a muslin veil across his face to stop himself being stung: but we soon realised he was completely motionless, and made of straw. And another, opposite the inn, was obviously supposed to be a poacher, with a gun over his shoulder, triumphantly holding up a brace of pheasant and several rabbits in both hands.

There was something strange, even hysterical, about it all.

"I think the whole thing's spooky," Nick said, gazing out across the green. "Remember what Miss Gossage snapped at us? *Our ceremonies will go ahead, you can't take that away from us!* It's like a huge celebration, isn't it? They're having a great time making all these guys dressed like jesters and poachers. And hanging everyone who lives at Kniveacres."

There also seemed to be piles of boxes appearing outside everyone's houses, many of them laden with twigs, like kindling.

Perhaps these were something to do with the ceremonies too. It was very intriguing indeed.

We were making our way back through the graveyard, past the tragic-faced clergyman, when I remembered I'd left our lamp in the church, on the pew next to where I'd been sitting.

"I won't be a second," I said.

Nick came with me into the porch, intending to wait for me until I'd retrieved the lamp; but when he heard my shout, he ran in to see what was the matter.

I had stopped in my tracks, just a few steps from the door. Sitting in a pew, right next to where we'd just been, was the jester.

It hadn't been there a few minutes ago, we were absolutely sure of that. It wasn't moving; it was simply sitting, bolt upright, in the pew. It was unmistakeable, in its colourful patchwork clothes of purple and red and yellow, its floppy cap with the two bells on the end dangling over its face.

"Nick," I said in a quaking voice, "it's the one we saw in the crypt."

"It can't be," he said. "It must be another one just like it." But, as we ventured tentatively back towards it, it turned its head slowly to look at us, and the bells on its cap gave out a tiny incongruous jingle as it moved. We stood rooted to the spot in horror. Its fleshless face stared straight at us from the pew, its jaw fixed in a lipless grin, its huge black eyes impenetrable and terrifying.

It was alive. And it had followed us up through the hole.

We fled the church, abandoning the lamp, and ran headlong down the path between the gravestones. When we got to the iron gate that led to the forest track, we stood gasping for breath. The guys were disturbing enough to begin with; but if they were going to start moving around on their own and following us, I for one had had enough. Even the hostile and oppressive surroundings of Kniveacres seemed preferable to this.

We were about to make our way through the forest gate and start running again, when we heard a shrill voice calling somewhere behind us. We'd have been convinced it was the jester coming screeching after us, if there hadn't been something familiar about the voice. We turned. A tiny figure had appeared in the distance at the far end of the churchyard, and was bustling down the path towards us.

"Oh! Nick! Mog! Wait!" it was calling, breathlessly.

"It's Fanny Nisbet," I said.

She hurried up to us, her face a picture of agitation. "Nick! Mog!" she gasped again. "Forgive me for shouting at you like that – I was beside myself wanting to get some sort of message to you, and then I saw you at the lych-gate, and thank goodness I did. I didn't know what to do for the best." She was holding her ribs, having run from the village green. "I don't want to say too much," she gasped, "because you can't be sure who's listening. But my dears . . ." She reached out a frail arm and grabbed my hand, squeezing it and swinging it in a state of panic. "My dears, you're in the most terrible danger. I can't say – but you mustn't go back to the Hall."

"Mrs Nisbet," said Nick, gently, "what on earth do you mean?"

"What kind of danger?" I asked. "Is it the guy in the church? The jester? Is that what you mean?"

She was still gasping for breath. "I can't – I mustn't say, not here," she wheezed. "I don't know about a jester. But you must believe me, both of you. I have overheard something – people talking at the inn. Your lives are in danger and you must stay away from Kniveacres, whatever else you do. Oh, my dears, I can't tell you – thank goodness I found you!"

"Mrs Nisbet," said Nick, "you're not making much sense. Why must we stay away?"

"If we can't go to the Hall, where can we go?" I asked. I kept looking nervously past her, up the path, expecting at any moment to see the jester coming out of the church and lurching towards us.

"My dears, I don't know, I suppose I – I'll hide you," she said. "If I have to, I can keep you safe, but you must beware. There are things – oh dear, there are such things! *Please* don't go back."

Nick looked at me, helpless. We both knew we had no choice.

"Mrs Nisbet," I said, "we *have* to go back. Bonefinger has locked up my dog, and I need him back. I can't leave him."

"Ohh," she wailed, "you must be careful, Miss Mog. You've no idea – things are getting so dangerous for you, I really fear for you, my dears, you *must* come with me."

Nick took both of Fanny's hands in his, and spoke reassuringly.

"Mog's right, Mrs Nisbet," he said, "we really must go back and find Lash. We'll be all right. We'll be careful, I promise. There've been terrible things happening at the Hall, but we've been all right so far. I promise we'll come as soon as we can."

"Oh, pray it's not too late, Master Nick," she wailed. "I can't warn you any more, you must both do as you think fit. But hurry. Don't stay at the Hall. Don't trust them!"

She stood at the gate, watching us go, wringing her hands. Once or twice, as we fled through the woods, we kept turning back to look; and she remained standing there until we'd gone so far that the trees completely obscured our view of her.

CHAPTER 8
THE SEARCH CONTINUES

We had no idea, of course, what we might be going back to. We reassured ourselves with the thought that Fanny might have misunderstood whatever it was she had heard. But also, we didn't entirely believe that things could get significantly worse. We had enemies in the village, and enemies at the Hall. The most extraordinary and frightening things seemed to be happening wherever we chose to go. What difference did it make where we were? The one thing I knew was that, when I found Lash, everything would be better. Not perfect, almost certainly: but better.

We went in by the courtyard stairs, without meeting anyone, and straight up to our rooms. We were starving: we'd had nothing to eat since breakfast, and it was now long past lunchtime. As we stood on the first-floor landing, fumbling for our keys, Nick volunteered to go back down to the kitchen and see if there was anyone there from whom he could beg a snack.

"I'll bring something up," he said, as he made for the stairs. "See you in there."

I let myself in; and stupidly, I suppose, allowed myself the half-hope that Bonefinger might have relented while we were out, and returned Lash to me, and that he would come bounding up to meet me as I opened the door, as he so often did. Although, deep down, I knew he wouldn't, the half-hope was just enough to give me a tangible thump of disappointment when the room turned out to be empty.

I sat down on the bed, and cried. I couldn't help it. I hung my head and cried until my entire face was wet and the tears were dripping from my nose and chin onto my clothes and onto the bedcover between my knees. There was nothing Lash liked more than licking the salty tears from my face when I cried, and of course that had always made me laugh, and made me feel better straight away. It was one of the most reassuring things I knew in my life, this transition from sobs to laughter; and one of the things which made Lash such a special, unique kind of friend. Much as I loved Nick, I couldn't imagine him ever being able to cheer me up so instantly and reliably, whatever he said or did.

My face was still pink and wet with tears when he came in with two potato pies.

"What's happened?" he asked.

"Oh, nothing," I said wretchedly, "but *you know.*"

And, to judge from his silence, I think he did.

When he'd finished his pie, which took about twenty-five seconds, he stood up and went through to his own room. I heard him pouring water from the jug into the basin, to wash his hands.

"What's this?" he said suddenly.

I sniffed. "What's what?" I called.

He came back in, holding a tatty piece of paper. "I've just picked this up off the floor," he said. "It must have been pushed in under the door."

"What does it say?"

He unfolded it. He was silent for a long time.

"Well?" I said.

"Mog," he said, "it's from Damyata."

"What?" I leaped off the bed and almost wrenched the paper from his hand in my eagerness to see it. It was written in a child-ish hand, very reminiscent of the notes Damyata had left us in London last year, with some strange spellings and a couple of alarming inky smears almost obscuring some of the words.

CLOY IS YOUR EMENY

it read.

HE DID IT BEST TO LET YOU DIE ONCE.
HE WILL DO IT BEST TO KILL YOU NOW.
BUT I AM WACHING.

And, reassuringly, the familiar Indian characters again beneath the line.

इम्यता

"Do you understand it?" asked Nick.

"I know what he means, but I'm not sure it makes much sense," I said. "*He did it best* – that should just be 'he did his

189

best', shouldn't it? But what does he mean? Sir Septimus did his best to let us die? Me die? You die? When? Does he mean the gargoyle?"

"It's very strange," agreed Nick. "But there's no doubt about that, is there? *I am watching.* He's been here, Mog, and he's still here, somewhere."

A sudden thrill ran through me. It really felt as though we had a secret protector; someone with real power, like magic, on our side. The words telling us we were in danger were in deadly earnest – just like Fanny's terrified warning this afternoon. We would obviously have to be very careful indeed. But knowing Damyata was somewhere close by was an enormous comfort.

"I'm going to put this away in the secret drawer," said Nick. "I just hope no one else has already seen it, like Bonefinger."

"If Bonefinger had read it, he'd have taken it away," I said, as Nick fumbled with the drawer down the side of the bed and slipped the piece of paper inside. "He wouldn't have left it here for us to find."

"I'm still hungry," Nick complained. He went to the cupboard, and threw me one of Fanny Nisbet's apples before biting into one himself. "What are we going to do?" he asked, with his mouth full.

"Keep looking for Lash," I said immediately. "We've wasted enough time already. I just hope Bonefinger hasn't hurt him." Nick was gazing out of the window, munching on his apple. "I – I'll go on my own, for a bit," I said. "It'll be easier – I won't be so conspicuous, on my own."

Nick seemed to agree. "I might go to the library and read a bit before tea," he said.

I was still convinced Lash couldn't be far away. I stood at the bottom of the stairs, in the courtyard, and listened carefully. The sounds of creatures were everywhere: the gentle rhythmic purr of a wood pigeon, the claque of rooks in the distance, the snorting of a horse behind one of the stable doors. I *thought* I could hear something which sounded a bit like a dog barking, but it was very hard to tell which direction it might be coming from: sounds could be very confusing here as they bounced off the high walls of the Hall. Nobody took much notice of me, as I wandered the gravelled yards and the muddy tracks around the stables and barns. At this quiet time of day, it was easy to disappear; and to be honest none of the servants or gardeners ever seemed to take much notice of us at any time. Yet I was extra-wary of meeting Bonefinger this afternoon, after seeing Damyata's letter. I crept among the low stone buildings, poking my head around the doors and calling Lash's name. Sometimes an answering rustle made my heart leap; until I realised it was just a rat, or on one occasion a litter of kittens, in the shadows. I went up to the kittens, who were jumping in and out of a pile of straw at the back of a long-disused barn. There were five or six of them, all but one of them jet black; and their eyes shone, in pairs, as I came close.

"Have you seen my dog?" I asked them, reaching down to pick one up. "He's a big silly boy, and he'd enjoy playing with you. He'd probably give you a bit of a scare, but he wouldn't hurt you."

The kitten squealed, in the tiniest imaginable voice, and dug its claws into my hand; and I let it flop back into the straw.

"A lot of use you are," I told them, as I left. But then, much more distinctly, the sound of a dog barking reached my ears.

It was coming from the woods. Climbing over fences, and paying little attention to the thorns in which my clothes kept getting caught, I ran towards the sound, having to pause quite often to be able to hear it again above the noise of my own breathing. As I got closer, and the barking got more distinct, I could tell that it was more than one dog; and after a few minutes' running I came upon a wiry little man, with two agile dogs like greyhounds or whippets, walking through the forest. He was one of the gamekeeper's men; and he regarded me with a suspicious scowl as I emerged through the trees. The larger of the dogs stopped in its tracks, and stared at me with wary, hostile eyes, just like its master's.

"You haven't – you don't . . ." I began, nervously, as I saw the dog stiffening. "The thing is, I'm looking for my dog. He's about that big," I said, pointing to the staring dog which had now started showing its teeth, "except he's kind of golden yellow, not grey, and sort of shaggy, not smooth. A mongrel, but a bit like a lurcher."

The man said nothing. I might have been speaking a foreign language for all the understanding his face betrayed. The dog began to emit a low growl.

"I don't suppose you've seen him?" I ventured, by way of further clarification.

"G'awn," he grunted – which at first I thought was his reply, but he turned out to be talking to the dog. He looked back at me. "Ain't seen'm," he said shortly; and with no further ceremony, he walked away, with both dogs trotting ahead of him.

I went back the way I'd come; but I must have taken a slightly different route without realising it, because the first building I came to was the old ruined chapel, which was some distance away from where I'd started. It had been built for the original owners of Kniveacres to hold their own private services without having to attend the village church; but it had fallen into disuse decades – perhaps even centuries – ago. The roof had fallen in, and all that was left were the high walls, with ornate but empty Gothic windows which had been letting in the wind and rain to batter and destroy the decorated interior over many, many years. We'd been warned that it wasn't safe; and it certainly didn't look safe, on the odd occasions when our explorations of the grounds had brought us this way and we'd peered in through the gaps in the broken-down walls. Rooks had built nests on the wall-tops and in the crannies formed by the few weathered old roof-timbers that remained.

I ventured inside through a hole in the old wall. This was far enough from the house for Bonefinger to be sure that a dog tied up in here wouldn't be heard. But there was no sign of Lash. All the wooden stalls of the original chapel had rotted away; but there were still alcoves and stone plinths built into the walls where statues or memorials may have stood, and, for all the weathering, the walls still showed traces of rich crimson wall-paintings which must once have made the chapel look very grand indeed. The flags of the floor were cracked and smashed, thistles and brambles sprouted from the corners of the walls; and in one place a tough little tree had grown through the broken wall, wrapped its mossy roots around the stones, and looked as if it was threatening to pull the entire wall down at any moment with a twist of its gnarled hand.

It was obvious Lash wasn't here, and I was about to make my way out, when I noticed something glinting on the ground nearby. The day was almost over and the light was fading, and I was lucky to have spotted it. I picked it up.

It was a tiny silver bell. As I shook it around in my cupped hand, it tinkled faintly; and when it did so I instantly knew what it was.

It had come from the jester's cap.

Now it had followed us all the way to Kniveacres! But what had it been doing here in the old chapel? I turned around, slowly and warily, the hairs on the back of my neck bristling, in case it was still here somewhere, watching me from the shadows. There were some strands of yellow straw lying around on the chapel floor, like that which had poked from under his cap like untidy hair – but no other trace of him.

As I held the little bell in my hands, something fell from the roof and landed with a soft thump on the ground beside me. I looked up. There were suddenly a lot of rooks gathering on the tops of the walls, and they were making a growing commotion. More rooks flew in to join them as I watched. Suddenly, another object, like a big bundle of black cloth, or a pair of bellows, plummeted to the ground; I had to move back to stop it from hitting me. Were the rooks *throwing* things at me? Over by the wall, near where I'd found the bell, another object fell.

It was only when I bent down to inspect the two things that had landed near my feet, that I realised they were dead rooks.

The squealing and squawking of the birds above my head

was growing into a cacophony. They bounced and flapped in tremendous agitation, as they were joined by more and more of their number, swooping in from the tree-tops and the chimney-stacks of the house. And more dead rooks began falling: thump . . . thump . . . All around the chapel, black corpses hit the ground, just a few seconds apart now, until the floor in places was thick with them. The noise of the rooks was grow-ing unbearable; they were almost literally screaming, hundreds and hundreds of them, blocking out the light. But as more and more rooks arrived, more and more were dropping dead and plunging to the ground. I stuffed the bell into my pocket and tried to step between the corpses, panicking now, revolted, dead birds glancing off my back as they spun through the air. I covered my head with my arms and ran for the hole in the col-lapsed wall where I'd come in. They were screaming and swooping, their huge black wings flapping around me; and all the time their dead bodies were falling around me, like can-nonballs in a battle.

I stumbled away, terrified, and ran until I reached the corner of another building, from where I could watch them, at a dis-tance. They were like a swarming cloud above the chapel. Something had driven them mad; and whatever it was, it was killing them, in huge numbers. One moment they were flying around and screeching, the next moment they died instantly on the wing, and fell out of the sky. Corpse fell upon corpse; the chapel floor must have been littered with dead rooks, within minutes of the first one falling.

Shaken, I walked back towards the house. I couldn't begin to explain what I'd seen, but I got the feeling it must have something to do with the jester. As though my simply finding the bell, and shaking it, had driven all the birds within sight of the chapel into a frenzy, and killed them.

Bonefinger had been strangely absent since my encounter with him this morning when he'd taken Lash away; and he didn't appear, as he often did, to supervise the serving of supper. Instead it was Melibee who moved silently in and out of the room at intervals, taking things to the kitchen, as Nick and I ate crusty bread with a gamey-tasting meat paste, and creamed spinach. In the intervals when Melibee wasn't in the room, I told Nick about the chapel, and the dying rooks. And I fished the little bell out of my pocket and put it on the table in front of us.

"It's definitely one of the bells off the jester's cap," I said, "isn't it?"

"I don't know," he said. "I didn't really get a good enough look at them."

"Oh come on, Nick," I hissed, "where else would a little bell like that come from? It makes the same noise we heard when we saw him in the church."

And, at precisely the same time as I picked it up and shook it to demonstrate, Melibee came back into the room. He said nothing; but I could tell from his face that he had heard the bell, and was straining to listen in case it sounded any more. We fell silent until he'd disappeared again.

"There's something weird about this," I said, once he was safely out of the room. "I'm sure it was the bell which made the rooks go mad like that."

Nick waited until he'd swallowed his latest forkful of food before replying. "You're imagining things," he said.

"Nick," I said impatiently, "I *saw* it happen. You weren't there. I picked up the bell, and shook it a few times, and straight away the birds started dropping dead around my feet."

"You're sure someone wasn't shooting them?"

"I *think* I'd have known," I retorted. "There was no gunfire. Just the rooks going crazy, and dropping dead one by one. It was like a kind of horrible magic."

Every time Melibee came in, we fell silent, and if one of us hadn't heard him come in and was still talking, we'd kick the other to shut them up. Once, conscious of our silence, Melibee attempted conversation of his own.

"You are both pensive," he said, "not your normal selves, Master Dominic, and Miss Imogen."

"We're all right," said Nick, slightly dismissively.

"Everyone in the house is upset, Melibee," I said. "We've been doing a lot of thinking. And I'm worried about my dog."

"What has befallen your dog?" asked Melibee, seeming genuinely not to know.

"Oh, he's been locked away by Bonefinger," I said, bitterly. "I don't know where he is."

"What reason did Bonefinger give for taking the dog?"

"That he'd found him in the chicken run," I said. "But I – don't believe him."

Melibee seemed to be considering his reply. "No doubt Bonefinger judged it the best course of action," he said, "for whatever reason. But you must not worry, Miss Imogen, he will not harm the dog. I will see to it that he is treated well."

Nick was sceptical. "Bonefinger does what he likes," he said, when Melibee had left the room. "He hadn't even *told* Melibeem about it. I don't see what Melibeem can do."

"Maybe he can find out where Lash is, and take him some food and things," I said. I badly wanted to believe in Melibee's goodness, after he had taken the trouble to reassure us. But I had an uncomfortable feeling that Nick was probably right: that the cunning Bonefinger routinely ran rings around his mild, blind, old fellow-servant.

It had been a long, bewildering day. I didn't want to abandon the search for Lash, but I wasn't sure I could stay awake for much longer; and I was starting to resign myself to the prospect of a night without his familiar warmth curled around my feet.

When I got back to my bedroom I heaved the bed aside so that I could hide the bell inside our drawer. I placed it on top of Damyata's letter, which was still just where Nick had put it. But, after sliding the bed back into place, instead of getting into it I took my quilt, wrapped it around myself, and went through to sit on Nick's bed so we could talk for a while.

"You never told me what *you* did this afternoon," I said, yawning.

"I didn't do much," he said. Then something occurred to him. "But I did find one thing out," he said. "I went to the library, and I found a book of Latin. Like a dictionary."

"Oh yes? And?"

"And," he said quietly, "I looked up the words on that tomb. You know, the ones the skeleton's pointing to."

"SCURRA something," I yawned.

"SCURRA CAELI REX MORTIUM," Nick obliged. "It

took me a while to work it out, and I'm still not sure I've got it right."

"What do you think it means?"

"Something like, 'The jester of heaven, and the king of the dead'."

There was a long silence. His words echoed in my mind, like the strange rushing sounds in the tunnel, as I curled tighter inside my warm quilt.

I expect Nick said something else, eventually; but I didn't hear him because I'd fallen asleep.

The cold woke me up. It took me a while to realise I was still on Nick's bed, lying awkwardly against the wall, only half-covered in my quilt. Nick was sleeping soundly, a gently-breathing hump under the covers beside me.

I sat up, wincing with cramp, climbed gingerly off the bed so as not to waken him, and stretched. It was pitch dark, and I had no idea how long I'd been lying there; but I gathered up my quilt, and was heading off to spend the rest of the night in my own bed, when I heard a dog barking.

I had to stand still, and strain to listen for a little while before I heard it again; but there it was, distant but unmistakeable, and I was more or less certain it was Lash's bark. And it seemed to be coming from within the castle.

I was about to rush out into the corridor when I realised I was nowhere near sufficiently dressed for a nocturnal dog hunt. The first thing I laid my hands on in my pitch-dark wardrobe was a silk dressing-gown, which had been among the things I was given when I arrived here, but which I rarely wore because it was

THE GOD OF MISCHIEF

too long for me. It would do. I grabbed it, pulled it around myself, and tiptoed out of my room.

The barking was intermittent; but out here on the landing it sounded much more distinct, and I could have sworn it was coming from upstairs, somewhere along the upper corridor where the servants' quarters were. Was Lash being kept in one of the servants' bedrooms – perhaps even in Bonefinger's own? My eyes still getting used to the darkness, I ventured up the staircase, clinging to the oak bannister, all the time listening.

I reached the top floor, and stood still for a while at the top of the stairs. I hadn't been up here since the morning Miss Thynne had been found dead. Everything had been tidied up, of course – or so I assumed. But, as I started to creep slowly along the passageway, I could see the door of Miss Thynne's old room slightly ajar, and a pale light coming from behind it.

I don't quite know what was moving me forward, now; whether it was sheer curiosity or something much further beyond my control; but I had the sense of pushing open the door and stepping through it *despite* my better judgement, *despite* my fear.

There was a lamp burning with a very low flame on a table in the corner. Perhaps a housemaid, cleaning the room or taking away linen last thing in the evening, had forgotten to put it out. It was sending a faint glow around the room, but its most noticeable effect was to create huge shadows as I moved, which probably scared me more than if there had been no light at all. The long red curtains were closed, and it seemed all of Miss Thynne's possessions had been moved out of the room, for the desk was bereft of her pens and neatly-stacked books, the photographs she had kept on the bedside table were gone, the cupboard doors stood open with no clothes on the hangers, and the big old oak bed was stripped bare. All that was left were the objects which, presumably, belonged to the house and had been here before she arrived. A small gilt mirror above the wash-stand; a couple of paintings, one a still-life of a dead pheasant and some lavender, the other a view of what looked like a for-eign harbour with strange-shaped boats and tropical trees. A statuette of an elephant: which, as I approached and inspected it, I discovered had been carved with another smaller elephant inside its belly, and that smaller elephant in turn had another much smaller elephant inside it, and so on – a seemingly end-less diminishment of elephants until the eye could no longer make them out.

And – the grandest object of all, I noticed as I turned around – a large and vibrantly-coloured peacock's tail, mounted on the wall directly behind the bed. At first I thought it was real; but on going up to it and taking one of the intricate, shimmer-ing feathers in my fingers, I found it was made of silk. It had been beautifully made: fragile and startlingly realistic, and some-how lambent, as though burning or shimmering with gold. The effect, I realised, was created by mirrors: a small oval mirror in the eye of every feather sent the light from the lamp back into the room, duplicated twenty or thirty times over.

All of a sudden, as I stood there gazing at the silk peacock, I felt the hairs on the back of my neck standing up. I could hear someone whispering.

I looked around. There was quite clearly nobody else in the room, and yet the whispering sounded extremely close, as though someone invisible were standing right by my ear. It was continuous; and I couldn't make out what it was saying, but it sounded like a woman's whisper.

It sounded like Miss Thynne's whisper.

Even as I realised this, and my skin began to crawl even more, her whisper was joined by another, and another, like a roomful of women whispering to me, indecipherable words but urgent and constant. It sounded as though they were trying to persuade me, to spur me on. I panicked. I tried to cover my ears to block out the sound, but I couldn't. There was a whole choir of women's voices, hissing something at me of which I had no understanding, a cacophony of whispers. Fighting the urge to scream, I clamped my hand over my mouth and fled for the door.

As soon as I emerged into the dark passageway again, the whispers stopped. I had to stand there for a few minutes, at the top of the stairs, listening to my own breathing to calm myself, clutching the silk dressing-gown tightly around me for comfort. I should never have got up. I could be snug in my soft sweet-smelling bed now, instead of standing here, terrified witless, in the cold.

And now, in the night silence, the dog barked again. I turned my head, and listened. This time it seemed to be coming from the other direction, away from the servants' corridor and down the passageways which led over towards the tower. Again it was intermittent, but when it came I was more certain than ever that it was Lash.

I followed the barking, through the dark passageways, find-ing my way by the small amount of light coming from the windows, if there was any, and by touch and memory, like Melibee, if there wasn't. The barking seemed to grow louder the nearer I got to the tower, and I realised this made perfect sense, because the tower was the one place we were forbidden from going. If we'd tried to enter the tower during the day to look for him, we'd have been stopped in no time. But now, in the dead of night, there was just a chance I might be able to get in without being found out.

Bonefinger and Melibee kept the only full sets of keys. But we had lived here long enough now to have discovered some of Kniveacres' secrets; and I knew that there was a key which habitually sat in the lock of a large oriental chest, on this floor, which also fitted the lock of one of the doors into the tower. They thought nobody knew this; but Nick hadn't lived among thieves in London for thirteen years without learning to try keys in locks, just in case. We also knew that the key which opened the summerhouse also opened the staircase down to the wine-cellar; and that you only needed one key to open all the store-cupboards on the kitchen corridor.

It took me a very long time, because I was trying to be completely silent, and even the operation of removing the key from the chest took two minutes, because I was terrified of making it squeak as it came out. Eventually, though, I was padding silently down the stone stairs of the tower in my bare feet; and the sporadic barking, which I now knew with certainty to be my poor lovely Lash, sounded closer than ever when it broke the silence of the night. From the pattern of his barking, I could even picture what he was doing. Trapped in a room somewhere, he was going to the door, barking a few times, and waiting for a response; when none came, he would go and lie down for a little while to have a scratch or a lick, before eventually deciding it was worth another go, getting up, and barking at the door again.

But I still didn't know where he was, and the way the sound echoed around in this stone stairwell made it hard to be certain which direction noises were really coming from.

I was standing, now, outside the door of Sir Septimus's study. The barking had stopped, and I needed to hear it again to be sure where I should go next. I had been so exhausted when evening came that I hadn't been able to stay awake; but now, in the middle of the cold September night, I felt wide awake, and more than naturally alert.

I was fairly sure Lash wasn't in the study, but I couldn't resist trying the door; and, to my astonishment, it opened with no resistance. The study was in total darkness, but the familiar fusty smell of Sir Septimus's books met my nostrils. Suddenly it seemed too good an opportunity to miss.

Maybe it would be easier, from inside the study, to work out where the source of the barking was.

Of course I knew it was utterly foolhardy and dangerous, but I was somehow drawn in through the oak door; and I walked around, silently, savouring the sensation of simply being in such a forbidden place, alone and undetected. My fingers ran along the spines of the books ranged along the shelves; I sat in one of Sir Septimus's leather chairs and it emitted a long, soft hiss of air. I went over to the desk and touched the battered leather surface, which I had stared down upon whenever Sir Septimus had summoned us for one of his uncomfortable conversations. There were bottles of ink and a tray of pens neatly positioned on one side of the desk; but all Sir Septimus's books and papers had obviously been tidied away.

I stood still and listened hard, for a minute or so, to reassure myself I hadn't disturbed anyone. There wasn't a sound from the rest of the house. The barking seemed to have stopped now; all I could hear was my own heartbeat. I was starting to feel cold. I retied the belt of my dressing-gown to wrap it more snugly around myself; but before I left the study, I decided to have a quick try of all the drawer handles on the front of the desk, just in case there turned out to be anything interesting in any of them. They were nearly all locked. The only one that turned out to be open was the top right-hand one, and it had nothing in it except a little bunch of keys which opened all the other drawers.

People are their own worst enemies, Nick often said: they may as well burgle themselves.

Most of the drawers contained nothing of interest; but in one of them I could feel several loose papers, which I gently pulled out. I was scared of lighting a lamp, knowing that any light in here could easily be seen from other parts of the house. As I stood in the dark room, full of the scent of ink and leather, I wasn't quite sure what I was going to do. I could take the sheaf of papers with me, but they would quickly be missed, and our rooms would be the first to be searched. But, as I stood there, the moon came out from behind a cloud for the first time that night, and it gave me the answer instantly. It was a full moon, give or take a day. Shining through the window directly onto the desk, it provided more than enough light to read by.

I sat down in Sir Septimus's chair, with the oriel window behind me and the moon casting its grey light in from my left;

and I began to inspect the documents I'd found. The top one immediately looked familiar: and sure enough, as I unfolded it, I found it was the chilling letter Damyata had left for Sir Septimus, which consisted of nothing but his name, in brown ink, in the middle of the sheet. I studied the writing on the other side: SIR SEPTIMUS CLOY, it said.

It hadn't occurred to me when Sir Septimus had shown it to us the other day, but now that I looked at it again something didn't seem quite right. The writing wasn't exactly neat, but compared to the smudgy scrawl Damyata had pushed under Nick's door yesterday, it was remarkably legible: and, come to think of it, even the Indian characters of his signature didn't bear much resemblance to the way he usually wrote them. Perhaps it was just because his notes were usually scribbled in frantic haste; whereas, the other night, most probably sitting at this very desk with Sir Septimus's creamy paper and elegant pens in front of him, he had had the leisure to make his words legible.

Turning over the next piece of paper, densely filled with small but bold black type, I could see straight away that it was a will.

I, Septimus Wellynghame Cloy of Kniveacres Hall in the County of Warwickshire do hereby revoke all former Wills and Codicils and do declare this to be my last Will, made this 23rd day of September in the Year of Our Lord One Thousand Eight Hundred and Twenty Eight.

I was intrigued. The date was only three or four days ago. It looked as though Sir Septimus had been drawing up a brand new will.

It was fantastically complicated. There were endless paragraphs about something called "issue", which I eventually understood to mean children, the gist of which was that neither Sir Septimus nor any of his brothers had any – at least, none who survived. It then went on to explain who stood to inherit Sir Septimus's estate. There weren't nearly enough commas.

> *I do hereby disinherit any blood Relative or illegitimate Issue or Party or Parties with similar entitlement under the Clauses of any foregoing Will and Testament now cancelled. I do devise and bequeath my entire Estate both real and personal to such of my loyal Retainers who shall be proven to survive me, namely Hieronymous Bonefinger and Anselm Archibald Melibee, if both in equal part, and do appoint them Executors and Trustees of this my Will.*

Trying to decipher the dense legalistic wording by the light of the moon was giving me a headache; and I was about to stop reading when another couple of lines, very near the end, caught my eye.

> *It is my Will and Stipulation that my Remains be buried at Kniveacres, unmarked, at the westernmost end of the yew-tree avenue, my sole Memorial to be the addition of my name to the Family Tombstone in St Moribunda's church.*

It might seem surprising, but when I read this I honestly just thought it was just intriguing, rather than hugely significant. Too many things had been happening in the past few days for my brain to have a hope of making sense of it.

I put the will aside and felt around in the drawer again. Beneath the few loose papers I'd pulled out there was a large leather wallet, containing a number of letters which had obviously been folded up and hidden away for safe keeping. Almost as soon as I had taken them out and unfolded them, a cloud snuffed out the moon, and I swore in a whisper, looking up at the window. Those ten minutes or so of clear moonlight, during which I'd been reading Sir Septimus's will, had been a brief interlude on an unsettled night. Thicker clouds were drifting in, and I was going to be lucky to have enough light to see these letters.

I had to wait quite a long time, but at length the moon reappeared, and I was determined to read as much as I could before I lost the light again. Now I could see that the letter on top of the pile was from a lawyer in London, addressed to Sir Septimus. Like the will, it was in highly contorted legal language, but it seemed to be discussing how much help Sir Septimus might expect in the event of someone else's family discovering something he had done, which he didn't want them to know about. There were a few sternly underscored sentences in the letter: <u>No word of this affair must be breathed to a living soul</u>, it read at one point. <u>This is not a matter in which you should feel at liberty to meddle</u>, it said further down.

Now, I knew, I was looking at real secrets. Sir Septimus's will was one thing, and I had really struggled to understand much of it; but I could instantly tell that these letters contained things I wasn't meant to know. Finding my fingers trembling, I leafed through some of the others. The paper on which the letters were written varied enormously, and some of them looked quite old, and faded, and were fragile to the touch. The dates ranged as far back as thirty years ago, and they were from a lot of different people: Col. G.H. Potts Mauberley; The Hon. Andrew W. Pugh; Mr Horace M. Smith-Chessingthorpe; Sir Lumley Sheets. They wrote from addresses in both England and India, and some of the envelopes which had been kept with the letters had Indian postmarks.

I was about to start reading another of the letters when the moon disappeared again. This was *so* frustrating; but I had already been in here far longer than I'd intended, and I decided it probably wasn't worth staying here any longer. The sky was black with clouds again: and without the moon, I couldn't read. It was simply too much of a risk to be here if I couldn't learn anything. I was cold, and tired, and I still hadn't found any real clues as to where Lash was, let alone freed him.

I hadn't put the letters back in quite the order in which I'd found them, but I thought I'd sorted them into a reasonably tidy pile, and I was just about to slide them all back inside their wallet and put it away when the moon emerged again briefly, and lit up the letter sitting on top. A single line leaped out of the page at me.

Regarding the case of Miss Imogen Winter

And the moon was gone again, as quickly as it had come. I held the letter right up to my face, but try as I might I couldn't decipher it without the light of the moon.

Maybe I should risk lighting a lamp, after all? Who would see it? Only someone who was already up, walking the courtyard or looking out of a window. It was the middle of the night: surely it was unlikely that anyone was watching, now?

I was sitting, chewing my nails with indecision, in Sir Septimus's chair in the complete darkness, when there was a clatter. I froze. The light of a lamp appeared at the door, and Bonefinger came into the study.

He stood still in the doorway, lifted the lamp, and looked at me for a long time, saying nothing.

CHAPTER 9
AN UNCOMFORTABLE WEEKEND

I blinked back into the bright light. The drawer beside me was wide open, and the pile of paper was still sitting on the desk in front of me. I couldn't possibly lie about what I'd been doing here. I was going to be flayed alive.

My grip tightened around the arms of the chair. Bonefinger came quite slowly and deliberately over to the desk, and placed his lamp on the edge. His expression in the orange light was impassive, not malicious – if anything slightly pitying. I was filled with simultaneous terror and loathing, and I dug my bottom teeth into my top lip to keep my mouth closed, because if I didn't I was certain I was going to scream.

Finally, he spoke, very quietly. "It's just you?" he said.

At first I didn't understand him. Then I realised he must have thought, when he heard someone in here, that he was going to encounter Damyata. He must have been quite afraid when he opened the door, and quite relieved to find it was me.

"Where is your brother?"

I looked up at him. "Asleep," I said. "I came looking for Lash, on my own. I thought I heard barking from the tower. What have you done with him?"

He ignored the question. "Perhaps you would like to explain," he said in a quiet voice, "what *possible* business you believed you might have in here."

"The door wasn't locked," I said sullenly.

Bonefinger nodded gravely.

"It was remiss of me to leave it open," he said. "It will teach me a lesson." He leaned over and snatched up the sheaf of papers from the desk, folding them into their wallet and tucking it inside his coat. "But you," he said quietly, "you must be taught a lesson too, Miss Imogen Winter." The chilling tone he gave to the last three words made it more than obvious he knew exactly what I had just been looking at. "It seems imprisoning your dog was insufficient warning against your wandering."

"I want him back," I scowled.

"That remains to be seen," he said. "It is out of my hands." He paused. "Sir Septimus must . . . make his own judgement," he continued, "on the basis of the report of your behaviour which he shall receive from me on his return. I find it unlikely that he will view your unauthorised presence in his study, and your quite calculated interest in his private papers, as an act of mere childish waywardness to be lightly or leniently dismissed. But that will be a matter for him. In the meantime, you will come with me."

He took the lamp and stood by the open door.

I got up slowly, and walked out. He closed the door behind us and propelled me down the stairs. When we got to the ground floor we turned not towards the door into the courtyard, but down another flight of stairs towards the cellar.

"Where are you taking me?"

"Somewhere you can be trusted to remain," he said. He was speaking with terrifying self-control. It would have been far less frightening if he had exploded in a rage and slammed me violently against the walls of the stairwell on our way down. We got to the bottom of the flight of stairs and we stopped outside a heavy wooden door. I'd never been down here before. It smelled damp, and it was colder than it had been upstairs.

"Is this where you've got Lash?" I asked as he unlocked the door.

I could have sworn I heard him stifle a chuckle. "You imagine I might give you and the dog the consolation of being reunited," he said. He grabbed hold of my upper arm and yanked me around so I had to look into his face. "Now why," he snarled, "would I do that?"

I panicked. He was going to lock me up, without Lash, without Nick. It was my own stupid fault. *Why* had I even risked going into the study? *Why* hadn't I left when I had first intended to? And now, who knew how long I was going to be kept down here, in this awful dark place?

On a sudden crazy impulse, I made a run for it. I leaped to the foot of the stairs and ran up them as fast as I could; but within a few seconds I'd lost all trace of light from Bonefinger's lamp, and I was stumbling up the steps by guesswork. If I could only get to the top floor and back out the way I'd come in – after that, well, I hadn't thought any further than that, but it was better than submitting to being locked up in this dismal cellar.

But the next thing I knew, I had got my feet caught in the trailing fabric of my long dressing-gown and fallen headlong up the stone stairs, grazing my leg painfully. For all his advanced age, Bonefinger could move remarkably fast, and he had caught up with me in seconds. It would probably only have been a few more steps before he'd have done so anyway, even if I hadn't fallen over.

He took hold of me now, and more or less dragged me back down the stairs, with his wiry powerful arm under my shoulder and his hand around my neck. I tried to wriggle, but I knew I was defeated. He threw me into the room and held the lamp up to show me where I was.

It was, at least, a room, not a dungeon: the floor was of stone, and there was even a rather thin rug in the middle of the room; but there was no bed, just a single chair and a wooden bench, like a pew. There was a small window high in the wall, behind a grating. I could see a porcelain chamber pot in a corner, but nothing to wash with.

"You won't need a lamp," he said, "there'll be light enough in the morning."

"I'll be cold," I said. "I've only got—"

"It was your own decision, to stalk around the house in your night-clothes," he cut in. He looked around the room, as if to assure himself that there were no unnecessary luxuries. "You might profitably contemplate your behaviour, while you're in here," he spat, as he turned to go. "Once you come out, you may find a shock in store for you. You are likely to discover that life at Kniveacres is no longer quite as you have been used to living it." The notion seemed to give him some pleasure. He took the lamp out, and closed the door behind him, and I heard him lock it.

I went up to the door, and banged on it for a few minutes, but it did no good. I had just gone and felt my way towards the bench to sit down, when the key turned in the lock again and he reappeared. He didn't say a word this time: he just tossed a large grey horse-blanket into the room, and withdrew immediately, locking the door again.

As I sat there in the darkness, with my foot on the bench so I could lick the blood from my grazed knee, I listened to the muffled sound of barking from somewhere; possibly a long way off, possibly only just behind the thick cellar walls. It hardly mattered where Lash was. My chance of finding and freeing him had just evaporated; and the tears welled in my eyes again as I realised my stupidity tonight had probably guaranteed the worst possible fate for all of us.

I somehow fell asleep on the hard little bench, and awoke what was probably only an hour or two later to find the grey light of dawn coming through the window high above my head. Now that there was light, I could see that this room really was about as much like a prison cell as it could be, almost as though it were reserved and furnished for precisely that purpose. This was the very oldest part of the house: the ancient walls were about six feet thick, and there were iron bars in the window, which was so high up in the wall I'd have had to stand on the shoulders of someone at least my own height to be able to look out. I had thought I might be able to attract attention this morning, especially if Nick came looking for me; and I tried shouting a few times, but I soon realised it was a waste of energy. I was in a cellar, whose only window was closed tight, and which in any case seemed to give out onto a side of the house where people rarely walked.

As the hours went by, and nobody came for me, and nobody knocked at the window, I sank into a state of chafing boredom and despondency. There was absolutely nothing to do except stare at the walls. Almost no sound penetrated to the little cellar: the barking I'd heard last night had stopped completely, there were no voices of servants or gardeners drifting through the pane of glass; I couldn't even detect any birdsong from outside. I began to feel increasingly sure that Bonefinger would have locked Nick up somewhere too. Nick's main purpose this morning would be to find me, and find Lash, and I doubted that Bonefinger would have given him the opportunity.

I was starving hungry, and cold, still wearing only my nightshirt, the long silk dressing-gown and the coarse old blanket Bonefinger had given me, which I had to keep wrapped around myself all the time to prevent myself shivering. One corner of the cellar was permanently wet, from a long shiny greenish streak of filthy water which dribbled slowly down the wall, and had probably done so for years if the build-up of algae and mould around it was any guide. My throat was already sore when I woke up, and before much of the day had passed I found myself coughing painfully. My ragged repeated cough was the only thing that broke the silence.

My heart leaped when, at last, there were footsteps and a murmur of men's voices outside the door, and the key turned in the lock.

Melibee came in. He was carrying a tray with a dish of soup, a jug of water and some biscuits. He came in without a word, kicking the door casually half-closed behind him with one heel, and placed the tray on the bench before returning to the door to lock it. I sat watching him. He was moving completely without urgency, apparently unconcerned at the door remaining open for so long. I could easily have escaped out of the door behind his back while he was laying the tray down. But I'd heard him talking to someone before coming in, and I was fairly sure Bonefinger must be lurking not far away.

"It will be remarked upon, Miss Imogen, if I spend too long in here," he said in a low voice, after locking the door, "but I may at the very least take the trouble to ask if there is anything you urgently require? I may be able to get it for you."

"Where's Nick?" I asked sullenly.

"Master Dominic is safe," said Melibee, "but has been – similarly confined."

"Have you seen Lash?"

"N-no," he admitted, "though I am aware of where the dog is being kept, and I know he is secure and nourished. I do not believe you will be denied your liberty for many days, Miss Imogen, but I fear I may not grant it personally."

"What time is it?" I asked.

"Approaching the hour of twelve," he replied. "The kitchen is not aware of your imprisonment and assumed you would both be taking lunch as normal. I collected it, and brought it down. I will be doing the same for Master Dominic momentarily."

"Tell him I'm all right," I said.

He lifted his head slightly to one side, in the habitual way he had, like a bird or a lizard, as though listening hard for tiny sounds which might give him information his eyes couldn't. "Your surroundings are – austere," he said. "Nevertheless, you may find sleep the most effective means of whiling away the hours. I will endeavour to bring you something to make you more comfortable."

"A pillow," I said, "and the quilt from my room."

He nodded, and moved back towards the door.

"I may not be able to return immediately," he said.

He unlocked the door, slipped out, and locked it again behind him; and the crashing silence descended again.

I ate the lunch in no time, and found my mood had lifted almost straight away. My conversation with Melibee had made me feel better too: not just because it was a straw of human company at which to clutch, but because there had been something genuinely reassuring about his manner. It was obvious he felt sorry for us, and I felt fairly sure I might be able to persuade him to do more to help, next time, if we were to be kept locked up in here for some days, as he had implied.

He'd said he might not be able to come back straight away, but I had only just finished eating by the time he was unlocking the door again and coming in with a neatly-folded quilt and a pillow sitting on top.

"When is he going to let us out?" I asked.

"I cannot say," he replied. "I have already advanced an argument in favour of your being freed."

"To no avail," I said gloomily.

"Perhaps not entirely," he said, mysteriously. I was about to say something else when there was a brisk footfall on the stone flags outside and someone rapped sharply on the door. Melibee put his finger to his lips. He picked up my lunch tray and went back to the door; and, sure enough, as he left I could hear Bonefinger's voice.

"Perhaps we may now regard their sustenance as taken care of, for the time being." Bonefinger's voice carried a chilly edge. "There are tasks upstairs which require our attention more urgently."

The door closed, and the voices died away. I lifted the pillow and the quilt over to the bench, and tried to arrange them. As I did so, I heard something tinkling.

I stopped and listened. I couldn't hear it now.

I shook out the quilt and laid it across the bench; then I picked up the pillow and tried to prop it up at a comfortable angle. And there was the tinkling again.

It was coming from the bedding: and it sounded like the little bell I'd found in the chapel. But I'd shut that away in the drawer in the bedroom, hadn't I?

I felt around the quilt, and I couldn't find any trace of it; but when I moved the pillow I could see that there seemed to be a strange, soft lump in the pillow-case. I reached inside, and could hardly believe my eyes when I pulled out the patchwork purple and yellow cap the jester had been wearing.

What on *earth* was it doing here?

It lay limply across the pillow, its two peaks crumpled underneath it. I smoothed it out, and immediately noticed that one of the bells was missing: there was just a short strand of loose thread sticking out of the cap's peak where it had come away.

How had Melibee got hold of this, and what was he trying to tell me by hiding it in the pillow-case? Had the jester been captured? Was Melibee somehow in league with the jester?

As I thought about it, though, I realised there was another possibility – and that Melibee may have had nothing to do with it at all.

Perhaps the jester had been in my room, last night while I was prowling around the castle, or some time today, while I was locked up in here – and had left the cap among the bedclothes, for me to find. Melibee had brought the pillow down, not even realising the cap was hidden there.

That would make far more sense. The jester must have put it there himself. But why – and who was he?

I was kept locked up in the cellar for the entire weekend. Night fell; Melibee came in with some supper, but he wasn't in a very chatty mood and, despite my attempts to get information out of him, he left quickly. I slept, occasionally, in short bursts, when I wasn't keeping myself awake by coughing; and I always woke up aching and stiff from the terrible discomfort of the bench. At one point I tried lying on the stone floor, wrapped in my quilt, thinking it might be preferable because I'd at least be able to stretch out: but I soon found it was far too cold. By the time Sunday dawned I was feeling ragged with exhaustion, grubby and hollow-eyed, my throat and limbs sore, my brain numb. I'd tried to use the hours to think through the events of the past few days, to try and make sense of it all, but, if anything, I felt more confused than ever. I couldn't bring myself to thank Melibee for the milk and fresh warm apple dumplings he brought in for breakfast. I knew he was trying his best; but I just wanted to be out of there.

And then, before he left the room, he placed a book on the bench.

"This may stave off boredom, at least temporarily," he said. "I had no time to make a considered selection. I hope it is not too dry."

He locked the door, and I listened to his slow footsteps as he climbed the stairs.

For a few minutes I left the book where it was, and hardly glanced at it. I ate the breakfast, feeling sorry for myself. Only when I'd finished did I look at the book properly; and when I did, I could hardly believe my eyes.

Melibee had brought me the very book Bonefinger had con-fiscated the other night: the big leather-bound *Chronicle and Description*, full of plans of Kniveacres, with the embossed coat of arms on the cover. Instantly, I felt much more awake. The light was so dim in here that I had to take the chair over and sit right under the little window in order to be able to see properly, but I began studying the book, trying to work my way through, page by page, and learn as much as I could about the house and grounds. There were so many things Nick and I hadn't explored, or didn't understand: I grew quite excited at the real-isation that this was my chance to find out some answers.

In the event, I soon found it wasn't as easy as I'd expected. There had been a surprising number of changes to the layout of Kniveacres since this book was printed; and even though much of it was in riddles, the extra notes in the little *Addendum* — which, of course, I didn't have — would have been very useful.

Nevertheless, the more I read, the more sure I was that Melibee hadn't picked up this book by accident. My conviction about his goodwill returned. He knew exactly what he was doing, bringing me this.

Progressive plans of the house over the years showed the house first of all in its original state, when it was little more than a great Hall with a few antechambers; then with three or four different stages of further building, until it had grown to more or less the shape we now knew. Along with the maps there were about a hundred pages of dense description and history, tracing the various owners of Kniveacres, its period as a monastic retreat in the 15th century, and its colourful role in the Civil War when it had been an important Royalist headquarters and often used as a hiding place. For most of its history, this had been a thriving family house, with almost all its rooms in use either by family members or by the cohort of servants who looked after their every need. More recently, as we knew, large parts of it had been closed off; new walls had been added, windows bricked up, and staircases taken out.

The other thing the book revealed, however, and by far the most exciting of all, was a veritable network of secret rooms and hidden passageways all over the house. Whatever had happened here down the years, it was clear that an enormous number of people had wanted to hide. There were secret chambers set into the chimney-breasts of grand fireplaces, stairwells which began behind the backs of cupboards, trapdoors under carpets, and passages behind wooden panelling – and here they all were, laid out in perfect detail in these plans. I was particularly intrigued, as I followed the lines and spaces with my forefinger, to see that there was a hidden corridor behind the walls on the top floor, which led all the way from Sir Septimus's bedroom in the tower – immediately above his study – to one of the servants' bedrooms in the east wing.

We had often wondered how Bonefinger managed to appear in rooms without having opened the door, or to get so quickly from one part of the house to another. Here was the answer. No wonder he had confiscated the book.

Of course, I lost no time in trying to work out whether there was a secret way out of the room I was now in. I found the room easily on the plan of the cellars, and was quite surprised to realise there were actually seven or eight rooms of a similar size down here under the tower. Disappointingly, however, there were no secret doorways marked in this room, and no tunnels behind the walls. According to the plans, it was just what it seemed: a featureless square space encased in thick, solid stone, unchanged since the medieval core of the house had first been built.

But, as I studied the next page, I had to stop myself letting out a cry of excitement as I noticed a tunnel marked on the plan which began at the butler's pantry. A footnote, with a little sketch, clearly explained the means of access down into the tunnel, by lifting the top step of the false staircase. *That* was why we couldn't understand where Bonefinger had gone, that afternoon, after we'd followed him in there. He hadn't gone through the stone wall, or up through a trap door in the ceiling: he'd gone *down*, through the top step, into a tunnel! According to this plan, it led underground to a long-bricked-up vault immediately below the kitchen, from where another tunnel then continued off the edge of the page, in the direction of the gardens. I remembered the fork we'd come across in the tunnel we'd explored, not long after we'd started making our way between the cave and the village church. If we'd taken the fork to the left, we'd probably have ended up in the butler's pantry.

I was alive with excitement, and I turned the pages more quickly now; but the further I read, the less I found of real interest. There were drawings of the chapel I'd been in only yesterday afternoon, showing how grand it had really once been: when this book was printed it had been intact, with an ornate ceiling and rich stained glass, and full of magnificent woodwork. But there was nothing in the description – how could there be? – to suggest a history of unexplained events, or a curse, or offer any hint as to why all those birds dropped dead. There was a plan, and detailed drawings, of the village church: so detailed, indeed, that I could make out the gargoyle above the porch which had so nearly fallen on Nick's head the other day. But the secret door in the tombstone, and the crypt, and the tunnel, were simply not shown. Maybe the person who had drawn these plans didn't know about them. Maybe, more than a hundred years ago, they hadn't even been there.

Still, I had learned a great deal more about Kniveacres than I had known when I was first locked in here; it made me *desperate* to talk to Nick and share what I'd found out, and it made the hours pass much more quickly. In fact, I almost forgot how wretched and miserable I was.

It was quite late on Sunday when there was a sudden flurry of activity: the sound of people running up and down the cellar stairs, locks being turned, shouting. I stirred: I'd been having one of my fitful naps in a sitting position, propped up against the arm of the bench. As I came to, I saw the door of my prison swing open and Bonefinger stood there, his face sour. He didn't come in: he merely loomed in the doorway, looking remarkably like the effigy of himself which the villagers had made and hung on the gibbet.

"Come," he said.

I gathered, from the voices I heard as I climbed the stairs behind him, and from the activity I could see outside in the stableyard as we reached the ground floor, that Sir Septimus had returned. Bonefinger made me wait at the bottom of the tower stairs for a moment. He was still saying absolutely nothing. He seemed to have less blood in his complexion than ever. Through the door into the yard, I could see horses being rubbed down and led back to the stable, Sir Septimus's carriage standing on the gravel, and a man heaving some boxes and pieces of luggage from the carriage to the house.

Within a moment or two, Melibee had joined us from the cellar, and he had Nick with him. Nick looked a bit tired, but not at all harmed. He blew air out between his lips to signal his relief at being freed.

"I thought they were never going to let us out," I murmured. "Are you all right?"

I nodded. "I've got—"

But Bonefinger cut short our conversation. "Sir Septimus wishes to see you both, in his study," he snapped. "Let's lose no time." And he chivvied us on up the stairs, with occasional sharp – excessively sharp, in truth – jabs of his fingertips against the backs of our necks.

Sir Septimus was standing, with his back to us, watching the activity in the courtyard below the study window. He didn't turn around when we came in, though he knew we were there. Bonefinger coughed.

"You may leave us," Sir Septimus said shortly, still without turning around.

When Bonefinger had withdrawn, he moved from the window and sat down, heavily, in the chair at his desk. He regarded us silently from under his eyebrows for a few moments.

"Mmy return home," he rumbled, "to reports that you have, mm, mabused your licence to roam the house and grounds. I believe I expressly said before I departed that I wished to hear of no, mmmm, *nuisance*, in my absence."

"Sorry, Sir Septimus," I said, "it was my fault. I was anxious about my dog. Bonefinger took him from me and locked him up. We were just trying to find him."

"Which is doubtless why you were caught going through my private papers in the middle of the night," Sir Septimus said. "You thought the dog might be in a drawer of my desk. Quite reasonable."

This was a shock. Sir Septimus had never been sarcastic in our presence before, let alone downright witty. I opened my mouth to say something, but he interrupted.

"Circumstances," he said, "have left you without much supervision or useful activity to which to direct your, mmm, menergies. I little thought your unemployment would lead to miscreancy in so short a time. Be that as it may, I have now taken steps to address this." He leaned forward across the desk. "Mmm, my did not return from London alone," he said. "Your new governess has arrived at Kniveacres this afternoon, mand

226

you will meet her in the morning. She has been instructed to make up for certain failures of Miss Thynne to rein in your more, mmm, spirited tendencies. How she sets about this task is a matter for her own discretion. My do not wish your discipline or occupation to be a concern which ever again distracts me, or my manservants, from our daily affairs. Do I make myself clearm?"

"Yes, Sir Septimus," said Nick quietly.

He looked at me.

"Yes, Sir Septimus," I said.

"Mrs Guisely begins her duties at dawn," he said. "Muntil then, I have instructed Bonefinger that you are to be freed. But you will remain in the east wing, and you will not be permitted to leave the house. Munderstood?"

"Yes, Sir Septimus," said Nick.

He stared straight at me again.

"May my dog be freed too?" I said.

He inhaled deeply. "Mrs Guisely," he said, "will be given the power to determine whether your dog is an appropriate companion, and how its welfare should be carried forward. Muntil she has had time to make such an assessment, I imagine it may, yes."

I closed my eyes. I was going to cry, I realised. I had to get out.

"Go," he said simply; and he stood up, and turned away from us again to look out of the window.

Nick hadn't really been told why I was locked up in the first place, and I'd seen him raise his eyebrows in surprise when Sir Septimus

227

mentioned my having been found going through his papers in the study. Once we were back in our rooms, and I'd spent a few minutes washing and putting some warmer clothes on at long last, he was desperate to hear what I'd discovered. But my revelations had to wait for a while, as Melibee then came knocking at the door to return our bedding, and I pressed him about Lash.

"Sir Septimus *said* he could be freed," I pleaded. "*Can't* you bring him, now? *Please* see if you can."

I went with him down the stairs, and hovered, near the kitchens. I had no idea whether Lash had been fed regularly over the weekend: I felt sure he'd be starving, because he nearly always was, whether he was locked up or not.

Melibee brought him round at last, on a leash. Darkness had fallen, and I could hear him yelping long before I saw him. As they emerged into the torchlight of the courtyard he gave such a wrench on the leash that Melibee lost his grip, and my enormous lovely gangly Lash came bounding up to me as I knelt by the door, with the biggest grin on his face I had ever seen, and licked me until I thought I was going to dissolve. The tears welled in my eyes, and I fussed over him, and hung on to his ears, and buried my face in the fur of his neck, and told him how happy I was and how I'd started to think I was never going to see him again.

After I'd got some food for him from the kitchen, and he'd wolfed it down, and I'd been to get some more food for him from the kitchen, and he'd wolfed that down too, his breath was significantly smelly, and I took him upstairs.

"Where was he?" Nick asked, as he fussed over the delighted dog.

I hadn't even asked, I'd been so excited at getting him back. Wherever he'd been, he'd emerged from his prison with no visible ill effects apart from a ravenous appetite. It was such a happy scene, this reunion in my lamplit room, and Lash was scampering around sniffing the familiar objects with such evident delight, that I cast all ominous thoughts completely to the back of my mind; but after a few minutes Nick brought them to the fore again.

"I don't like the sound of this new governess," he said.

Neither did I; and it was what Sir Septimus had said about Lash that worried me the most. It was going to be up to her to decide whether Lash was "an appropriate companion". What on earth did that mean? That he might be taken away? The memory of his words made me reach out and hug Lash tightly. I never wanted to let him out of my sight again.

"You know," I said, "when he locked me up, Bonefinger said something about life at Kniveacres never being quite the same again. He seemed really pleased about it, the vile man. He said we'd got a shock waiting for us. Maybe this Mrs Guisely is going to be bad news."

"Did he really catch you in Sir Septimus's study, going through his drawers? What were you thinking of?"

"I don't know," I said, rather ashamed. "I honestly did go looking for Lash. I woke up in the middle of the night and heard him barking, and I found my way into the tower because I thought it was coming from there. I didn't expect the study to be open, but when it was, well – would *you* have been able to resist?"

"You didn't have a light in there, did you?"

"Of course not, I'm not that stupid. I read his letters by the light of the moon. And Nick, I'd found out a few things by the time Bonefinger came in. Sir Septimus is a very bad man."

Lash sat between my knees, and I stroked his head while I related my adventures to Nick. I told him about the accusing letters, and the one from the lawyer saying no one must breathe a word about what he'd done. I told him I'd seen my name – or rather, our mother's name – on one of the letters. I told him about the will, by which Sir Septimus provided for Bonefinger and Melibee to inherit his entire estate. And I told him how Bonefinger had found me, and locked me in the cellar; and how Melibee had brought me the big book about Kniveacres, and some of the things I'd found out from it. Nick's eyes widened especially when I told him this.

"And Melibeem brought you it?" he said. "Just like that? You mean, actually *gave* you it?"

"Completely out of the blue, first thing this morning," I said. "To stave off the boredom, he said."

"*That* was one in the eye for Bonefinger," said Nick.

"He more or less said it was the first book he'd had time to pick up, and he hoped it wouldn't be too dull," I said. "But I think he knew exactly what it was."

"I'm sure he did," agreed Nick. "You can tell Bonefinger and Melibeem hate each other. It's become more and more obvious. I heard them talking when I was in the cellar, and they were – well, *frosty* isn't the word."

"Don't you think Sir Septimus and Bonefinger have fallen out, too?" I asked. "They were barely speaking to each other this afternoon. Sir Septimus seemed completely contemptuous."

"Sir Septimus is always contemptuous," said Nick. "But Bonefinger looked very shocked when Sir Septimus came back. You know he wasn't meant to come back until tomorrow? I think Bonefinger was up to something while Sir Septimus was away, and he can't get away with it now he's back. What are you looking for?"

I was feeling around amongst the bedding Melibee had brought in. "I wanted to show you something," I said. The jester's cap seemed to have gone missing – until I remembered I'd folded it up and put it in the pocket of the dressing-gown I'd been wearing. It was hanging over a chair; and as I pulled the colourful cap out of the pocket with a tinkle, Nick's eyes widened again, and Lash ran up to sniff at it, fascinated.

"Where did you get that?" he gasped.

"Did you know it was here? In the house?" I asked him.

"Of course not!"

"It was stuffed inside my pillow-case," I said. "I asked Melibee to fetch my pillow and quilt, because I was so cold, and the bench was so hard in that awful cellar. And when he came down with it, this was stuffed inside. I thought you might have found it, and put it in my pillow-case as a kind of message."

"I've no idea what it was doing there," he said, taking it from me.

"Then I thought, maybe the jester had been in here. In this bedroom. Looking for the missing bell. Maybe he knew I had it."

"What, and then he dropped his cap as well?"

"Or *left* his cap," I said, "on purpose. Like a kind of calling card."

Nick was inspecting the loose thread where the other bell should have been. He squeezed the cap tightly in his fist. "This is very strange," he said. "The jester follows us out of the crypt, comes to Kniveacres, loses one of his bells in the chapel, and then leaves his whole cap in your bed." He was thinking. "I have a feeling it's not *us* the jester is trying to scare," he said.

"What do you mean?"

"I don't know, I haven't really worked it out yet," he said, thinking as he spoke. "But what if – what if Damyata dressed up as the jester, just to scare Sir Septimus? And say every time he appeared here at Kniveacres, leaving him notes and prophecies, he dressed up? To taunt him. And the rest of the time he could hang around the village pretending to be just another scarecrow?"

"So this is his way of saying he means us no harm?" I said. "Leaving us his cap?"

"It could be, couldn't it?" said Nick. "In any case, I think it might not be too long before we find out what's going on."

I yawned. I was tired, and hungry. "Isn't it time for supper yet?"

"It can't be far off. Unless they've decided we don't deserve any."

"They can't do that," I said. "They didn't feed us properly while we were in the cellar. And they didn't feed you, did they, Lash?" I looked into his face and fondled his ears, and his tongue darted out to lick my nose. "Did a horrid man lock you up?" I asked him in a silly, soothing voice. "Did you bark, and bark, and nobody came? You poor boy. You poor, lovely boy."

I remembered something else.

"Nick," I said, "before I went into the study on Friday night and got caught, I did a bit of exploring upstairs. I thought I heard Lash barking up there first of all. So I went into Miss Thynne's old room."

Nick stared at me.

"It was one of the scariest places I've ever been," I said. "I could hear her voice, Nick, whispering and whispering, like she was still there, trying to tell me something . . . and all sorts of echoes of other whispers, like a lot of – ghosts. I couldn't tell what they were saying. There was this peacock – all made out of mirrors."

I realised I wasn't explaining myself very well; but Nick had pricked up his ears. "A *peacock?*" he said.

"A silk one," I said.

He got up. "Hop off the bed," he said.

Intrigued, I stood up, and watched him manoeuvre the bed away from the wall and crouch to open the secret drawer.

"One thing I did manage to do yesterday morning before Bonefinger locked me up," he said, "was get this back." He pulled out the *Addendum*, and came and sat down on the bed again.

"I thought he'd have hidden that!" I exclaimed.

"Yes, well, it was just in the library under some other books, more or less where I left it. It took me about ten seconds to find. Maybe he's not as clever as we think." He scanned the yellowing pages rapidly, looking for something in particular. "Here! Remember this bit?" He handed it to me, with his finger on the relevant paragraph.

"*In this room,*" I read, "*you would do well to observe the peacock, as the obverse may be true.*"

"In other words," said Nick, "watch out, because the peacock is watching you."

"They were spying on Miss Thynne," I gasped. "Weren't they?"

"Who knows what they've been doing," said Nick, rather wearily. And as he said this, I was flooded with a sense of the unfathomability of it all. Everywhere we turned, we seemed to uncover evidence of wickedness. Sir Septimus's whole family was loathed. When you asked anyone to list the reasons why, they hardly knew where to start. Sir Septimus kept letters hidden upstairs from countless correspondents over many years, alleging dishonourable behaviour. A clever and virtuous woman with family links to the Cloys had died, in this very house, this week, with no explanation. We'd nearly been killed or badly hurt by falling gargoyles, a dumb-waiter, a dangerously loose window-sill, a gaping open well covered up with flimsy branches – all of which looked like accidents at the time, but could quite easily have been nothing of the kind. Bonefinger went out at night and buried bodies, disappeared down secret passageways, met strangers with whom he conducted shady conversations in inns, threatened people, locked up dogs and children out of malice. They all covered up for one another. Only they knew where it began, and where it ended.

"There's the supper bell," said Nick.

"About time too," I grumbled.

He got up and slid the *Addendum* back into the drawer. "We couldn't work out what this meant before, could we? But no wonder we'd never seen the peacock, if it was up there."

We had to leave Lash behind, which was agonising. I tried to reassure him he wasn't going to be on his own for long this time; but he seemed quite happy in his familiar surroundings, and he grinned at me as we went out of the door.

We fell instinctively silent as we came out. Melibee was attendant at supper, and I felt a bit more relaxed about talking openly, though Nick was still glaring at me to be wary. But Melibee maintained a dutiful discretion in response to everything I said. I should have realised he'd be more discreet, here, where someone else could have walked in at any minute. I had been intending to find out if he might tell us any more about the mysterious Mrs Guisely; but he was in no mood to be drawn. We ate our supper in almost complete silence.

Afterwards I rushed back to the bedroom, not wanting to leave Lash for more than a few minutes after his ordeal of the past few days. As so often, Nick wanted to while away an hour in the library before bedtime. But Lash wasn't allowed in the library.

"I'm going to stay here," I said. "I might just go to sleep, actually, I'm so exhausted."

I did fall asleep, within minutes of Nick leaving the room, and Lash fell asleep in his customary place on my bed at my feet; and I could have been forgiven for thinking a calm and restorative night's sleep was in store. It was what we needed, after all.

But Circumstances, as Sir Septimus called them, had other surprises to spring.

The way Nick described it to me, later, was this. He had gone to the library, and had curled up in the big sofa with a couple of books he'd been reading on previous evenings. He'd been there for about twenty minutes when he heard someone coming in. Sitting quietly, not moving a muscle, entirely hidden by the back and arms of the huge sofa, he worked out that they didn't realise he was there. He couldn't be sure who it was until he plucked up the courage to peep far enough around the sofa-arm to see their reflection in one of the big dark windows. Sir Septimus was moving around the room, looking for something on the bookshelves. Occasionally he'd take something over to the table, where we used to have our lessons with Miss Thynne.

Sir Septimus was silently reading at the table when the door creaked open, and Bonefinger joined him. Bonefinger's reaction suggested he hadn't expected to find his master here; and Sir Septimus's response suggested this was obvious.

"Did I startle you? My apologies."

"Not at all, Sir Septimus, I – that is, I – should have realised you were here."

"Perhaps you were counting on my being, mm, melsewhere altogether tonight."

"I – am not sure I comprehend you."

"I was pursued, in London," came Sir Septimus's murmuring voice. "My knew before we even arrived that I was being pursued, because I was observed, at Edgware, and I, mobserved myself being observed."

Bonefinger made a nervous little noise, halfway between a chuckle and a cough.

"All weekend, I had little choice but to mobserve," continued Sir Septimus drily. "Carriages outside the Oriental Club. Men at the bottom of stairwells, and behind newspapers in lobbies. Your friends have much to learn about discretion, Bonefingerm."

There was a croak, like something swallowing an insect.

"*My* friends, Sir Septimus? I trust you are not implying . . .?"

"I'm not a complete fool," retorted Sir Septimus. "One of them was quite plainly that buffoonish Fastolf, or Fastall, or whatever his name is, mmm, whom you engaged to silence that person from Ockham the year before last. And in Mayfair whom do I encounter but Bullock."

There was a significant silence.

"He pretended it was a coincidence," Sir Septimus grunted.

"I can assure you—" began Bonefinger, but Sir Septimus cut him dead.

"You can assure me of nothing," he snapped, "except that this, mabsurdity, will cease. What curs you may have set loose which you now have to call off, I neither know nor care, but see that you do it, or I may be forced to reconsider some decisions to which I have lately put my name. I think you understand very well to what I refer."

Another sullen silence.

"We have tasks to accomplish here," Sir Septimus reflected grimly, "which call for cooperation. This *prankster* still dances around us. My imagine you have been too busy directing your silly cloak and dagger puppet-show to root *him* out this weekend. And the children have been allowed to find out far too much. Far, *far* too much. Your imprisonment of them had the smack, mmm Bonefinger, mof barricading the stable door long after the horse had gambolled into the hills."

Bonefinger cleared his throat. "Mrs Guisely arrives at an opportune time," he said.

"Mrs Guisely." Sir Septimus echoed the name with a faintly

bitter edge to his voice. "I should have grasped the nettle, Bonefingerm. My thought I had done so years ago, but I should have been more ruthless and more thorough. Now, mm, we put our trust in someone neither of us has met until today, who comes with some highly dubious recommendation from the least honourable man either of us knows in the whole of London."

"His recommendation, in this field, ought to count for something," Bonefinger countered.

"He says whatever comes into his head that he thinks will get him off whichever hook he happens to be wriggling on," growled Sir Septimus. He was quiet for a while, and he seemed to have calmed down slightly when he next spoke. "Min any case," he said, "I trust my breath will not have been wasted."

"Rely on it, Sir Septimus." Bonefinger's reflection bowed, with absurd self-abasement.

"I am going to bed," Sir Septimus announced. He teetered towards the door. "Then the regime of Mrs Guisely begins," he said, still with an air of sarcasm. "It's the most fatuous name, Bonefingerm. Who concocted it?" He didn't wait for Bonefinger's reply. "My expect you thought it rather clever. We shall see how clever the whole enterprise turns out to beam." He sighed. "What's her real name, remind me?" he asked.

"Muggerage, Sir Septimus," came the reply.

"Muggerage," said Sir Septimus, chewing the word. "That was it." He pulled open the door. "Pleasant dreams," he said; and he staggered out into the passageway.

CHAPTER 10

THE FIRE CEREMONY

Nick shook me awake. He was moving around the room with an urgency verging on panic, gathering things up, stumbling into things in the dark and cursing.

"What's going on?"

"We've got to get out," he whispered. "Get up, and put some clothes in a bag."

I sat up, bewildered, and Lash jumped off the bed and started to stretch and yawn. "What do you mean?" I asked.

"We've got to be quick," he said. "Mog, it's the new governess. It's Mrs Muggerage!"

"What are you talking about?" I retorted. "He said she's called Mrs Guisely."

"So he *said.* But I've just overheard Sir Septimus talking to Bonefinger. She's not really called Guisely at all. It's a made-up name. And we're not staying here another minute."

"Where will we go?" I wondered, anxiously, getting out of bed.

"To London. I don't know, anywhere but here." He flung my clothes at me from the cupboard. "Put something on." Then I heard a scrape as he pushed the bed back to get at our secret drawer. "We'd better take a few other things too," he said, "if we can carry them."

I couldn't quite believe this was happening; but I pulled on my clothes in the dark as hastily as I could. Lash gave a low woof of excitement, knowing we were going out somewhere; I shushed him. My sleep-numbed mind was trying to catch up with Nick.

"How do you know it's Mrs Muggerage?"

"Because they *said* it's her," he said. "I heard them talking about her. They came into the library while I was sitting in the big sofa, and they didn't know I was there."

Nick had found a big carpet-bag and was scooping things out of the drawer into the bottom. I pushed a few spare clothes in on top of them. Feeling around on the bed, in case I'd left anything important, I found the jester's cap.

"Better not forget this," I said, folding it up and putting it in my pocket.

"Right, are we all set?"

Nick led the way down the stairs, tiptoeing so as to make as little noise as possible. I was desperately trying not to cough. When we got to the door leading out to the courtyard, and he grasped the handle to open it, he gave a low groan.

"What?"

"We're locked in."

Sir Septimus had said we mustn't leave the east wing: and he'd taken steps to make sure we couldn't.

"There might be an open window in the kitchen," I said.

It was worth a try. The big kitchen door opened easily; but

the windows were high up in the wall, and they were the type which were designed not to open more than a chink at the top before being stopped by an iron catch. Although Nick stood on a table, and yanked at the frames with both hands, he couldn't get them to open far enough for us to stand any chance of crawling out.

He jumped down. I was racking my brains, trying to remember whether there were any other doors or windows down here we could try. As Nick felt his way back from the window, he accidentally kicked a big fish-kettle which was jutting out from underneath one of the big kitchen benches. It made an almighty clatter, and the lid skidded across the room and came to a halt with a resounding clang over by the range. Nick swore.

"You idiot!" I hissed. "You'll have the whole house after us!"

As we emerged from the kitchen, desperately trying to work out what we were going to do, there were thuds from high above us; and, as I turned my head to look up the stairs, I could see lamplight and shadows on the walls, right at the top of the stairwell on the servants' landing.

"There *must* be a way out," said Nick through gritted teeth.

After his carelessness the other night, I knew Bonefinger would have done his job thoroughly this time, making sure he locked up every possible escape route. I could hear voices at the top of the stairs. We were going to be caught. I felt panic welling up; until the mental picture of Bonefinger going round with his keys made something suddenly occur to me.

"Nick!" I hissed. "The butler's pantry!"

"What?" he whispered. "But there's no way out of there."

"There is," I said. "Let's just see if it's open. Go on!"

Footsteps were coming down the stairs now. We ran along the kitchen passage until we reached the little pantry door. I hardly dared turn the handle, fearing that it would turn out to be locked; and I could hardly believe our luck when it gave way. Bonefinger had left open the one escape route he thought we wouldn't be clever enough to find.

Better still, there was a lamp in here. It probably wasn't many minutes since Bonefinger had been in here himself.

"Come on," I said; and, as the echoing footsteps came nearer and nearer to the foot of the stairs, the three of us squeezed ourselves into the little pantry and closed the door behind us. I jumped up onto the second step of the apparently pointless little staircase leading up to the blank wall; and bent to grab hold of the edge of the top step. Up it came, like the lid of a box, just as the drawing in the book had said it did.

"Mog, what are you doing?" Nick asked, baffled.

"Ssssh!" I stuck an exploratory foot into the hole, and found a solid little wooden ledge inside, with another beneath it, like the rungs of a ladder. "Bring the lamp," I said, "and follow me."

I disappeared down into the hole, hoping we weren't going to have to climb far down this ladder: Lash wasn't very good at ladders. It turned out that the bottom of the steps was only about five feet down, after which I was able to step back on what felt like a solid stone floor. I looked up. Nick was holding the lamp into the hole now, amazed at what he could see.

"How did you know about this?"

"Just shut up and get down here." I reached up and took the lamp from him.

"I'm going to pass you Lash first," he said.

Lash wasn't especially keen on the idea of being passed; but when he realised we were both coming down and staying down, he let Nick sort of spill him over the edge of the hole, and I caught him as he scrabbled head-first down the ladder.

"Pull the lid down after you," I said, as Nick scrambled down last, with the bag. Whoever had come to investigate must have gone into the kitchen to look around first: but they wouldn't stay in there for long, and someone had probably already been into our rooms to find us missing. The further we could get before anyone worked out where we had gone, the better.

I led the way this time. At first we had to go down a few short flights of stone steps to roughly the level of the cellars. Then the tunnel levelled out a bit, though here and there it still seemed to dip downward as it led away from the foundations of the house. Lash trotted behind me, his muzzle occasionally making contact with my fingers as I reached back to make sure he was there. Nick brought up the rear.

"This tunnel was marked in the book I got from Melibee," I explained, breathlessly, as we hurried on. "I think it links up with the one we were in on Friday."

"It's a good thing you read about it," came Nick's voice. "I thought we'd had it, back there."

Before long we came to the point where the tunnel joined the other. We actually had to duck, and slither down a little slope, to get onto the floor of the longer tunnel. Presumably, it had been almost impossible for whoever dug it to tell whether it was at the right level to join up with the other one, and they'd miscalculated by about two feet.

Now we were on familiar ground. We wanted to get as far

away from Kniveacres as we could, as quickly as we could; and we hurried through the tunnel towards the church, sploshing right through the middle of the muddy pools on the floor rather than slowing down to skirt around them. It wasn't too long before we arrived, panting, in the little crypt. Lash went to sniff nervously at some of the bones, and came back whimpering with uncertainty. Needless to say, the jester was nowhere to be seen.

"Sorry, Lash, old boy," Nick said, "we'll have to do a bit of heaving again to get you through the hole." He reached for the iron ring in the wall, and turned it; and, just as before, the stones above our heads moved apart with a long grinding sound. I jumped up, and helped pull Lash up into the gap while Nick heaved him up from underneath. Then Nick followed us up.

The church was empty; but there was a strange and eerie glow flickering through the windows, which you'd have expected to be completely dark at this time of night. Ruby-coloured shadows danced on the walls and columns of the church. "I hope there aren't people out there with torches, looking for us," I said, suddenly afraid.

Nick had climbed up onto the Letherskin gravestone to close the entrance to the tunnel with the lever behind the skeleton's eyes. The two halves came together with a rumble.

"Surely they couldn't have got here already?" he said, jumping down.

I chewed my lower lip. "They could," I said, "they could have jumped on horses and been here in half the time it's taken us. Nick, what if they're waiting for us?"

"Don't worry," said Nick, "they won't *dream* we've found the tunnel. I expect they're still running round the house, trying to work out where we're hiding. It'll take them ages to work out we've come this way."

Nevertheless, it was with the utmost trepidation that he opened the heavy church door, at first just a crack, with Lash and myself hovering anxiously behind him, to see if the coast was clear enough for us to creep out.

There didn't seem to be anyone in the churchyard, as far as we could see; and we stepped tentatively out into the porch. There was a fiery glow coming between the trees, from the direction of the village; and now we could hear a hubbub of raised voices in the distance. Something was burning. We could smell it too. Smoke drifted across the churchyard on the westerly breeze.

Nick ran to the lych-gate, and we followed a few paces behind.

There was a gigantic bonfire on the village green, and it seemed that almost all the villagers were gathered there, watching it, standing in clusters or dancing. The guys had been taken down from their gibbet just in front of the lych-gate; and, as we took in the scene, we could see rows and rows of them, sitting or lying on the grass near the bonfire, as though they too had gathered to watch.

Catching the excitement in the air, Lash stood up with his front paws on the top bar of the gate, and gave a woof.

"The ceremonies," said Nick. "This must be what Mrs Gossage meant."

Nobody had seen us. We stood under the cover of the lych-gate, watching, for a long time. Bright sparks rose from the fire, up into the night air where they cooled and disappeared. The children who had thrown things at us the other day were all gathered, and were dancing round the bonfire in a chain with linked hands. We could see that most of the people closest to the fire were the village women; whilst, on the grass in front of the Cloy Arms, most of the menfolk were standing, drinking, and milling in and out of the inn.

Suddenly I clutched Nick's arm. "Look," I said.

He followed my pointing finger. There, among the other guys ranged near the bonfire – I could make out the sad-faced vicar, the huntsman, the poacher, the flying witch – was a slumped figure in a multi-coloured coat, with a bony domed head shining in the firelight.

The jester. Without his cap.

I put my hand in my pocket and my fingers closed around it; I squeezed the little silver bell between my finger and thumb.

"He doesn't look very scary, sitting there, does he?" Nick said.

"He just looks like a straw man," I said. "Do you think he really *can* be Damyata, Nick?"

But before Nick had time to reply, we were suddenly aware of the sound of voices behind us, in the churchyard.

I turned. There was someone standing under the porch of the church. Two people: and as they emerged into the light of the fire I could instantly see who they were. A man, in a familiar black cloak that lay across his back like a pair of folded wings, turning his head warily from side to side to make sure he wasn't being observed. And, by his side, a more solid figure altogether, towering over him, whose purposeful gait betrayed no trace of fear of anyone or anything.

It was Bonefinger, and Mrs Muggerage. They had come after us through the tunnel, and now they were coming down the path. And any minute now they were going to spot us.

"Nick," I said, "Nick!" I tried to pull the gate open but Nick was leaning against it. "Nick!" I shouted again. "Look behind you!"

There were a few seconds of blind panic, which I barely remember; we simply couldn't move fast enough. I hauled Lash out of the way and we almost vaulted over the gate; but the movement had attracted our pursuers' attention, and there was the sound of running footsteps behind us now.

"The bag!" I shouted. "Get the bag!" Nick had to yank the big bag through the gate, but it got caught between the gate and the gatepost, and we wasted three or four seconds in freeing it – which was almost enough for the terrible pair to catch up with us. As I slammed the gate closed, and turned to run, I saw Mrs Muggerage's face lit up by the flickering firelight, and my head swam as the full horror of it hit me again. It was a face I could never forget, but which I had never wanted to see again, however long I lived. Broad and masculine, like a bull-dog, its mean features were clustered into the centre of a giant, flat slab of flesh and bone. It was the face of a prize-fighter. Her hair had evidently been shaved in whichever prison she'd been sent off to; she had a scar across one cheek, several layers of double-chins, and her neck was even wider than her head, which had the effect of making her head look almost triangular. Her top lip was lifted in a kind of fascinated grimace, as she approached; she'd probably thought she'd never lay eyes on the two of us again either, but the light of the fire in her eyes suggested a horrible pleasure in the prospect of renewing our acquaintance.

We ran across the green, not knowing but little caring where we were going, as long as we were going away from Mrs Muggerage and Bonefinger. We could have run out of the other end of the village and just kept running, and never stopped until we got to Wales. The noise was mounting: there was sporadic chanting breaking out among little groups around the bonfire now, as well as dancing. Few people took any notice of us; we ducked among the crowds and it was our pursuers who attracted the attention and indignant comments, as they elbowed villagers aside in their haste to get at us. Lash was barking excitedly, finding it the most tremendous game he had played for many weeks. Even with a cumbersome bag, we were lighter on our feet than they were; and by doubling back at one point, and running right back around the bonfire in the other direction, we managed to wrong-foot them completely. As we ran in a large arc, back towards the church, we saw the cluster of low wooden beehives ahead of us.

"Down!" shouted Nick; and we skidded to a halt, and took cover in the deep shadows between the hives to get our breath back, in a position which gave us a clear vantage point across the green.

Bonefinger and Mrs Muggerage had split up, and were prowling in opposite directions around the bonfire, looking carefully among the crowds to try and pick us out. Bonefinger was stalking, with his ridiculous gait and thin legs, like a huge black insect. Mrs Muggerage was marching a few paces, then stopping to look around, then marching on a little. She stood silhouetted against the fire, her frame wide – almost impossibly wide. Sloughter Cripps would have thought twice before wrestling with her. She hadn't seen us, but at one point she came within five or six yards of us, as she walked around the fringes of the crowd. Lash lifted his head and began a low growl, which I had to silence by stroking the top of his head and hissing in his ear. He'd had a couple of encounters with Mrs Muggerage in London, and I felt sure he must remember her as clearly as I did. I wondered what Nick was thinking, on the other side of the hive, watching the woman he had called "Ma" for most of his life, and for whom he had had the utmost loathing. I hadn't the slightest doubt that we were doing absolutely the right thing, running away from Kniveacres. My brief acquaintance of Mrs Muggerage persuaded me that she was the cruellest woman I had ever come across. Bonefinger's comment, that the new regime would not be quite what we had been used to, was a grotesque understatement. Life with her in charge would be nothing short of a living hell, whatever name she had chosen to call herself.

As we lay in the grass, we could tell they'd worked out that we weren't in the crowd. They began signalling to one another, shaking their heads and pointing. There were probably no more than a hundred people around the bonfire altogether, and they soon knew that, despite the darkness, they couldn't have missed us if we'd been there. Bonefinger came over to join Mrs Muggerage and they had a low conversation which was impossible for us to hear through the general hubbub; but it was clear from the way they looked around them, towards the edges of the green and the cottages, that they were about to start to widen their search. The hives were bound to be more or less the first place they looked, before they moved on to search behind the garden walls. I crawled backwards and moved around the other side of the hive to whisper to Nick.

"We can't stay here! They're going to find us any minute!"

"There's nowhere else to go," came Nick's reply.

"We've got to risk running," I said.

Suddenly Lash made a noise somewhere between a woof and a sneeze; and I became aware of something slumping towards us through the grass from the darkness behind the hives. A badger? It was too big. It was moving quickly on all fours, so quickly I had no time to get a proper look at it before it was upon us. I stifled a scream as it clutched my leg.

Nick realised what it was before I did.

"Lamb?" he whispered.

Emerging momentarily into a shaft of firelight between the hives, the sad eyes and gaping bat-like nostrils of Lamb Nisbet. He must have seen us being chased, and taking refuge here. He gave a low grunt, and beckoned us back with both hands. He wanted us to follow him. I glanced towards the bonfire again, and saw Mrs Muggerage and Bonefinger setting off in different directions for a renewed search, away from the crowd: Bonefinger towards the cottages on the other side of the green, Mrs Muggerage heading straight for the hives.

We had no choice.

"Come on," I said to Lash, and to Nick.

Keeping low, like animals, on our knees and elbows, we followed Lamb across the grass towards Orchard Cottage, Nick dragging our bag behind him. By the time Mrs Muggerage was standing among the beehives, looking determinedly around her, we were on the corner by Mrs Nisbet's cottage garden, and Lamb was leading us around the back to the parlour where a soft light burned. He had saved our skins – for the time being.

Once we were inside, he motioned us to sit down, and began to fuss over Lash.

"We're being chased," I said to him. "Did you see them? Bonefinger and a woman."

Lamb nodded. He puffed up his chest and stuck his elbows out, to signify a large, powerful person.

"She's called Mrs Muggerage," I said, "and you don't want to meet her. She'll kill us, Lamb. They both would, if they caught us. We have to get away. Do you think you can help us?"

Lamb looked at us. His distorted expression rarely changed, but his eyes were darting from one to the other of us, as he thought quickly. Sitting on the settle, he held out his arms and did an impression of someone driving a carriage, jolting up and down on the seat.

"The stagecoach?" said Nick. "Do you mean the stagecoach?"

Lamb nodded.

"The stagecoach doesn't come through until the morning," I said. "Where are we going to hide till then?"

Lamb stood up, and went to the longcase clock that stood against the parlour wall. "Nnnng, aaaah," he said, and pointed up at the clock face. He pressed his finger against the bottom edge of the dial.

"Six?" queried Nick. "Six o'clock? Is there a stage at six o'clock?"

"Nick, there is!" I said. "I remember Judith or someone mentioning it at the Hall once. On Monday mornings there's an early coach, that gets to London by nightfall. But only in summer. Is it still going? Will it go tomorrow?" I asked Lamb; and he nodded excitedly.

"It's nearly midnight already," I said, biting my lip. "It's not so long to wait."

"But they're searching the cottages," Nick said. "It won't take them long to get here. We need somewhere to hide."

"Mm." Lamb ruffled the fur of Lash's head, and slipped out of the back door, returning a moment or two later with a little wheeled cart, which he pulled right into the parlour. Then he disappeared outside again; and came back in after a minute or so with some horrible old clothes and a fistful of straw torn from a bale. He pointed at us, and then at the cart.

Nick stared at the cart, then up into Lamb's face; and broke into a broad grin.

There was still a great hubbub around the fire as Lamb pulled the cart, with the two of us in it, out onto the village green. We had dressed ourselves up to look as much like scarecrows as we possibly could, putting on the mouldy old clothes, stuffing straw down our necks and into our sleeves, and smearing cold grey ashes on our faces. It felt itchy and disgusting, and the cart was appallingly uncomfortable; but we were holding out the hope that in the firelight we'd look sufficiently unlike ourselves to arouse no suspicion in our pursuers. As a finishing touch I clamped the jester's cap on my head, and we jolted out towards the bonfire, sitting as still and stiff as we could possibly manage. Lash had been shut in the parlour and given something to eat: it was impossible to disguise him.

Nobody gave us a second glance as Lamb moved through the crowd. A few people greeted him; one or two whispered behind their hands and laughed. Most people were too busy in conversation, or watching the fire, to pay him any attention. He wheeled us around the opposite side of the bonfire, to sit in the cart next to the other scarecrows, lined up in stiff rows facing the fire, like an unresponsive audience. Once he had positioned us, he moved off, not wanting to draw attention to us by standing close by.

We sat there, not daring to move, for a long time. It was very tempting to look around and see if we could see Bonefinger and Mrs Muggerage, but we had to resist the temptation to turn our heads. Occasionally I saw one or the other of them, walking past the fire on their way to search somewhere else. Bonefinger came out of the lych-gate at one point, having obviously been to search the church and the graveyard again. He was looking grim and frustrated.

I felt a sudden movement behind me, and realised that Nick had leaned over to one side, imitating a scarecrow slumping over. He was sitting at a strange diagonal angle now, in the back of the cart, with his head on his shoulder.

"Careful," I said, trying not to move my lips. "Don't get cocky."

"I was getting cramp," he said between his teeth.

As we sat there, the murmur of conversation around the fire gradually began to die down, and the villagers seemed to turn, as one, to look at something that was happening at the other end of the village. Our view was obscured by the bonfire; we just had to sit still and watch everyone's reactions. They were standing still now, in their groups, or on their own, all facing the western end of the village, and the only sound was the roaring and crackling of the bonfire. The ceremony was nearing its climax.

Soon, we were able to see what they were watching. From the mill house came a man dressed in a long gown, with a barrel on his head. The barrel was blazing with fire; and he walked slowly, grasping it with both hands as he came. He was followed by another man, with another flaming barrel; then another. In a procession, out of the old mill, came seven men holding burning barrels above their heads, walking slowly towards the bonfire. The villagers remained still and silent as they watched. Bonefinger and Mrs Muggerage, too, were forced to stand still, though they were looking around anxiously, fearing that we might be taking advantage of the stillness to escape.

As the procession of men neared the fire, a low hum began. At first I thought it was in my head; but then I realised it was the villagers. They were humming the men home; a kind of ritual drone, taken up by every man, woman and child on the green, their lips together, their eyes still fixed on the parade of flaming barrels. Wordlessly the men moved between the crowd and the bonfire, so they were standing in a pattern, seven of them all around the fire's edge, equidistant from one another. Now, one by one, they lifted the barrels of fire down off their heads, and placed them on the grass. Each man turned to the next, to signal that it was his turn; then stepped back away from the flames. The humming of the crowd continued until all seven men had placed their fires on the ground; at which point silence fell.

For a few moments, there was no sound but the roar and

crackle of the enormous fire, and no movement but the dancing of the flames and the bright weightless sparks streaming up
into the air. The entire crowd stood still, as though in some kind
of collective religious reverie. Soon, though, one of the cloaked
men moved from his position, stepping quickly through the
static crowd to where the guys sat in their stiff rows. He bent to
pick up the nearest guy and, holding it out in front of him at
arm's length, he moved back towards the bonfire with it, as
though performing a strange dance. When he got within a few
feet of the bonfire he turned, to demonstrate the guy to the
watching villagers, and then flung it high into the air so that it
landed among the flames.

The crowd erupted in excited chatter. The burning had
begun. There seemed to be a strict order to things, which everyone understood. No one in the crowd moved from where they
were standing until all seven of the cloaked men had taken a
guy, one by one, and flung it into the bonfire with the same
kind of flourish as the first; and the cheer from the crowd grew
louder with each new guy that was burned. They burned where
they had landed, blackening and twisting on the roasting fire;
their clothes shrivelled and were consumed, their straw bodies
disintegrated to orange cinders. Soon the entire front row of
waiting guys was gone: the poacher, the huntsman, the big
pumpkin-headed guy Mr Greywether had made.

The seven men melted into the crowd, their part in the ritual
complete; and now it was the bystanders' turn. Members of the
crowd moved forward and began picking up guys from the
rows, taking it in turns to cast them flamboyantly into the fire
to rising cheers. One by one, in their varied sizes and costumes,

the effigies were added to the pyre. Although we were scared, we couldn't stop watching. Fanny Nisbet had told us the guys were supposed to absorb the evil spirits from the village and bring good luck for the coming winter. This burning ceremony, presumably, was supposed to get rid of the evil spirits that had inhabited the guys: to cleanse the village of its demons as the smoke rose into the dark sky. The crowd was in a frenzy. I didn't dare turn my head for fear of giving us away, but I was aware that the number of remaining guys around us was diminishing, and it wouldn't be long before someone came for us.

My whole body prickled with sudden terror. "Nick!" I said, through clenched teeth. "We're going to end up on the fire. Lamb's tricked us, Nick!"

And even as I said it, to my horror I saw Bonefinger heading towards us with his purposeful stride; and, not far behind him, the grim-faced Mrs Muggerage, her eyes flaming with the light of the fire. They reached the dwindling array of scarecrows and began yanking them up, carrying them towards the fire and flinging them in with dreadful enthusiasm. Other villagers were picking up guys too, and we watched helplessly from our cart as the grabbing hands came nearer and nearer. Before long, we were among the last six or seven guys left; and between the forest of villagers we could clearly see Bonefinger and Mrs Muggerage coming back towards us, making straight for our cart. Their faces were horrifying, unsmiling, rigid with determination. They had singled us out. I had no idea whether they'd worked out who we really were, but there was no doubt we were the next guys they were going to throw, and they were bearing down on us fast.

Suddenly, the most extraordinary thing happened. The crowd's excited chatter ceased, and everyone turned towards the fire again. Running into the firelight came the jester, in his colourful harlequin cloak, the bare grinning skull that was his head uncovered for all to see. It hadn't even occurred to me that he was missing from the group of guys. He was carrying what looked like a big sheaf of straw; and as he ran close to the fire he swept the end of it through the flames, so that when he pulled it away it was burning like a torch. Nick and I could only stare from our stock-still positions in the cramped little cart. He was certainly not just another slumped straw man any longer. The jester lifted the torch to his skinless face and blew; and a huge jet of fire leaped forward, making the crowd gasp and the children squeal. Nearby, Bonefinger and Mrs Muggerage were rooted to the spot, as unprepared as anyone in the crowd for this mesmerising interruption. Around and around the fire he went, dancing, his arms moving gracefully, exotically up and down as he moved sideways like a crab on widely-parted feet; and every few moments he blew fire, like a purple and yellow patchwork dragon, in brief bright spurts which turned to billowing black smoke and rose into the night air. He blew fire in all directions, at every group he saw standing around the fire; sometimes the flames he spat came so near the people that they leaped back, or had their skirts or even their hair singed where they stood.

When he had danced among the flaming barrels for a few minutes, and completed three or four circuits of the bonfire, he came running over towards us. I froze, even more rigid and still than I had been so far. He was staring straight at me with his giant dark empty eye-sockets. My heart leaped into my mouth, and it was all I could do to keep from screaming, as he sprang towards me and snatched the two-pointed cap off my head, clamping it onto his own bare skull, and provoking a swell of excitement amongst the onlookers.

But in some sections of the crowd the fascination was turning to fear. There were disturbed murmurs now, and people started to move from where they had been standing, to talk anxiously, to wonder to one another who this mysterious figure with the death's head might be. He wasn't part of their ritual. Where had he come from? What kind of black magic had produced him?

And, the silence over, the jester's spell broken, Bonefinger saw his chance. He sprang to life. Before I really knew what was happening, the gnarled fingers of the vile old servant had grasped me by the upper arms and swept me out of the cart, and as I kicked and screamed I could see Mrs Muggerage towering over Nick, preparing to pick him up too.

But my face was suddenly full of flame, and the jester was there again, standing in front of Bonefinger with his burning straw torch, blocking his way to the fire. At first Bonefinger tried to shield himself from the flames by holding me out in front of him; but I was becoming too much of a weight for his old limbs and, as the jester kept up his challenge, Bonefinger was forced to drop me to the ground to defend himself.

I crawled out of the way and watched them, horrified. Bonefinger and the jester were in hand-to-hand combat now, wrestling with one another. The crowd parted to let them grapple, too scared of the jester's magic to touch him, too full of loathing for Bonefinger to try to save him. The crazy harlequin figure, with the jingling cap and the gaping eyes of a skull, was getting the better of the wiry old man. He was backing Bonefinger towards one of the blazing barrels. They were going to collide with it in a moment; and if they did, they would both be badly burned.

I could hardly bear to watch. I was no longer concerned about being taken for a scarecrow. In desperation I looked around me, to see if anyone was preparing to intervene and stop them; and suddenly, diving to the ground by my side in the dark, was Nick. And he had Lamb with him.

There was a gasp from the crowd, and a crash as Bonefinger was hurled against the burning barrel of tar. Fire had caught his clothes and he began to scream. Still the jester parried and tried to wrong-foot him as he lurched forward. It was a fight to the death, now.

Nick took hold of my head in both his hands and turned it towards him so he could speak directly into my face. The light of the fire burned in the black centres of his eyes.

"We've got to run," he was shouting.

The crowd was so engrossed in the dreadful struggle that no one gave us a second glance as we ran, with Lamb lolloping a pace or two ahead, back across the village green towards Fanny's cottage. Our backs had only been turned on the scene for a few moments when there was a sudden bright glare of flame, more gasps and shrieks from the crowd, and a blood-curdling scream which didn't stop. The blood pounded in our heads as we ran for our lives, and our breath came in gasps, but nothing could snuff out the dreadful continuous sound of screaming, of a man being burned alive.

As we staggered breathlessly into Fanny's parlour, Lash greeted us at the door, snuffling and almost dancing with excitement; and Fanny was there, her face grey with shock.

"Thank God," she said, and embraced us both. "Forgive me, my dears, I didn't know you were here, but Lamb came to find me. Something terrible has happened, hasn't it? The Devil himself has come, and no mistake. But thank God you're safe."

"Where did Mrs Muggerage go?" I asked Nick.

"I don't know," he said, uneasily. "I really thought she'd got me. She came *this* close. I thought she was going to fling me onto the fire. But as soon as the jester appeared, she kind of froze – and then suddenly, next time I looked, she'd gone."

Fanny had been watching from the window of her little front room, and we joined her to peer out at what we'd left behind. There was confusion in the crowd on the green: they seemed to gather into tight circles for a few minutes, and then fan out again. Women were crying, some were ushering their children back towards their cottages as quickly as they could, out of danger. Men's voices were raised in angry shouting for several minutes outside the Cloy Arms, but it wasn't clear what had happened until the crowd began to disperse properly, and the villagers retreated to their gates and doorways to watch, and talk. Only now could we pick up the odd snatch of conversation from the people who passed outside the window.

No one had been able to save Bonefinger. He had been burned alive in the tar barrel; and, in the commotion, the jester had disappeared – until someone in the crowd suddenly cried out that they'd got him. Yet, as the men descended on the slumped figure with the bells on his cap, they quickly realised he was just a limp, insubstantial thing of straw. A scarecrow.

Something unforeseen and terrible had happened here tonight – and there was already talk that the only explanation lay with those children at Kniveacres, who had been seen running away. And this only a few days since they were mixed up in the death of poor Justina Thynne. Two sinister killings in one week.

Fanny began to bustle, and organise us. Her mind, and her lips, were moving quickly. "You can't wait all those hours for the stagecoach," she said, "you're not safe in the village, now. You must go, as far away as you can, and quickly." She picked up the carpet-bag we'd left on the parlour table and began laying fruit and bread inside, on top of the clothes. "Take some provisions with you," she said. "Get on the road out of the village, by the path across the south field, and pick up the stagecoach as it comes by at first light. You should be able to get as far as the turnpike. I'll tell the coachman to watch out for you. You must climb aboard, and don't you worry, your passage will be paid."

There were hugs, and tears in Fanny's eyes, and we were gone. I took Lash by his leash and Nick carried the bag. Lamb led us first through dark back gardens and briar lanes, so as to avoid appearing anywhere near the inn and the bonfire; we crossed the village green at the far end, and again ducked through cottage gardens into the fields beyond. We said little as we scuttled along, the extraordinary events of the night having all but hypnotised us into pensive, disbelieving silence.

Lamb left us when we got to the road. We thanked him, and shook his hand, and Lash licked him effusively; and he turned back into the field and shuffled into the darkness. We could hear his footsteps receding through the undergrowth for some time after we'd lost sight of him.

"Well," I said, "I feel awful. I want to get rid of these clothes."

"They're not very nice, are they?" Nick admitted.

We stood under a high hedge, in the darkness, and took off the mouldy, stinking old coats and breeches Lamb had provided for our disguise, gratefully pulling the straw out of our hair and changing back into the comfortable and familiar clothes we'd put away in the bag. Nick decided to sit the horrible old clothes up in the hedge, propped up by hawthorn branches like two tramps, watching the road.

"We haven't got time to mess about," I said. "Fanny said we had to get as far as the turnpike by daybreak."

"What *happened*?" Nick asked, as we walked along the road.

I shook my head, at a loss to explain. "I can't even be sure I'm really awake," I said. "This whole week has just been – one unbelievable thing after another. But that was the strangest night of all."

If we turned around we could still see the glow in the sky above the trees from the bonfire we were leaving behind; and even the hubbub of voices was still audible for the first little while. But no one came after us. We met no one on the road going in either direction, until the first grey streaks of dawn appeared in the eastern sky, and we came to the wide patch of muddy, churned-up ground where the road from the village joined the main turnpike highway. We were tired, and relieved to stop. Nick hadn't slept at all, and I'd only slept for a couple of hours before Nick had woken me.

"The stagecoach should be passing any time now," said

Nick. "I hope Fanny's right, that it will stop for us."

We heard it before we saw it: a kind of muffled drumming sound, which became more distinct the moment the coach came over the crest of the hill. We had plenty of time to stand up and gather our belongings; it was a dull morning but no longer dark, and it was clear the coachman had seen us from some distance away. He pulled up the horses. Spatterings of mud spun through the air from their hooves, and from the big coach wheels.

"On top," he shouted. Another man hopped off to help Nick with the bag.

"Sorry, the dog's a bit muddy," I said; but the man heaved Lash up into the air with both arms under his belly, and deposited him on the top of the coach where he sat next to Nick with his tongue hanging out, watching me as I clambered up.

It was difficult to tell how many people there were inside the stagecoach: several of the benches seemed to be full, and there was a lot of noise of gossip and laughter coming from within as we rumbled off. We sat among the luggage, bracing our backs against a large trunk; I wedged our carpet-bag against the side-rail and it made a tolerable head-rest. More passengers were due to embark as we proceeded; but at present we were the only people riding on top, apart from a young man wearing pin-stripes under his overcoat, who clutched his luggage as we swayed along, and regarded us knowingly. The morning hadn't been cold when we set off, but speeding along up here we found we had to turn our collars up around our necks and huddle down among the bags to stay warm.

The coach lurched along, rocking alarmingly from time to

time when one wheel or another bumped through a ditch or pot-hole. The road was straight, and the surface had recently been improved, and coaches along this route had developed a reputation for trying to outdo one another in speed. The passengers seemed to be quite amused by all the lurching and jolting, and a collective whoop of laughter went up from the crowd inside whenever there was a particularly alarming bump. It wasn't very long before I started to feel decidedly sick, as the coachman drove the horses on relentlessly; but I found that closing my eyes helped matters, and I was so tired that I soon nodded off, snuggling close to Lash for warmth, my head on the carpet-bag.

Just as I had started to doze, however, our companion on the top of the coach chose his moment to break his silence.

"Going all the way?" he asked Nick; but he didn't wait for the reply. "All the way to Paddington, me," he continued. "Got myself a little position as an articled clerk, wouldn't you know. At Lincoln's Inn. It's a good address. My employer turns over thousands. The big cases," he said, tapping the side of his nose. "Ones you'd have heard of, if I could talk about 'em."

Perhaps he thought we'd be interested in finding out about his employer's cases, and would ask him lots of questions; but Nick just smiled at him, and I positively glared at him, before shifting my position and rearranging the bag under my head to make it more comfortable.

The coach trundled on, and the young man turned to watch the passing fields and churches. I had just dropped off again when his voice piped up, as though it had taken him ten minutes to think of his next comment.

"Anyone ever tell you two you look alike?" he asked.

"Wouldna been able to tell you apart, when you first come aboard. Looking at you over time, I can see some subtleties, but they ain't there for all to see. You need an eye for physiognomy." He winked at Nick. I lifted my head and glared at him again. "Brothers, I imagine, are you?" he ventured.

"Twins," replied Nick. I groaned inwardly. Don't encourage him, Nick, I thought. But the young man didn't seem to have much of a response to this; he tapped the side of his nose again in a self-satisfied way, and fell silent.

We had gone another few miles, and I had just fallen asleep again, when the voice piped up a third time.

"Curious the characters you meet on a journey like this one," he said. This was becoming completely intolerable! I sat up, and glared at him again wordlessly. "Do this journey a few times a year, me," he continued. "See a few people in my line. Blow me if just before you got on, at the inn there, where it looked like they'd been having a rare old bonfire, there wasn't someone came aboard what was up in court not long ago, in a case I had a small part in. Couldn't tell you the name, too many names come and go in my line, but I can't say I'll ever forget the face. Woman as looks like a man. Up for handling stolen goods, I remember. Couldn't tell you what she got. Terrible face, but you'd never forget it. That's why I noticed when I seen her."

I was pulling my coat around my ears again and burying my face in Lash's fur; but Nick leaned forward, suddenly intent on the young man's monologue.

"Excuse me," he said, "but did you just say a woman, who looks like a man, got on this coach at the inn before it picked us up? And that she was in court not long ago for receiving stolen goods?"

The young man beamed, and pointed down at the roof of the coach.

"Sitting below even as we speak," he said. "Curious-looking woman. Enormous."

I was bolt upright now, and sleep was suddenly the last thing on my mind. "She can't be," I said.

"She can," murmured Nick. He had gone white. "After what happened at the bonfire she'll want to get away, won't she? And fast."

I pictured her awful bulk sitting inside – perhaps even immediately below our feet. Surely she would have seen us climbing aboard at the junction? She'd be sitting there, biding her time, smiling to herself, casting her gaze up to the roof above her head, waiting for the moment when she could get her hands on us. When we climbed down at the next stage, there she'd be, waiting to receive us and tear us limb from limb.

I suddenly wanted to be anywhere but on board this stage-coach. Looking down at the ground moving rapidly beneath us, I contemplated whether we'd be able to leap off without killing ourselves.

"What are we going to do?" I wondered.

"We'll have to get the coach to stop, and then make a run for it," said Nick, thinking.

"But how will we get off without her realising? We'll still have to climb down past the window!"

"We can run faster than she can," reasoned Nick. "Maybe we can lose her. But we can't just sit here all the way to London, with her down below. Even if she hasn't seen us, she will do, next time we stop."

I gazed in desperation at the fields and woods either side of the road. "There's nowhere to go."

"I know. But anywhere's better than where she is."

I scrambled to the front, and yelled at the coachman. "Can we stop? I need to – I need to get off."

He turned his head and yelled back up at me.

"Five or ten minutes, be at Daventry," he said. "Scheduled stop. Let you off there, young sir."

We sat, clutching the side-rail, sick with worry, as the churches and clustered roofs of the town appeared ahead of us.

Chapter 11

Reunion and Return

The moment the stagecoach pulled up, we leaped off at the back. We'd been hoping we could get out of sight by the time the other passengers disembarked from inside; but Mrs Muggerage was quicker than we expected. Sure enough, she'd seen us, and had been waiting for her chance; and she made sure she elbowed all the other passengers aside and made it off the coach first. By the time we'd stumbled to the ground outside the coaching inn, taken hold of Lash, and set off through the streets, she was really not far behind us at all. The town was busy, but it wasn't like ducking and diving through the crowds and narrow streets of London, and it was remarkably hard to lose her among the inns and yards and smart house-fronts.

"In here," said Nick, suddenly ducking through an archway.

We ran down a narrow brick passage, which led into a yard behind the main street and towards a low building from which there was the most offensive stench. Breathing through our mouths, we ventured inside – and found ourselves in the town abattoir. Men were wheeling carts across the floor, from which the limbs of dead animals poked at unlikely angles. Another man was using a long broom to push pools of bright red fluid down a gully. There was blood everywhere, some of it running across the floor, some of it congealed. The gullies led down into drain-holes, and a short distance away there was a six-foot drop into the yard, where enormous iron bins stood collecting the more solid animal waste from the slaughtering process – fat and car-tilege and internal organs and chips of bone. Everyone we could see was covered in blood from head to toe, as though they'd been in battle. There were no live animals in here at the moment but, from all the evidence, there had been quite a lot, and not long ago. I gripped Lash's rope tightly. I felt my gorge rising.

"I can't stand it in here," I said. "Let's go somewhere else."

"No, this is a good place to hide," insisted Nick, "I bet she won't follow us in here."

But she already had. Her giant frame loomed in the same doorway we'd walked through less than a minute ago. She must have seen us cutting down the passageway from the main street. Nick darted up a flight of stone steps, past a roughly-painted sign which read KEEP OUT; and we followed him up to a second storey, which turned out to be just a vast, empty, floor-boarded attic space under the rafters of the building. It was warm up here, where all the heat from the slaughterhouse floor rose into the roof-space; and the air was revolting. A brief glance around was sufficient to reveal we'd made a fundamental mis-take. There was absolutely nowhere up here to hide; and, worse still, there was no other way down.

Nick swore under his breath. "What now?" he murmured.

What now, was that the sound of heavy footsteps began echoing ominously up the stairway after us. I could hear the voices of one or two of the slaughterhouse workers shouting, "Oi, you can't go up there!" But it seemed unlikely that, when they realised who they were dealing with, any of them would press the matter very far. We looked around in desperation; but no amount of looking was going to provide a hiding place, up here in this completely empty room.

Mrs Muggerage's head appeared at the top of the stairs. She paused, almost imperceptibly, when she laid eyes on us; and then she kept climbing, until she was standing there, blocking out the light coming up the staircase. Only now that she was standing in the room did she permit herself a smile.

"Well well well," she said quietly. "Oo'd a thought it? After it looked like we was never going to see one another again."

Nick said nothing. We were standing, our backs against the brick wall, about ten feet away from her. Lash stiffened and began to growl. I was holding grimly on to his leash. She wasn't scared of him, and she would have thought nothing of throttling him if he went for her.

At first she didn't bother approaching any closer. Standing there at the top of the stairs was, after all, the most effective way of trapping us.

"Thought you was rid of me, did you?" she said. "Livin' the grand life now, in the country, no need to think about the people what brought you up. But I'm back, Master Nick, and dear brother Mog, or dear sister, or whatever it is you wants to be these days. I ain't that easy forgotten. After I brought you up, all those years," she said to Nick, "it's sweet to get another chance, ain' it, Nick?"

Nick's face was shot through with fear and hatred. She cowed him, as she had always done; but after more than a year of living without her vicious and violent temper, he was more defiant than he had been.

"Where did they find you?" he asked bitterly.

"Oh, you never mind that. Connections, is what they calls it. Connections is wonderful things. No need to go into it now. There'll be plenty of time for catchin' up, when you comes back to Kniveacres with me."

"We're not going anywhere with you," Nick said with a scowl. "You don't own us. When you were locked away they said you were an unsuitable guardian and I'd never have to spend another day in your company."

"They said cruel things, Nick," whimpered Mrs Muggerage. Her face hardened and her eyes shone with a horrible resolve. Now, for the first time, she took a few paces forward. "No more runnin' away," she said. "The chase is over, Nick."

"Not yet it's not," he shouted at her. "The chase isn't over till you catch us. Come on, Mog."

Lash and I followed him, at a run, our feet thudding across the floor of the attic, until we were standing at the opposite end, fifty or sixty feet away from her. We knew we had to get past her to make it down the stairs; but we also knew fine well that, for all her formidable strength, what she lacked was agility. If we could keep her running round the attic after us, we might be able to duck past while she was over on this side, well away from the top of the steps.

"You can play yer silly games," growled Mrs Muggerage, her grating voice echoing in the empty room, "but all I got to do is wait for yer."

"You'll wait for ever," called Nick.

"You'll starve, meantime," she said, with a sudden smile as though she found the prospect a pleasant one.

Nick put his hand on my shoulder to signal that he wanted to whisper something. His face came close to my ear.

"She'll come for me every time," he said. "I'm going to try and get her away from the stairs, and I want you and Lash to run. I can get away. We're all much faster than she is."

I was terrified. Ducking past her was all very well in theory; but a swipe from those powerful arms would knock anyone out cold. And Nick was probably quite right to say he could outrun her – but perhaps not when he was carrying a heavy bag.

He strolled, very slowly, over the floorboards towards her. She waited for him, not moving. He got quite close to her, and then tried to wrong-foot her by dodging from one side of the attic to the other – making it look as if he was going to try and break for the stairs. She held her arms out, and bent forward.

"Come on then," she sneered. "Come to Ma."

Those arms had knocked Nick senseless many times, delivered countless bruises, pinned him up against walls, on one occasion broken his nose. But he knew how she moved and how she thought; over the years he had become an expert at dodging her casual violence. And Nick had grown, this year: he was no longer the slight, cowed little boy she had been accustomed to flinging and cuffing around. She was already nervous. Her eyes were darting from one to the other of us, as though she hadn't expected us to split up; trying to plan her moves in case we should both make a run for it at the same time. There was what seemed like a lifetime of stalling, as Nick stood six feet away from her, taunting her, pretending to launch himself this way, then that. I grasped Lash's rope, my whole body buzzing with anticipation, awaiting my chance.

Now Nick made his move; and her brain simply wasn't up to it. He darted forward, getting within reach of her for a split second before ducking back again. She instinctively took a step forward, and lunged for him; but of course she lost her balance and he was past her in no time, diving for the far corner of the room, away from the top of the stairs, and simultaneously shouting, "Go, Mog!" As I ran for the stairs, Mrs Muggerage had her back to me, trying to coordinate her giant bulk to spin around and come after me; but she simply couldn't keep her eyes on both of us when we were at opposite ends of the room. Nick sent the bag spinning over the floorboards and it met me as I neared the stairs. "Take the bag!" he shouted.

My heart pounding, I picked up the bag; and now Lash and I were on the stairs, running down them, not stopping until we reached the door of the abattoir, where we waited with increasing anxiety for Nick.

"What's going on up there?" a bloodstained man shouted at me. "What do you kids think you're doing? It's not safe up there."

"He'll be down any minute," I said.

"He'll get a piece of my mind," said the man angrily. "There's a sign there says keep out. If I'd known you was sneaking around—"

There was the most almighty thumping from above us, as Nick led Mrs Muggerage in another crazy, clumsy dive across the attic floor. Suddenly there was a sickening crunching sound;

and a kind of explosion in the ceiling as the wooden floor burst under Mrs Muggerage's weight. The men down here on the floor winced and ducked; planks and splinters flew in all directions, and Mrs Muggerage plummeted, a drop of twenty feet, straight down through the ceiling into a huge bin of blood, discarded organs and intestines which stood beneath. The viscous, vile-smelling stuff was sprayed everywhere as she landed in it; and we weren't sure whether to stare over at the blood-filled bin in which she now seemed to be drowning, or up at the gigantic rip she'd left in the ceiling.

Nick practically fell down the stairs. "We're going," he said.

"Not so fast!" the slaughterhouse man said. But he wasn't quick enough to grab hold of us, and faced with a choice of pursuing us, or going over to investigate the enormous woman drowning in a two-ton bin of offal, he chose the latter.

We ran until we were back on the main street, and could see the stagecoach still standing outside the inn. It was only supposed to stop here for half an hour. I was sure it must be leaving again any minute.

"Shouldn't we have gone back to help?" I gasped, as we reached the back of the coach and stood clinging on to the handrail to get our breath back. Nick looked at me as if I were insane.

"Help? *Help* Mrs Muggerage? She would have killed us, Mog."

"What do you think will happen to her?"

"Well she never could swim," said Nick, "and I don't suppose she floats."

"You two coming back aboard?" the coachman asked, emerging from the inn and climbing into the driving seat. "Better get back up on top; neither of you smells so good. Some sort of accident was it?"

I looked down at my clothes, and realised we'd failed to avoid the almighty shower of blood which Mrs Muggerage's belly-flop had sent around the abattoir. Even Nick, who'd been upstairs at the time, had some of it in his hair.

There was a lot of bustle, as passengers rushed to take their seats at the last minute. "Just get going," I muttered, turning my head anxiously to look back down the main street. At any moment I expected to see Mrs Muggerage, bloodsoaked but undeterred, emerging from the slaughterhouse passage and marching menacingly towards us.

The young articled clerk was back on board, winking at us as we sat down. He had just been sitting in the coaching inn, taking refreshment and waiting for the journey to resume. We were still out of breath, and we must have been a frightful sight, sitting there covered in gouts of blood; but he was behaving as though everything was perfectly ordinary. At last, everyone was ready; the coachman gave a sharp click, and the coach pulled away, past the faces of the townspeople who'd come to see off family members, or simply to watch out of curiosity.

It was only when we left the streets of the town behind us, and the long straight road opened up ahead, that I really allowed myself to believe we were safe. I relaxed, and slumped back against the carpet-bag again, stroking Lash's neck as we lurched along.

Now the articled clerk piped up.

"That's good ale, there," he said. "The veal and ham pie's all right, but the ale's the best." He smiled to himself slightly dizzily, as though he had sampled a little too much of it. "If you don't mind," he said, "I think I might try and have a bit of a sleep. Not that I don't enjoy a chat, as the journey goes. Always interested in people, that's me. But right now I think I feels slumber coming on. I'd appreciate it if you two didn't make conversation, for the time being."

And, as I stared at him and then at Nick in astonishment, he laid his head on his arm across the heavy trunk beside him, and closed his eyes.

It was just getting dark when the stage pulled up outside the Golden Cockerel in Paddington, with perceptible relief on the part of horses, coachman and passengers alike. Lash had become tremendously excited at having the smell of London in his nostrils, and I couldn't help feeling a rush of happiness, mingled with slight trepidation, at the movement and the crush and the black brick walls and the smoke and the dirt and the billboards and the shouting, which were the familiar ingredients of the life I'd lived since before I could remember. We were back; and it felt very strange to be here, as though almost the whole of this year, since we'd come away to Kniveacres, had been some sort of dream, some interruption of normality.

The articled clerk was fortunate enough to have transport arranged as far as Lincoln's Inn, and he generously invited us to share it. Nothing about London had changed, I reflected as we trundled falteringly through the streets. How could it have? Just as Kniveacres had its habits and its familiar layout which had been unchanged for centuries, so did the city; and however many new people arrived, or new buildings appeared, or old ones were destroyed by fire or dilapidation, or new fashions were introduced, the life beneath the surface remained the same.

We took our leave of the young man, and made our way on foot past the dark walls and lighted windows of Gray's Inn towards Clerkenwell. I had no idea whether Mr Cramplock would still be at work; but we had decided to make the little printing shop our first call, and as we came around the corner into the square I felt the most peculiar shiver. So much had happened here. The blank, singed window-frames of the vacant, ruined Charnock House stared down at us, as they always had; how much more we knew, now, about who had lived there and what it had contained. Propped up against its solid northern wall, the humble brick structure that was Cramplock's shop was still showing a light. Lash knew his way around perfectly, and seemed to think it was the most natural thing in the world to be back here. He couldn't understand why we rang at the door of the shop, and waited in the dark to be admitted, rather than just going straight in; he looked up at me, whimpering, and nosed at the door, trying to get me to open it for him.

Mr Cramplock's face was black with ink, as usual; he peered out, opening the door no more than a crack, looking slightly irascible at being disturbed at this time of the evening. But when he saw the three of us standing there, his eyes nearly fell out of his head.

"Mog! And Nick! And Lash! What are you – can it really be – what brings you . . .?" Lash had squeezed past him as the door swung open, and was already making himself at home in the back room where the big iron presses stood, surrounded by piles of paper which Cramplock had been working on. We fell into spontaneous embraces at the door, and it was some considerable time before Cramplock stopped asking unfinished questions and remembered to invite us inside. He pulled up stools for us around the inked-up press and, as we sat down, Lash continued his systematic prowl around the workshop, sniffing to make sure everything was still where he had left it more than six months ago.

"We've got so much to tell you I don't think I know where to start," I said. "I suppose we've come to ask for help." Although I didn't say so, I had the strong sense that we'd come back for good. Plunged back into old familiar surroundings, Kniveacres seemed to belong to another life entirely, and I knew Nick was thinking the same: that, after all that had happened this week, it was the last place we wanted to be just now.

Cramplock leaped up again and went over to the hearth. "I was letting the fire go out," he said, "because I was going to shut up for the night soon. But let me – there now." The fire glowed gratefully, as he shoved the embers around with a poker and piled more wood on top. "I've got something to drink in here," he said next, going over to a cupboard and rummaging for some bottles of ale. "Not much to eat, I'm afraid, but I expect I can find something for Lash. I want you to sit down and tell me everything that's happened. Goodness me, what an extraordinary surprise!"

We did tell Mr Cramplock more or less everything, and the lamps of the printing shop burned late into the evening as he listened, and gasped, and exclaimed, and laughed, and occasionally asked questions. And whenever we talked about our fears and suspicions of Sir Septimus, and the mysteries of his role in our past, and the terrible events of the past week, and the reappearance of Damyata, he nodded his head gravely; and his eyes occasionally twinkled with understanding, and with the hint that some of what we were telling him might not be as much of a surprise as we thought.

"And look, Mr Cramplock," said Nick, climbing down off his stool and opening the carpet-bag we'd brought with us. "We found this in the library at Kniveacres, and we've been taking it with us wherever we go. It was printed here, wasn't it?" He pulled out the *Addendum*, by now rather shamefully bent and dog-eared, from under the clothes and the squidged-up remains of the bread in the bag. Mr Cramplock's eyes lit up when he saw it.

"You *found* it," he said, thrilled. "How *clever*. And tell me, how much of it do you understand?"

"Well – some of it," Nick admitted.

"It's told us a whole lot of things," I said, "but we only really got the hang of it the other day. It's all in riddles. As though it's not really *meant* for people to understand it, at first."

Cramplock was nodding. "That's exactly it," he said, "exactly it. What clever young men – I mean, forgive me, Mog, it's still a little hard to remember sometimes! But you've understood that much, at least. The whole point was that no one just glancing at it would realise what it contained."

"So you know all about it," said Nick, fascinated. "Do you know what it all means?"

"My father printed it," Cramplock said. "You know by now, don't you, that the Cloy family at one time lived here, next door, in the burnt old house? Kniveacres was their country seat and Charnock House was their town house, until – ooh, until about ten years ago, I suppose it would be, when it burned down. Well, having his shop where he did, my father used to print documents for the Cloys, and for their lawyers. He had a lot of legal work in those days, which I've rather let go, I'm afraid. Well . . ." He stopped, thinking hard about how he might explain it. "The point is," he continued, "my father knew all their business. He was party to all their secrets. And he thought these secrets were too important, and too terrible, just to be hushed up and never spoken of again."

We sat, intently, listening to him. Waiting for him to elucidate.

"Yes?" I said eventually. "And what were their secrets?"

He gave a short chuckle. "Where would you like me to start?" he said. He got up and went over to the fire. "You've learned a lot of things already," he said as he stoked it. "You've told me what you found out from your governess. You've told me about the letters you saw in the study in the middle of the night. And you've told me about Damyata, coming back to settle some sort of score. That's the most extraordinary part of all." He came back and sat down. "Last year, when you discovered you were twins, and you found out about your mother's letter, Mog, and where you had really come from, Damyata was here in London, wasn't he? I didn't know that, at the time. I knew there were some sinister people looking for you, and leaving threatening notes everywhere, but I never imagined one of them might be *him*. If I had, I might even have been able to help him." He regarded us both, as we drank in his words. "Didn't you ever wonder how Sir Septimus came to be discovered so suddenly, and how it came about that you were sent off to start a new life?"

"What I think is *odd*," I said, "is that Sir Septimus turns out to have known our mother, all those years ago, and known Damyata, and even known about the two of us being born – and yet, we'd never heard of him until this year."

"Well, that's because he never wanted you to hear of him," said Cramplock. "You're related to him. You were one of his family's biggest secrets. And when you found your brother, and found your mother's letter, and worked out what it meant, the secret started to come out. He couldn't deny your existence any longer."

"But *you* knew who he was," I said.

"Yes, I did," he admitted, "and I knew who *you* were, Mog."

He could tell we were still baffled.

"Listen," he said gently, "I think you should sleep. And tomorrow, we'll go to Kniveacres."

I stared at him. "But we've just run away," I said. "Why do we want to go back?"

"Back to *Sir Septimus*?" put in Nick. "And back to face the villagers, after what happened last night? I don't think so, thanks all the same."

"Trust me," said Cramplock, "I think it will be all right. It will be a lot easier to explain everything when we're there. And I think you'll be glad to go back, in the end."

There was an autumnal chill in the air at Kniveacres. The creeper along the south walls of the Hall was turning a vivid scarlet, but the afternoon light was flat and muted as our carriage came around the drive towards the front of the house.

Nick and I hadn't approached Kniveacres this way since we first arrived, all those months ago, and we were struck again by how grand, but how melancholy, the house looked from its front aspect.

We had taken more than a day to get here, in slow coaches and hired carriages, and had had to spend last night at an inn at Towcester. We'd been away from Kniveacres for nearly three days, during which time September had given way to October. There was very little sign of life as we approached, and I found myself wondering, for the first time, really, what had happened here since the dreadful night of the bonfire. Bonefinger's demise, and Mrs Muggerage's disappearance, not to mention ours, must have left the place completely at sixes and sevens; but we had been too intent on our own journey to think about just what we were leaving behind.

At first, nobody greeted us; but after we had climbed down, and Nick had gone round to the stableyard to look for someone, Melibee came slowly down the front steps. He looked distressed, and short of sleep. He couldn't work out who the carriage belonged to, and when I spoke his face showed relief.

"Miss Imogen," he said, "I am glad, indeed I am, to hear your voice. Is Master Dominic with you?"

"Yes," I said, "he's gone round to the yard. Melibee, we have brought a friend with us from London, Mr Cramplock, my old employer."

Melibee bowed, in the direction he imagined Mr Cramplock to be, which was roughly correct; then he put his old hand to his face in a gesture of despair.

"Miss Imogen, things are not right, not right at all," he said.

"I wonder that you have returned, to such unhappiness. You heard about the tragedy on Sunday night?"

"We were there," I said. "We were hiding, watching. It really happened, then?" The recollection of the events around the bonfire was so surreal that I wouldn't have been at all surprised to find Melibee telling me I must have been dreaming them, and Bonefinger stalking out of the house behind him.

"The servants have deserted," Melibee continued, anxiously. "They all believe Kniveacres is cursed. And sometimes it's easy to believe it might be. Oh, Miss Imogen, as if this weren't enough, Sir Septimus is not well at all. Since the night of the fire he has been distracted out of his wits. He has taken to wandering, and talks all the time, but makes little or no sense. Perhaps you and Master Dominic can calm him. Really, things are most dreadfully awry."

We went inside, Melibee helping with the bags. Nick met us in the entrance hall. "The place is deserted," he said.

"You find Kniveacres in a state of deep unhappiness," Melibee explained. "I have never known things so out of their proper shape."

There was something different in the air, as we went up to our rooms. The house felt exhausted, silent and lifeless; but somehow completely unthreatening, all its danger evaporated. It was as though someone or something had sucked out all its venom, as if from a snake-inflicted wound. Mr Cramplock was shown to a guest room and Melibee said he would arrange for refreshments. We washed, and changed, and after half an hour or so we joined Mr Cramplock in one of the sunnier drawing rooms at the front of the house, which we hadn't usually been allowed to frequent. Melibee was quite right that the house felt unhappy; but the sense of liberation was tangible.

As we sipped tea and ate up a three-day-old mincemeat tart – for which Melibee apologised, the kitchens having been abandoned for most of the week – Mr Cramplock talked to us more about what he knew, and what he had brought us here to tell us. His father, H.H. Cramplock, had learned about all of it from the Cloys' legal papers, and naturally he had picked up snippets of it himself as time went by. It was the most extraordinary story.

Our mother, Imogen Winter, had spent most of her teenage years in India. The Winter and Cloy families were already connected by marriage, and Imogen was at one time intended to be married to one of Sir Septimus's nephews. But she resisted such a match for some years, and eventually fell in love with a man called Damyata, to the fury and embarrassment of both families; and when she found she was to give birth to his child, she was sent home to England in an attempt to keep the scandal as quiet as possible. During the voyage home, she gave birth to not one child, but two – myself and Nick. She also fell fatally ill.

Knowing she was going to die, she wrote a letter to the nearest relative she could think of who might be in a financial position to look after us. This was Sir Septimus's wife Harriet – who was herself a Winter, actually the cousin of Imogen's father. When we arrived in London, two weeks old, we went with our mother to a hospital where she died a few days later. The plan was that we would be taken from there to Charnock House, into the care of Sir Septimus and Harriet, Lady Cloy, as our mother had pleaded.

We were, however, destined to experience anything but the secure and comfortable childhood our mother had envisaged. Sir Septimus had grown up out in India, the seventh son of an important East India Company family, and far and away its least disciplined member. He wasn't military in disposition, and he had idled away his youth and made his father despair of his ever building a proper career; though the family money meant he was still too wealthy for his own good. Documents which Mr Cramplock's father had seen, in his capacity as legal printer, made it clear that the young Septimus had committed a large number of crimes and misdemeanours which the family had tried hard to cover up. He had gambled, he had stolen, he had thrown his weight about and acted above his authority; and he had a reputation for highly improper behaviour towards the girls of other Calcutta families, not to mention servants and other natives. The girls he had wronged at various times in his life, it seemed clear, included our mother, even though she was fully forty years younger than he was; and Imogen Winter and Septimus Cloy had come to hate one another. Imogen knew all about his misdeeds, and he lived in constant fear that she would reveal them.

It must have been an especially desperate decision for Imogen, therefore, to write to the woman Sir Septimus had eventually married, and ask for her help and forgiveness. While Harriet had accepted the duty she owed to the daughter of her cousin, and was all prepared to bring up Imogen's two babies as her own, Sir Septimus had other ideas. He had no intention of having two children growing up in his life who would remind him constantly of Imogen Winter. He collected us from the hospital after our mother's death, but instead of taking us home he took me to an orphanage, and Nick to another charitable foundation where he was eventually adopted by Mrs Muggerage and her partner, the dreadful drunken bosun. He destroyed all the documents which provided a record of our identity – and went back to Harriet with the lie that Imogen's poor little children had died in the hospital too.

But, unknown to him, a page of the original letter she wrote to Harriet had been preserved, completely by accident, and wrapped up with the meagre bundle of things the baby Nick took with him. Nick had kept it, the only memento of his real mother he had ever known, apart from a silver bangle.

"Do you mean to say," I said, my voice breaking with emotion, after we had sat in silence listening to Mr Cramplock's account, "that Sir Septimus could have brought us up in his house, with all his money and all his comforts, from the very beginning – but he deliberately abandoned us?"

"His wife wanted you," Mr Cramplock said. "He deceived her. He deceived everyone, all the time. The other thing he did, of course, to cover his tracks, was burn down the house."

I gasped. "*He* burned it down? On purpose?"

"When he came back from India for good, he knew a lot of the documents that incriminated him were kept in Charnock House. So he set fire to it. Well, it was never proven that he did it, but I knew he had, and I think his brothers knew he had, though they've all taken it to their graves."

There was silence as we took in the enormity of Sir Septimus's wickedness.

"My father was enraged by all this," continued Mr Cramplock, "most especially by the story of the orphans, which he found out all about and which he thought was utterly unforgiveable in this life or the next; but he didn't see what he could do, as a mere printer, to put things right. But he told me about it, and he kept as many papers as he could. When my father died I went through all the papers I could find, and I was able to use them, Mog, to find out which orphanage you were in. It was hard, because none of the documents contained your names, and all I knew was that I was looking for a girl and a boy. I thought if I could rescue the Winter children and maybe give them work in the printing shop, I'd be doing my best to make amends. I brought you out of the orphanage, Mog, six years ago now it must be. And, you know, I thought you were the boy. But there were simply no documents that told me where the other child might be found. You had disappeared into thin air, Nick."

"And it turned out you were only a few streets away," I said. "But even after I came out of the orphanage it took me five years to find you!"

"You've never told us this," Nick said to him. "I never knew you rescued Mog. I thought she came to work for you, sort of by accident."

"It was too complicated," said Mr Cramplock. "I was waiting until Mog was older before I told her. When she found you, and you discovered things about your past, I thought I might tell you the whole story – but even then I didn't know whether Sir Septimus was alive, or whether he could be compelled to look after you. And it all seemed too difficult to explain."

"So if Sir Septimus was so hateful to us, all those years ago," said Nick, "why did you have us sent back to him after all this time?"

"Because I discovered," said Mr Cramplock quietly, "that there were no living members of the Cloy family who had a greater claim on the inheritance than you two. And it seemed only right that you should claim it. Sir Septimus is the last in his line. All his older brothers died, most of them in rather strange and tragic circumstances, and most of them without heirs – you could say that the family is more than usually unfortunate in this respect. And with the sudden death of his only surviving nephew last year, the nearest living relatives are the two of you. Of course, if nobody here knew who you were, or where you were, you couldn't have inherited the estate. Now you can."

"Wait a minute," I said, "I don't think we can. I've read Sir Septimus's will, and I'm sure it says Bonefinger and Melibee inherit half each."

"Not if a living relative comes forward within a month of Sir Septimus's death," said Mr Cramplock. "Perhaps you didn't read it carefully enough."

"Well, it *was* very complicated," I said doubtfully.

"And you were reading it in the dark," put in Nick.

Mr Cramplock got up. "Come and look at something," he said.

We followed him through the house. He was leading us up to the main passageway towards the bedrooms in the west wing, the grand old family quarters.

"Have you been here before then, Mr Cramplock?" I asked.

"No," he said, "but my father came, more than once, I

believe. And he told me some secrets. Now then – which one is it?"

We went into a beautiful bedroom, with a huge window looking out onto the gardens, hung with golden cloth, furnished with golden mirrors and embossed gold-coloured coverings on the walls. We had never been in here before.

"Is this the Gilt Bedroom?" Nick asked.

"It is,"said Mr Cramplock. "And these wall hangings," he said, "were restored on the orders of Lady Cloy – Harriet, that is – not long before she died; so they're really quite new, and splendid. But there's something here very few people know about. Do you have any idea what I'm talking about?"

We stared at him blankly.

"You've read the *Addendum*," said Mr Cramplock, "but you probably didn't understand what you were reading. Now then – *please* let them still be here." To our astonishment, he began to fumble in a corner, and gradually pulled aside the ornate covering from a big expanse of wall. It was like a huge sheet of fabric, hung from a rail just beneath the ceiling, with the furniture placed back against it. All four walls had similar decorative hangings.

And on the bare wall behind were pasted sheets and sheets of paper, covered in print, and even what looked like some handwritten letters. Mr Cramplock went around the room, lifting the corners of the hangings here and there, and revealing that the papers continued all the way around.

"My old father did do one useful thing to help you before he died," he said. "He plastered the whole story of the Cloys, and their misdemeanours, and their cover-ups, and their deceptions, here under their very noses, in their own house. And Sir Septimus never realised. Even though the clue was there in the *Addendum*, in his library, all the time."

Nick was staring, incredulous. "The story behind the hangings," he said. "This is it."

"Of course it is," said Mr Cramplock. "Can you pull that curtain aside a bit, Mog? That's better." The late afternoon sun was directly opposite the window and, as Mr Cramplock held up the gilt hanging, the sun fell upon the yellowing sheets of paper pasted on the plaster wall. "Sir Septimus thought his secrets had been obliterated in the fire next door," he said, "but he reckoned without my old father. I've no doubt there's a whole load of information here I've never known about, and which Sir Septimus will have hoped the whole world had forgotten. But look, it's just come to light."

CHAPTER 12

DAMYATA

We were making our way back to the east wing, suddenly feeling exhausted and keen to get some proper rest before dinner, when the sound of raised voices from outside attracted our attention; and a quick glance out of a window onto the courtyard revealed two figures outside on the gravel.

It was Sir Septimus, and Melibee; Sir Septimus was talking, and occasionally shouting, and Melibee seemed to be trying to calm him down.

"What's going on out there?" Nick wondered.

"Melibee said Sir Septimus had gone out of his mind," I said. "Do you think he needs some help?"

We went down into the courtyard, and, as we hovered uneasily by the door, we could hear what was happening a bit more clearly. Sir Septimus was getting highly exercised by something.

"He's trying to kill me, I'm telling you," he was saying. "He got them to come after me. There they were, boom! I turned the corner, and what was I supposed to do? After me, they were. That rascal. That rascally man!" His eyes went glassy now, and he stood in the middle of the courtyard talking loudly into thin air. "Did you know what they said to meem? They said I could never keep it quiet, but I was too clever for them. That father of hers, he's a fool and will never be Prime Minister, whatever he thinks. She didn't mind, you know. She said she didn't, at the time, but they all change their minds later. Boom! What was I supposed to doom?"

"He's *completely* loopy," whispered Nick. "What on earth is he talking about?"

"Trying to have me killed!" Sir Septimus shouted, waving his finger at Melibee now. "You won't have it, but it's true! And to think I was going to give him everything! Everything! That man!" He moved forward, took hold of poor Melibee, and began to shake him. "Nobody will listen!" he shouted.

"Come on," I said.

We ran over and tried gently to pull Sir Septimus back.

"Sir Septimus, you'll hurt someone," I said, "come away, try and calm down." Melibee staggered slightly as he was freed from Sir Septimus's unexpected grasp; he adjusted his rumpled clothes.

"These are the children of that other girl," Sir Septimus ranted. "Mmm . . . mmm . . . that girl, do you remember her name? They wanted me to have them, but I wouldn't. What, and haunt me? Haunt me to the grave? There are her eyes, look. Twice over. Brrrrr! They told her all sorts of lies, that day. You weren't there. How do you know? Mmmm . . . but I can't help it," he said to us. He began shaking his head, repeatedly, from side to side, like a tiny stubborn child. "They're wrong, they're all *wrong*, all of them, wrong, wrong, it wasn't like that, they're *wrong*."

"He's been like this since the other night," said Melibee. "Something terrified him, the night Bonefinger died, and he's never been well since. It was before we even knew what had happened in the village. I heard him screaming in his room, and he was pointing into the dark and talking about a cap with bells on. It didn't make much sense to me, but he appears to have reverted to talking about incidents from his youth, all mixed up with other quite disconnected events."

"I never did half the things they said," Sir Septimus piped up again. "I never did them. Never did them. Never did them. They liked it, anyway. You weren't there. You've no idea, all of you, standing there. How do *you* know what I did?"

"He should see a doctor," I said to Melibee.

"A doctor came, yesterday," Melibee said, "and said if his condition worsened I should call him again. I must say, I believe this is the worst he has been."

Attracted by the shouting, Mr Cramplock appeared at the door.

"Come and help us, Mr Cramplock," I called.

"Who's this?" Sir Septimus asked, as Mr Cramplock came up to us. "Looks like that printer next door." I gasped. "Looks like him," he said. "Can't be, though. Mmmm . . . he died. Didn't like me. *Died*," he repeated, staring into my face, "like the others."

"I think we need to get him back inside," I said to Mr Cramplock. We managed to lead him back to the door at the foot of the tower; and suddenly he slumped, as though something else had been inhabiting his body and had left him. His strange ramblings stopped, but he seemed to crumple, and become just a grey, fearful-looking husk of a man, whom Melibee and Mr Cramplock carried between them, up the stairs towards the tower bedroom.

Doctors came, and lawyers, from London. There seemed to be a general acceptance that Sir Septimus was about to die, and all his papers were gathered and scrutinised in great detail as he lay in bed, oblivious to it all. Melibee and Mr Cramplock gave assistance where they could. Nick and Lash and I walked in the grounds, thinking and talking about what the past week's events had thrown up. We had the freedom of the house, too, at last. Doors which had been closed to us ever since we arrived were unlocked, and left unlocked. Curtains which had probably been closed for years were opened.

Late on Thursday afternoon, we were asked to join one of the lawyers, and Mr Cramplock, in the study. It felt very strange, walking in and seeing someone other than Sir Septimus sitting framed in the oriel window. The lawyer, Mr Lilicrap, was in the large chair, with dusty bound files and large piles of paper arrayed on the desk in front of him. Clean-shaven, his hair neatly oiled close to his scalp, and exuding a faint smell of pencil sharpenings, he looked up and greeted us with a demeanour that was efficient, but not unfriendly.

"Dominic, and Imogen," he said, "sit down, if you'd be so kind." He gathered together the papers, and his thoughts, and looked up at us again. "We haven't involved you, up to now, in the process of ordering Sir Septimus's affairs. But we find there are one or two matters with which we can make limited progress without information from you. You might not be aware," he continued, "that two men were apprehended in London last weekend. They were acting suspiciously, and were in possession of certain incriminating documents. They have since made a full confession, and it is clear they were under instruction to murder Sir Septimus."

We stared at him.

"I need to know," he said, "if you have overheard any conversations, or witnessed any unusual behaviour, on the part of Sir Septimus's late manservant Hieronymous Bonefinger."

Where to begin? I looked at Nick, and he raised his eyebrows.

"We've – we always found Bonefinger a strange character," I said. "He was unusual in lots of ways."

Mr Lilicrap permitted himself a smile. "Perhaps what I mean, then," he said, "is any behaviour which seemed unusual to you, even allowing for Bonefinger's customary eccentricities."

We told him about the burial at the yew-tree avenue; our suspicions about the gargoyle, and the dumb-waiter; the meeting I had witnessed between Bonefinger and the men at the Cloy Arms; Bonefinger's imprisonment of us; and his conversation with Sir Septimus which Nick had overheard from the big sofa. Mr Lilicrap seemed especially interested in the first of these, and the last.

"What did you believe he might be burying?" he asked us.

"It was wrapped up," I said, "so we didn't see it properly – but it looked like a dead body."

"What made you think that was what it might be?"

I shrugged. "Its size," I said. "Its weight. The way he carried it."

"The fact that he was burying it," said Nick. "I mean, it

looked a bit like a roll of old carpet, but people don't bury carpets."

"I think we need to send someone to dig it up," said Mr Lilicrap to Mr Cramplock. "Would you be able to show us, you two, exactly where to dig?"

We nodded. "It's not hard to see," put in Nick. "The grass hasn't grown over it properly yet."

"Tell me more about the conversation on Sunday evening," said Mr Lilicrap. "This would be just before you left the house, and a couple of hours before the fire ceremony on the village green?"

Nick related, as he had related to me, the words both parties used, as accurately as he could remember them.

"So you formed the impression," said Mr Lilicrap, "that Sir Septimus was aware of having been followed?"

"Oh yes," said Nick, "and cross with Bonefinger because he suspected him of arranging it."

"Afraid?"

Nick thought for a few seconds. "Contemptuous," he said. "The men had made it rather obvious they were watching him. He kept saying things like, 'if you must play your ridiculous games'. What did he call it again? 'Your silly cloak and dagger puppet-show'."

"Bonefinger underestimated his employer," said Mr Lilicrap. "Sir Septimus was certainly never supposed to return from London; but he outwitted his pursuers, and had them arrested to boot."

"So," I said, beginning to understand, "Bonefinger was trying to have him killed, because he wanted the estate?"

Mr Lilicrap gazed at me, and reached for a large document on the desk in front of him. "Bonefinger's motives can now only be guessed at," he said, "but it is far from unlikely that he wished all of you removed from the picture, so that the estate might be his. Indeed. This is Sir Septimus's last will. You all stood in the way of Bonefinger's inheritance – Sir Septimus, the two of you, and Melibee too, if it comes to that."

"But I thought Sir Septimus changed his will," I said. Mr Lilicrap stared at me. Reddening slightly, I elaborated. "I came across a will, dated just last week," I said. "I could swear it clearly said all previous wills were cancelled, and that Bonefinger and Melibee got half each in any case."

Mr Lilicrap seemed intrigued. "Where did you find it?" he asked.

"In Sir Septimus's desk. Bonefinger caught me reading it, in the middle of the night, and he took all the documents and put them in his pocket."

"In that case, I can only conclude they ended up in the fire with him," said the lawyer. "No such will has come to light. Perhaps he still had it in his pocket at the time of the – accident."

"Bonefinger must have thought he was protecting it, by keeping it on his person," said Mr Cramplock. "Little did he know what was going to happen to him."

"It's fortunate for you two," Mr Lilicrap said, unfolding the papers in front of him, "that this will here is the most recent version we have. We will, of course, perform a further thorough search – but unless the other can be found, this one must stand." He leafed through it for a few moments. "There will be a formal reading when the legal implications have been decided," he said, "but this is the relevant paragraph, I think:

In the event of no legitimate Issue surviving at the date of my death nor any other blood Relative being found to survive nor any claim by any illegitimate Issue or Party or Parties with similar entitlement under the above Provisions being lodged within one calendar month of my death, I devise and bequeath my entire Estate both real and personal to such of my loyal Retainers who shall be proven to survive me, namely Hieronymous Bonefinger and Anselm Archibald Melibee, if both in equal part, and do appoint them Executors and Trustees of this my Will.

"Which means," he continued, "that Bonefinger's claim is void on two counts. For one thing, you two are likely to have the prior claim. And secondly, of course, he has not survived."

I couldn't take it in. I wasn't at all sure, sitting here in this fusty-smelling study, that I wanted to inherit Kniveacres. What on earth would we *do* with it, if we did?

Mr Lilicrap turned back to some papers on the desk in front of him. "We also have some evidence," he went on, "that Bonefinger dressed up, in a strange costume, to scare Sir Septimus. He posed, several times we believe, as an old enemy from India, whom Sir Septimus had not seen for twenty years. He left forged notes, and tried to intimidate Sir Septimus by means of an old prophecy."

I looked at Nick, crestfallen. "Are you saying," I asked Mr

Lilicrap, "that Damyata – the jester – was actually only Bonefinger dressed up?"

"Who else did you think it might be?" smiled Mr Lilicrap indulgently. "The *real* Damyata? Come from India to haunt him?" He chuckled. "There's no evidence," he went on, "that this man Damyata is still alive, or even if he were, that he might be in any position to pursue his old enemy to England. I fear that is the stuff of paranoid fantasy. But it appears to have worked. Bonefinger's murder plot may have misfired; but he has succeeded in scaring Sir Septimus out of his wits."

"So who was it on Sunday night, then, who fought Bonefinger at the bonfire?" asked Nick, incredulously.

Mr Lilicrap looked uncomfortable. "Well," he said, "the truth of *that* is rather difficult to arrive at. The talk in the village is all of supernatural forces. I believe investigations into that may be ongoing for some time to come."

I suddenly felt adrift: unsure of what to believe and what not to believe. Surely Damyata's notes, and tokens, and signals to us, hadn't merely been left by Bonefinger as a deception?

"Of course," said Mr Lilicrap, "Bonefinger himself is no longer around to corroborate any of this, and he will never stand trial. Sir Septimus is hardly in a position to give reliable evidence either. Conjecture must remain conjecture. But the picture is emerging."

"What about Miss Thing?" asked Nick. "I mean, Miss Thynne – the governess? She died here last week. Did Bonefinger want her out of the way too?"

"That we may also never know," admitted Mr Lilicrap. "Her past associations with Sir Septimus have been looked into, and there is without doubt more to them than meets the eye. She was in Calcutta at the time of some of his most unsavoury exploits. She certainly had information which it would have been – inconvenient for Sir Septimus, let us say, to see widely revealed. And she may have been one of the only people still alive who was in possession of it."

"It appears," put in Mr Cramplock, "that Justina Thynne was one of your mother Imogen's closest friends, when they were girls."

"She *never* told us that!" I exclaimed, looking at Nick.

"It's unclear why she accepted the position as your governess, given her past dealings with the Cloy family," Mr Lilicrap said. "Perhaps she too felt she owed some duty to the two of you, on behalf of her childhood friend. Although Sir Septimus may very well have brought her here with the ultimate purpose of containing her or – *in extremis*, I suppose – silencing her. Nonetheless, I fear she, too, has taken the truth of the matter with her to the grave," he sighed.

"But she was being spied on," I put in. "In her room there was a big silk peacock's tail, covered in mirrors. And there's a room behind the wall where someone can hide and peep through, without being seen. It's mentioned in old Mr Cramplock's *Addendum*. I wouldn't be surprised if that was Bonefinger too."

"We can get someone to look up there too," said Mr Lilicrap to Mr Cramplock, who nodded. "There may be clues." He was about to write a further note in the book in front of him, when there was a sharp rapping at the study door, and Melibee appeared in a state of considerable fluster.

"I do apologise, gentlemen," he said, "forgive me, but – it's Sir Septimus. He has gone wandering again, and I am – unable to find him."

Mr Lilicrap stood up. "You've been most helpful, Imogen, and Dominic," he said. "Thank you. Now – perhaps we can all assist in searching for Sir Septimus."

Melibee had gone to Sir Septimus's room to take him a drink of weak tea, and found the door wide open and the bed rumpled and empty. We were all given an area of the house to search – I had to look in the servants' quarters and the kitchens – and when that yielded nothing, the grounds were divided between us. There wasn't much light left, and there was a sense of urgency about our quest. The kitchen garden and summerhouse were my responsibility; and when after twenty minutes I'd found nothing, and it was getting too dark to search any more, I suddenly heard shouts from the edge of the wood, not far away.

Mr Cramplock, seeing the white-clad figure of Sir Septimus at a distance in the twilight, wandering near the lake, had pursued him through the trees and up to the yew-tree walk. He had been moving at quite a pace, muttering to himself, in his night attire. Suddenly, as Mr Cramplock thought he must be catching up, he'd heard a crashing sound and a cry; and had rushed to the top of the crater on the edge of the wood, to find himself staring down the slope at the gaping hole of the well.

I knew from the way Lash sniffed his way down the slope and around the well, whimpering, that the worst had happened.

Torches were brought, and help was called for. Seven or eight men arrived from the village within about half an hour: gardeners, and men who worked on the estate, mainly, but they had also brought with them the strongest person they knew. With increasing awe we watched Sloughter Cripps, his shock of hair waving from the top of his head, working furiously by firelight to dig steps and heave branches and secure long ropes. After working for a while, they were able to lower a man down the well to investigate; and, when they had brought him up again, he delivered the grave news that Sir Septimus lay at the bottom, and that the fall had killed him.

We were sent back to the house to bed, as the men continued to toil to bring Sir Septimus's body up. Nobody said so, amid the shock and turmoil; and it didn't occur to us until we were back in our rooms; but this terrible final mishap meant the old prophecy had come true.

"It would have been his birthday tomorrow," Nick said.

I went and sat on Nick's bed. Lash jumped up beside me. "So he was cut off," I said, grimly, "at threescore ten and seven."

"In his last three or four hours of being seventy-seven," said Nick. "Just like the book said. It gives you a bit of a chill, doesn't it?"

"He was convinced it would come true," I said. "That morning last week, when he saw the prophecy, underlined. You could see it in his eyes. He was terrified, because he believed it."

"The question is," said Nick, "who underlined it, and left it for him to find?"

"Nick, Mr Lilicrap *must* have been wrong," I said. "Surely it wasn't Bonefinger all along, leaving those notes? Dressing up as the jester to scare Sir Septimus? Damyata really did come back, didn't he? Just like he really did come to London last year, even though no one believed it then?"

Lash suddenly sat up, and pricked up his ears. He gave a short woof.

"What?" I said to him. "Is someone outside the door? Lie down, you daft boy."

Nick was quiet. "I don't know what to believe about Damyata," he said. "I really just don't know, any more. But I know something. This place is ours now. We're the heirs, Mog. Think about that."

I could hardly fathom it. It was too unreal, the thought that Kniveacres belonged to us. I was much more interested in the thought I'd been harbouring for several days now, and which I had clung to with more and more conviction: that our father was alive, and somehow with us. His presence meant more than any gigantic creaky old house or estate. And suddenly, today, there was the fresh suggestion that he didn't exist after all: that we'd been dreaming him; that we'd been fooled.

I shivered. "I can't possibly sleep," I said. "I'm going to get my quilt. Do you mind?"

Lash slipped off the bed and came with me. There was no lamplight in my room. I went in to pull the quilt off the bed, and was about to take it next door, when I noticed something in the near-darkness on the table beside the bed, which I didn't remember having left there.

I picked it up. I definitely hadn't seen this before.

It was a little silver comb.

Suddenly the hairs on the back of my neck stood up, and I

felt the most peculiar, dizzy sensation; as a whisper behind me said: "It's yours, Mog."

I hardly dared turn around. I didn't know if I was thrilled, or terrified. Slowly, I turned my head; and there was a tall figure standing in the deep shadows near the bedroom door. I should have screamed; but I was mesmerised, frozen. It was as if my heart was in my throat, making it impossible to utter a sound.

Lash was standing, rigid as I was; he stared at the figure in the darkness, and took a little step backwards, staying right up close to me; but he was completely quiet.

"You know what it is, don't you?" the whisper said. "You must have it."

"You really have come," I said, in a strangled voice. "You found us."

"I found you a long time ago," said the shadow. "I watched and waited. I knew this moment would come, Mog."

"So did I," I whispered.

"Mog?" called Nick from the other room. "Who are you talking to?"

"Call him," said Damyata.

"Nick, come in here a minute," I said.

There was the sound of padding feet. Nick appeared in his nightshirt, a silhouette at the door; he stopped dead, clinging to the door-frame.

"Who's there?" he hissed.

"Someone, and no one," said Damyata from the shadows. He was no longer whispering. "You know my name, Nick. You have known my name for many years. Even when you had no idea what it meant, my name was with you."

"You did come," Nick said.

"I did," he replied. "And I have achieved my goal, of seeing justice for you, and justice for the man who wronged you. All of this should have been yours from birth. You have been very cruelly wronged. But it is now come right."

My eyes were getting more accustomed to the darkness of the room and I could make him out more clearly now. An imposing, self-possessed figure with a high forehead and sharp features, and bright eyes which seemed to catch and distil the faint traces of light from the doorway and from the night sky through the window. His jester costume had gone, and he was wearing a dark cloak with a collar turned high against the autumn cold. He looked like someone who was travelling.

"What did you do?" I asked.

"What did I have to do? Almost nothing. Others helped you. I watched them, and I watched things going right, and things going wrong. I warned you of danger, and I tried to reassure you of my intentions. What I did? You must decide."

"Did you kill him?" Nick asked, still standing at the door.

There was a long silence. "You saw what you saw," came the eventual reply.

"We saw the jester fighting with Bonefinger," said Nick quietly, "and pushing him into the flames. And then the jester turned back into a scarecrow. How can you explain that?"

"In the village they believe in evil spirits," Damyata said, "just as they do in India. And what is real? What you wish and believe to be real, is real. Anything that *seems* to explain what you see. I had to protect you."

"So are you an evil spirit?" I ventured. "Can you do magic?"

"How do you do it?" asked Nick.

He laughed, a quiet chuckle, not menacing. "Silly tricks," he said. "Warnings and signs. Snakes and music; conjuring tricks. Not evil. Your mind must be open. It's about what you believe you see, not what is really there. You walk into a house, and you find it in another time, when it contained people and objects quite central to your story. Empty skulls and straw limbs come alive and dance. They are real for you, but who can say how they appear to others? Conjuring tricks," he said again.

I was starting to feel a flood of inexplicable joy. I wanted to laugh out loud. I suppose it was sinking in. This was our father we were talking to.

"What about rooks?" I said.

He laughed louder this time. "It's not difficult," he said. "It was just mischief."

"I was scared," I said.

"People are often scared of what they cannot explain," he said. "It may take the wisdom of many lifetimes to banish fear."

There was an awed silence. He took a pace or two towards us. Nick moved from the door, and came to stand at my shoulder.

"Is it all true?" Nick asked. "What we've been told, about you, and our mother? And Sir Septimus? The whole story behind the hangings?"

"I loved your mother," he said. "More dearly than I have ever loved anything or anyone or ever will. She was a most special person, and you are more special than you will ever know, just by being hers. Cloy also fell under her spell, except that his love was covetous, not generous. He wanted to possess her. He was a jealous, furious man. Truly wicked. And she hated him. *Hated* him."

"He was jealous of you," I said.

"Oh – without question," said Damyata. "And her whole family believed she had done a quite terrible thing, and that I must be a most evil creature. But look at what Cloy did, after she died. What sort of love is that? A man full of hatred and jealousy and evil, who can make babies suffer as punishment for their mother's rejection of him. He was your enemy from the moment you were born, you two, he made your lives misery for years when you had never even heard of him. Yet he could have made you comfortable, happy, wealthy. You are well rid of him. I do not mourn him and no more should you. Be glad. What was his, is yours, at long last."

"And what about you?" Nick asked quietly. "Will you share it with us now?"

Damyata stood in the darkness. "My work here is done."

"No," I said, my fist closing around the silver comb. "You must stay, now, after all this."

"Think of it not as abandonment," he said. "I will remain with you. Reality is what you wish and believe. I have seen you inherit your absolute birthright, to which you have infinitely more right as a result of evil that was done to you. My protection has been spiritual, not – what is it? – corporeal. It will not go away, even though I do."

"Stay," said Nick.

"Love," said Damyata, "remember it. Love is the most real thing, and without it life is not life. I can trust you to know it, in your hearts, you two of all people on earth. You may not know it, but there is more love in you than in whole nations. I am proud of you, Mog and Nick. I will never be otherwise."

"You can't—" I began; but I was speaking to an empty room. One moment he was there, the next he had gone. We rushed out into the corridor, but there was nothing but silent air, and a lingering scent of something sweet.

Arrangements were laid for a funeral. With Bonefinger and Sir Septimus both gone, the village's fears began to subside, and gradually the servants' curiosity got the better of them and they returned. Mr Lilicrap was in evidence at Kniveacres for several days, and he wasn't the only lawyer who came and went, and spoke to us in language we barely understood about the technicalities of our inheritance. The air buzzed with talk of trusts, and ages of majority, and executors; and while they sorted it all out we lived, with everyone making a great fuss of us, as though we were the joint master and mistress of the house. The pieces of paper telling the story behind the hangings were carefully steamed off the walls of the Gilt Bedroom, and stored for legal purposes, presumably as evidence of our right to the estate. The grave which Bonefinger had dug at the top of the yew-tree walk was excavated, and, after further investigations in the local area, there was at least a working hypothesis about what was going through the deceased Bonefinger's head.

Just as he had wished our deaths – which had never quite come to pass – to look like accidents, he was determined that Sir Septimus's death should look entirely natural. He had paid the hapless murderers to get rid of Sir Septimus in London and dispose of his body somewhere where it could never be discovered; but he knew that the security of his inheritance would depend on his not being found out. It seemed his plan was to pretend to the whole world that Sir Septimus had died of natural causes. In accordance with his wishes, he would say, Sir Septimus had been buried in the yew-tree walk. So, when he heard that a man from another village some miles away had fortuitously died of natural causes at the age of not quite eighty, a fortnight or so before his horrible plot was due to come to fruition, he went to the trouble of obtaining the corpse. If something should go wrong and the murder ever be suspected, Bonefinger calculated, by the time anyone came to exhume Sir Septimus to find out the truth, the bogus corpse would be sufficiently decomposed as to be unidentifiable, except as a man of roughly the right age and build.

Mr Cramplock took his leave the day after Sir Septimus's death, and returned to London to tidy up his business. We had become aware for the first time, this week, of what a gigantic debt we owed him, and the goodbyes on the gravel drive were effusive and tearful; but he travelled back to Kniveacres a few days later for the funeral, and he was to become a regular visitor. Sir Septimus was buried, just as his will specified, in the grave which Bonefinger had dug. The house resumed its age-old routines: Judith organised the domestic staff, Melibee took sole charge of the finances, and the pervasive air of wickedness and death slowly diminished; but I was very unsure indeed whether it could ever be a comfortable place to live.

Nick and Lash and I at least knew we had the freedom to roam, the freedom to bring the pleasant quarters of the house back into use, the freedom to have whoever we liked to come and visit; and the freedom to show our faces in the village, since everyone there soon saw it as our triumph that the terrible Cloy dynasty had come to an end, and we were suddenly regarded with great affection.

And all this was insignificant, compared to the memory of one dreamlike conversation, in half-darkness, one October night. We rarely talked about Damyata; but we both thought about him nearly all the time, if we were honest; and we were in no doubt that he would stay with us for our entire lives, just as he had told us he would.

"I wonder where he is now," I said to Nick one afternoon, a few weeks later, as we came in from a frosty walk with Lash, to find a fire roaring in the massive medieval fireplace of the great hall, and Melibee appearing with two steaming mugs of hot tea and honey.

"He's where we wish and believe him to be," Nick said; and despite the twinkle in his eye I wasn't sure whether he was being serious. Melibee wished us a good evening and melted quietly into the darkness of the passageway.

"I suppose we'll never really know if he was real," mused Nick. "I mean – physically *there*."

"He was completely real," I said. "It sends a shiver up my spine. He was more real than I could ever imagine."

"But in a way that other people aren't," Nick said. "That's what I mean, really. We couldn't see him properly, but we both knew he was there, and he sort of – filled us, didn't he? More so than anything we *can* see ever could."

"Ye-es ," I said, "I know what you mean, I think."

"I mean," Nick said, still grasping for a way to put it, "we could both have, sort of, *imagined* him, couldn't we? It wouldn't mean he wasn't there."

"You know," I said, "one day, I might try and write all this down. The only trouble is, I have a feeling no one would believe it."

I took my boots off, placed them beside the chair, and put my feet on Lash, who had curled up on the rug in front of the enormous fireplace, in a warm and familiar patch of his own hair, and who, even though his eyes were open, had started to make a noise which sounded like a snore. He looked utterly at home. And, in a strange way, for the first time in my life I felt at home myself.